Goon Girl:
The Minors

© 2023

Written by Colin Moreland

Audiobook narrated by Eva DeBaie

Contents

About this book

This book was authored to be consumed as an audiobook. You, the reader, may prefer to consume the stories as an ebook instead, but this work was written to be read. The oral history of Penny is told in the audiobook by an alumni of the Canadian female hockey program, and is produced to provide the *most* authentic Goon Girl experience we can accomplish. If you're considering the book, we suggest considering the audiobook available on Audible as an alternative, to enjoy the stories the way we intended them to be heard.

Most of the stories are told chronologically, but every single chapter is intended to work as a standalone narrative while also fitting into the whole. Others look at the backstory of specific characters or key moments in their lives.

You, the reader and listener, can safely skip any chapter you don't want to listen to or re-listen to without worrying about missing key parts of the story. We have deliberately avoided ending chapters in cliffhangers, so you can play one chapter while driving or working out and not worrying about getting cut off midway through a critical plot arc.

We have done this to make the most use of the smart platforms that are the mainstay of publishing now, and to give you unprecedented control over your literary experience.

Dedication

This work is dedicated to three parties:

To my wife and children, for their patience and support through the authorship and production process

To my parents, Brian and Sandy, for their constant support of my lifelong literary amibitions

And to the female athletes of all sports who continue to break down barriers and challenge expectations to compete and thrive in organized sports all around the world. Stay fierce.

Land Acknowledgement

The contributors to this work acknowledge that we live and work on the lands of the Blackfoot people of the Canadian Plains and pays respect to the Blackfoot people past, present and future while recognizing and respecting their cultural heritage, beliefs and relationship to land. Our homes in the City of Lethbridge are also home to the Métis Nation of Alberta, Region 3.

Content Advisory

This work contains strong language, violence, underage alcohol and drug use, and same-sex relationships that some readers or listeners may find disturbing. Reader and listener discretion is advised.

This book and all stories, characters and organizations within it are works of fiction. Any similarity to figures or situations real or deceased is unintentional.

1. First Season

When Penny turned ten she won an argument that she and her mother had having since Penny had learned to skate. Penny, inevitably, wanted to play hockey. Her three older brothers had all played andne still did. For most of Penny's young life she had spent early mornings and weekends at the rink watching her brothers grow up and become players of the game they had all loved.

Penny's mother, on the other hand, did not love hockey. With one son banned from his league and another permanently out of the game due to injury, it wasn't hard to understand why. Not that either of those things had been true when Penny first asked if she could play, but little had happened in the subsequent years to change Mrs. Davies' position.

The best outcome Penny had achieved in the past had been to convince her mother to let her play ringette. From 6 to 9 she played in the local rec league and showed herself to be a capable player with good senses and solid skating ability. But Penny's town of Maple Creek Saskatchewan didn't have a U11 Ringette team and that meant that when she aged out of U10 she had to quit the sport. That left the local girls U15 hockey squad as the only other alternative. Mrs. Davies tried her best to redirect Penny's interest to another winter sport like figure skating, snowboarding, or even curling, but Penny was not interested. She wanted to keep playing and it was now hockey or bust. So what was a parent to do? Mrs. Davies agreed that Penny could join the U15 female team.

Penny's first experience with the new team was a not what she expected. Penny had grown up going to her brother's practices and seeing how the boys program evolved over time. When she showed up on her first day ready to start the same skating and shooting drills that helped coaches sort boy players by their various skill levels, she was faced with the complete shock of there only being a single team available to play for regardless of a girl's skill level. Even that team was going to barely meet the minimum league requirements for number of players. Aside from the returning veteran players who'd been with the team in the previous season, most of the new girls had never skated before, and those that had were more interested in showing off moves from their figure skating than showing how quickly they could skate a suicide.

Penny also found the coach's mentality tough to reconcile. Again, used to her brothers coming home in tears after practice sometimes after being ridden so hard by their coaches, the two moms coaching her team seemed more concerned about praising her team's lack of failure at rudimentary skills than they were about excellence or winning. The team had placed second last in their league the previous season, putting up 8 wins and 22 losses that finished with no hope of the playoffs. The coach told the team that her "stretch goal" for the season was for the team to improve to 3rd last and win at least 10 games this season.

Penny was one of three new girls on who had elder brothers who played the game. They quickly became the core of the rookies because they knew the game the best. The coaches leaned on them to help the other girls learn the game and develop while the coaches put their attentions at on the first and second liner veterans who would get most of the ice time that season.

Overall, it was a role Penny felt comfortable sliding into. It gave her focus and purpose at practices and let her get to know the other rookies. It also gave Penny something to focus on aside from the coach's vision, which Penny had rephrased for herself as "don't lose more than three quarters of your games this season". Instead, Penny was able to focus on her little group of rookies and making them into a group that could one day become the heart of a much more competitive squad. Working from the ground up she and the other two rookie leaders were able to establish solid fundamentals of skating, passing, and shooting early, and worked with their teammates on being the best they could at those skills every practice.

Meanwhile outside the rink, Penny's home front was a different story. For her dad, having a kid simply meant being part of the minor hockey ecosystem. Girl, boy, it didn't make any difference. Penny being the fourth in line was just the last and youngest of the kids to go through the system.

Penny's mother had a different outlook. A reluctant hockey mom at the best of times, her mother had not found many reasons in the last decade of having 3 boys in the sport to let go of her reservations about having her kids participating. A view that girls should be sugar and spice and everything nice further didn't line up with her only daughter participating in such a rough sport. When Penny first told her parents that she wanted to join the female league, her father had just asked when the registration was. Her mom had disappeared to her bedroom and cried.

Penny's brothers were the ones who really stepped up to help Penny's hockey career. Paul, nearly a draft pick in the CHL, would run shooting drills with her when he had time. Pat, Penny's oldest brother though, was still trying to figure out who he was after his own hockey career had abruptly ended the previous season. Pat drove Penny to her practices and gave her frank criticism after each one on things to improve upon. Pat made sure he and Penny went to at least two open rink sessions each week to work on skating and conditioning skills. And Pat spent as much time as Penny at Mr. Bennet's backyard rink playing pick-up and helping his sister's game evolve. Pat quickly became more of a coach to Penny than either of the ones on her team, and she listened closely to each piece of advice he gave her. If not for Pat, Penny figured her mom would probably have tapped out on her hockey dream after the one season, but Pat made sure Penny both showed up for every practice on time, and that she became one of the top rookie prospects on the team.

Penny, along with every other girl at "tryouts" had been selected to the team. She was officially a member of the South Saskatchewan Minor Hockey League Hungry Beavers. She'd seen the name at tryouts and thought it was a joke. A few of the older girls on the squad quickly taught her that, no, it wasn't a joke, but a long time throwback to when the club's major (well, only) corporate sponsor had been the Hungry Beaver Bar, and that was because one of the club's alumni parents had been assistant manager there. The veterans educated her that none of the players referred to their team by its actual name. Instead, they referred to themselves as the Beavs.

One older girl in particular, Fleur, took on helping Penny and the other rookies get used to the team. Fleur was a forward and she was in her second year with the team. She didn't get a lot of ice time but had a bubbly and outgoing personality that made her feel like a big sister to Penny and the other younger girls.

Alongside Penny in the rookie group was Penny's best friend Siobahn – Shiv – who had played Ringette with Penny and aged out at the same time. She had been the team's goalie on the ringette team, but the Beavs already had a veteran goalie so Shiv was now playing defense. Penny landed a spot on the 2nd defense line and Shiv on the 3rd. Both were paired with veterans on the team.

Penny's defensive linemate was Rebecca "Becks" Milton. Becks was a third year member of the team in her final year before she would have to "graduate" to the Junior Female league. Becks was a solidly built girl with flowing ginger hair and freckles she had yet to outgrow. Penny was fairly certain Becks vocabulary consisted of f-bombs and as few other words as possible.

There were a pair of Jessicas that found themselves paired up as forwards. Jess H and Jess M – affectionately referred to as "Jess-uh" and "Jess-mm" could have been twins with tall, lanky frames and perfectly straight long blonde hair. Between them at center was Jennifer, who went by Jenn. Jenn was a tough five-foot-nothing bull in the China shop. Her dark hair had never seen a comb in its life and her native features made her that much more ferocious when bearing down on you at full speed.

Li was a Chinese girl who was part of the rookie squad. Looking at her, you'd think that a tough breeze might blow her over, but as soon as she put on a pair of skates there was no catching her. She'd barely picked up a stick before tryouts, and had a long way to go to figure out shooting and passing. She freely shared that she pretty big in the junior figure skating community until she got banned for a season. She'd earned the ban by knocking her doubles partner off of the podium after he tripped her and they placed third in a tournament. Li's parents refused to come to any of her games, not the least of which because the partner she'd shoved off the podium had been her twin brother Xin.

And then there was Kelly Brick. Brick, or "Bricks", was appropriately the team's goalie and had held that position for her first season with the team. Bricks was a big girl who had originally been born in one of the Dutch agricultural communes in southern Saskatchewan. Her mom had married into the community after meeting her father, but divorced him and taken Kelly with her when Kelly was still a small child. Bricks grew up in her father's image though, with tough, broad shoulders and thick muscle tone. She couldn't skate to save her life and handled the puck as if it was a hot potato, but in pads she covered more of the net than anyone else and didn't seem to bother having freezing rubber slapped at her for hours on end, so that made her uniquely qualified for net anyway.

Those were Penny's people on the team. The ones she got to know and made friends with. There were ten other girls filling out the roster for the season, but Penny wouldn't get to know them that well.

Their first game had been against the league leaders from the previous season, the Big River Baronesses. It had been a blowout with Penny's team losing 11-0.

Penny had only seen about three shifts a period in that first game, and been surprised – not by the poor play of her own team – but by the poor play of the Baronesses too. She only had her brother's teams as a point for comparison, and neither team looked like the U15 Minor teams Penny had seen in the boy's league. For a group that were the defending champs, their passing and skating seemed just as choppy and broken as the Beavs' was. Despite the loss, Penny left that first game with a giant shot of confidence that having just seen the "best" in the league, her team may not be as far behind as her coach made them out to be.

The Beav's second game Penny got her first penalty. Coming onto her shift with a 3-3 tie at the beginning of the 3rd period, the Beav's had set up a good puck cycle in the opposing zone and were looking dangerous. Penny missed a pass back to her spot on the point and the puck caromed off the boards towards center ice and the empty rink behind it. Penny dug her skates in and raced towards it, seeing a flash of the other team's red jerseys in her peripheral vision. Knowing she wouldn't win the race, Penny dove forward, reaching with her stick and managed to poke check the puck across the blue line and towards her team's goalie – but more importantly away from the stick of the opposing forward beside her. As she executed the poke check, the other skater planted a skate squarely atop Penny's stick and tripped, going down and just catching herself with her hands in time to avoid a full faceplant. There were conflicting cheers from Penny's bench and roars of disapproval from the opposing bench. As Penny got to her feet, she saw the black-and-white striped referee skating towards her, pointing to the penalty box. She made a downward motion with her arm as if picking snow up off the ice, indicating the penalty was for tripping.

Penny skated over to the penalty box, which one of the parent volunteers already had open. She sat, breathing hard, with the blade of her stick pressed up against the glass and a knot of apprehension in her stomach as the power play she had given the other team unfolded.

The goal came late in the power play. Bricks had been on her back after making a pair of saves and there was a scramble for a loose puck in front of the net. The other team had gotten a stick on it and put it up and over the goalie to score. Penny skated back to the bench with her head hung low. She caught her coach's reproachful glare as she got back to the bench and felt worse. She was surprised a moment later when Fleur came onto the bench off the PK team. She patted Penny on the helmet. "Don't feel bad!" Fleur said with her usual energy. "Yes, maybe you could have kept the puck in the zone but once it was out, that penalty stopped a goal. It was the right play to make." Penny didn't look up but felt a lot better. Until the final buzzer went and she realized she had lost her team the game.

The locker room was quiet after that game. Penny caught several glances from her teammates in her direction while they sat and cooled off. The coach leaned against the wall reading something on her phone. The silence overwhelmed Penny and she stood up.

"Look everyone, I know I lost us the game. I'm sorry." Penny blurted out in a rush. "I made a dumb move and I'll do better next time." She then sat down and hung her head. She was preparing herself for the jokes, or the jeers, or insults for her mistake. Anything but what happened.

"Sorry everyone, I lost us the game." Fleur said, standing. "I missed that open net back in the 2nd period. Sorry."

Penny and the other players were raising their heads now as a new wave of energy shot through the room.

"I'm sorry everyone. I should have stopped that 2nd shot." Bricks said.

"I shouldn't have taken that penalty in the first." Jess H. added.

Laughter rippled through the room and one by one everyone in the room offered a reason why they had lost the game. The last few explanations were drowned out by an uncontrollable fit of giggles from the room.

When it had at last died down the coach leaned forward from the wall and put her phone down. "Alright everyone sit down. Now that we've shown that we're all Spartacus, the takeaway from today is that **no one person** can win or lose a game for us. Win, lose, or tie, this team succeeds or fails as a unit." That elicited another round of giggles. "Grow up. We're all going to make mistakes and nobody here is so talented or untalented they can single handedly decide the outcome. If any of you had that illusion coming into today, check your egos at the door next time because it isn't true. Now get your gear off and go home to think about that." The coach left at that point to go do whatever coaches have to do after a game is over, leaving the room with the simmer giggle train dying down, but the players looking awkwardly at one another.

"OK!" Shiv finally shouted at the room. "That was some real kum-bai-ya wax-on, wax-off mojo, but someone here want to tell me just who the hell Spartacus is?"

The rest of Penny's first season with the team had lots of ups and downs, wins and losses. Some of those are stories in their own right for another day. But when Penny looked back on her first season it was that locker room confessional session that took the Beavs from being a group of girls playing together to a team for the first time. Penny thinks about that moment a lot more than she ever thinks about the missed play or her first penalty.

2. First Goal

Penny Davies of the South Saskatchewan Minor Hockey League had a problem. It was December, a full two months into her first season with the Hungry Beavers (the Beavs) and Penny was the only girl on the team who hadn't scored yet, goalies aside of course.

Penny played defense and that didn't give her the best opportunities to put the puck in the net, but Penny felt, and her teammates regularly reinforced, that this was no excuse. It didn't help that every other defender on the team had managed to find the back of the net by now. Nor did it help that her best friend on the team and fellow rookie defender Siobahn, Shiv as she went by on the ice, had scored in her second game and managed to tally up a total of 5 goals already.

Penny on the other hand had over forty shots on goal to this point but was still sitting with the ugly *zero* in the goals column of her stat card.

Penny had been a solid point producer on her ringette team before joining the SSMHL and the Beavs. She had regularly found the net and landed a full dozen goals in her last ringette season before aging out of the league that operated in her hometown. And it wasn't that Penny had a bad shot either. She wasn't the hardest shooter, but she *was* accurate at hitting the net and decently skilled at putting the puck where she wanted it to go. She just wasn't getting the puck past the goalie.

Pat, Penny's brother, had assured her it was nothing to worry about. "When I was in U16," he told her driving her home one day, "I put up thirty-two goals." Penny had heard this fact many times and rolled her eyes.

"Uh-huh." She said, not feeling any better.

"Well what I *don't* talk about is I went fourteen games that season *without* a goal. In a row." Penny had to admit she hadn't heard that part of the story before. "Yeah, right in the middle I just couldn't find the back of the net to save my life."

"What'd you do to finally break the streak of bad luck?" Penny asked.

Pat assumed a sly look. "Ok this is going to sound pretty stupid so don't go sharing this around."

"No promises." Penny replied. "If it doesn't work, guaranteed I am making sure the world knows."

"Cold." Pat observed. "But fair." He took a deep breath as if considering the ultimatum then continued. "When you tape your stick you tape it the same way, right? Every time?"

"Yeah, just like dad taught me." Penny nodded. "Why?"

"Well, when I was in my drought, my coach told me to wrap my stick backwards."

"That's it?" Penny asked, incredulously.

"Yep. The dumbest part of it? It worked. I wrapped my stick backward and **the same day** I scored twice."

"Do you still do it?" Penny asked, still disbelieving.

"No." Pat said. "I did it for three or four games then once I felt the slump was over I went back to the old way of doing it."

"I'll have to try that." Penny nodded.

The next game however, Penny forgot about the advice until well into the first period. She skated onto the bench after ringing a wrister from the point off the cross bar and remembered Pat's advice. In her mind, she kicked herself for the oversight. Coach mom 1 came over while she was sitting on the bench. "It's just a case of the yips." She told Penny. "Just keep tossing the puck at the net, it'll find its way home and then things will go back to normal."

"The what?" Penny asked.

"Just call it a case of nerves." The coach said. "Lots of athletes go through slumps, you're just having a tough start this season."

"Thanks, Coach." Penny replied, mimicking the short Rastafarian from the movie *Cool Runnings*. Coach patted her helmet hard on her head, completing the scene.

Penny took the intermission to unwrap her existing tape job as quickly as she could, and then retape in the opposite direction. Instead of starting with the tip and ending at the foot of the blade, she wrapped foot-to-tip. It was awkward going since she had never, not once, in her entire life done

13

this task this way, but she managed to get it finished by the time the team had to go back on the ice. Granted, it looked like a kindergartner had done the tape job and there were spots of exposed blade in some areas and big uneven blobs of folded tape in others, but at least it was done. And most importantly as Penny stepped out onto the ice, she felt *different*. She was very conscious of the new tape job and how it made her stick feel on the ice.

Her first shift of that second period Penny felt less comfortable on the ice than she had in years. She suddenly felt like her body's natural motions skating and handling the puck were all wrong. Everywhere she stepped it felt like the freshly resurfaced ice wanted to give way under her blades and make her fall. Her stick felt like some extra limb that weighed and dragged at her as she struggled to keep her body upright. Her "hockey brain", the zone she got into mentally which let her keep up with the game and the players around her, was totally shut off and Penny nearly ran into other players at least twice that shift.

Back on the bench, she shook her head violently trying to clear her mind of the discomfort she'd just felt on the ice. Her mind was running through all the mistakes she'd made. She started to feel dizzy and realized she was breathing in deep heaving breaths. She became aware of Fleur shaking her shoulder.

"Are you ok?" Fleur demanded for the third time.

Penny finally looked over at her. "I'm." She took a deep breath. "Okay." And then took another breath, as if the entire effort of saying the single work had exhausted all the oxygen she had in her body.

"Bullshit." Fleur glared. "You look like you're about to faint." At Fleur's insistence Penny sat down on the short bench behind the other players. Fleur sat down beside her. The two moms coaching the team saw this and started to come over, concerned looks on their faces, but Fleur shot them a look that kept them where they were.

"Ok Pens, just take it easy for a minute." Fleur directed.

"Feels like I can't breathe." Penny gasped.

"Stop trying so hard." Fleur commanded. "Small, short breaths." She demonstrated, looking like she was about to have a baby in the process. "Now you." She told Penny.

Penny fought her body's desire to suck in as much oxygen as fast as possible, and did her best to mimic Fleur's breathing.

"Now count to three in between each breath." Fleur instructed once Penny had more or less got down the first part. Penny did as she was told, clearly struggling less with this step than the first step. "That's good," Fleur observed. After another few seconds she asked again, "Are you ok now?"

Penny locked eyes with her and Fleur saw resolve there. "Yes." Penny replied. "I'm ready to go again." She didn't seem to be struggling to breathe anymore and Fleur stood up and patted her on the helmet.

"Good cause it looks like your D-line is almost up." There was a whistle and sure enough the coaches signaled a line change. Penny got ready to hit the ice, Fleur tapped her again, "Remember your number one job out there is keeping pucks *out* of our net." She gave Penny as playful smack across the numbers and Penny was off.

Back on the ice Penny still didn't feel comfortable. Her stick still felt like a giant caveman club she was dragging around with her, but her feet were doing what they were supposed to again and she could tell her game sense was coming back.

She came on shift to a faceoff in her own zone that Becks lost. The other team started to pass the puck around their end of the ice and Penny saw their center was looping around to get loose in front of the net. The rest of her squad had been pinned against the boards trying to tie up members of the opposing team. The puck came loose from the corner and slid towards the opposing center who was just getting to the front of the net waiting for it.

Penny was already on the way. She skated as much *through* as *past* the center, bumping her hip in the process and knocking her aside. Penny grabbed the puck and looked for someone to pass it to but found nothing but… a wide sheet of open ice between her and the opposing goalie.

"SHOOT!" She could hear the coaches shouting from the bench and Penny did. She dug her skates in hard and pushed off, skating with the might of all the expectations she and her team had on her. She sped out of her own zone and into the neutral zone. In her peripheral vision a defender had broken free and was trying to catch her, but the defender was skating up the boards and Penny could already tell she wasn't going to have the speed to get to her before Penny reached the net.

Penny focused ahead of her as she crossed center and approached the other blue line. She locked eyes with the other goalie, who was already in her ready position aggressively forward of her net. She was smiling and Penny wanted nothing more than to wipe that smirk off her face with the puck. Penny deked right and the goalie shifted her body to the right.

Penny deked left, cutting hard and spending some of her lead on the defender still racing to catch up to her. The goalie came left, skating back a few feet to the edge of her crease, eyes still locked on Penny's. And that was Penny's advantage she realized.

Penny deked a final time as she came up to the left hash mark and cut back to the right. She lined up a point blank slap shot and the goalie's body slid across the net matching her perfectly. The goalie froze as Penny stopped and slapped her stick against the ice letting the slap shot go. The goalie followed where Penny's stick was aiming and got her glove up with lightning speed.

And that was when the puck Penny had *not* carried into the third deke or fake slap shot with her slid across the goal line and into the net. The referee whistled, the red goal light came on and the goose honk of the goal horn sounded. Penny stood disbelieving for a second but then her teammates caught up with her and she was swallowed in a surging huddle of bodies around her.

"You finally did it!"

"What a goal!"

"You didn't even have to shoot!"

Her teammates erupted in praise and hugged her and patted her helmet and back. Jenn gave her a shove from behind and Penny started skating, seeing her team leaning over the bench with their hands stretched out expectantly.

The world caught up with Penny and she let out a massive, animal *roar* of relief and accomplishment. "Yeeessssss!!!!" She skated past her bench bumping fists with all of her excited teammates and made sure to loop around to catch Bricks' outstretched hand at her team's blue line.

The coaches signaled for a line change and Penny skated off the ice. As she passed Fleur coming off the ice, Fleur pumped her fist in the air and called out, "Knew you could do it!"

Coach mom 1 came over when she was back on the bench and leaned over, telling Penny "There we go! The hard part is over! Way to show those yips who's the boss!"

Penny nodded and thanked her. She looked back and out into the stands. Pat was sitting in his usual seat in a row just above the height of the glass. He was smiling and when she looked at him he flashed her a loud thumbs up. *Proud of you, kiddo.* Penny could almost hear him saying in her head.

At the intermission, Penny ripped the tape off her stick as quickly as she could and retaped it the proper way. It had served its purpose and now it was just screwing with her mind too much having it taped wrong. As she went through the *very familiar* process of retaping it the *right* way, she finally felt a wave of relief and gratitude wash over her. Her drought was over. She'd done it.

That wouldn't be the only time in her life Penny would experience the yips. Every few years she'd find that something that used to be second nature would just abruptly become difficult. Usually it went along with there being a lot riding on the outcome of things – like an exam or an important promotion at work. But after that first experience, Penny knows now what to look for and how to beat them. Learning about the pattern early will over time become one of the most important *life* lessons Penny will take away from her hockey career.

3. Paul's Broken Arm

When Penny was young her older brother Paul broke his arm. Not that there was anything too exceptional about that. Penny grew up with 3 older brothers, all of them played hockey, and so someone was always in a splint, cast, or sporting a shiner. Injuries were part of the reality of Penny's upbringing, and it usually fell to Penny to play nurse and maid to her brothers while they were recovering from their latest sacrifice to the altar of ice and puck.

To Penny, these were some of her favorite times with her brothers. When they were healthy, they had practices to go to and friends to see and school to get to and they spent their remaining free time over at the neighborhood rink. Busy boys with busy lives who found it easy to overlook a baby sister who idolized them and just wanted to spend time with them. But when they were injured, Penny got them all to herself. Penny loved the long lazy evenings of Disney movies and board games that came with one of her brothers being injured.

But the *best* parts were when she could get them to tell her about their hockey lives. When Penny was really lucky, she'd get to spend the evenings or weekends with the injured brother listening to them tell her stories about their games, about the great and awful people they'd played with and played against, and the grand excitement of their victories over the years. After Pat broke his arm, this was how Penny found out about what happened and how it had changed his and Paul's hockey careers forever.

Pat and Paul were eighteen months apart in age. Pat was eldest and Paul was younger. Peter was a full 3 years younger than Paul, and then Penny was the youngest another 2 years down. The two eldest brothers had always shared a special bond. They weren't twins, but Paul had grown up faster than Pat so since Paul was about 5 the two had been roughly the same height. Both had their mom's happy, rounded face and their dad's glacial blue eyes. The two were also close enough in age that Pat couldn't remember life without Paul in it, although he could remember what it had been like when it was just him, Paul and their parents before the other kids were born.

The age gap meant that Pat and Paul had been inseparable at home. When Peter came around they would come up with all sorts of imaginative games and tricks to play on their young sibling. When Peter was just learning to speak for example, the two had corrected him every time he said "please" to "cheese", such that well into his fourth year Peter would innocently walk about asking for "more food cheese" or "can I play with my brothers cheese?"

When Pat started playing Timbits, Paul wanted to come to every one of his games and couldn't wait to start playing just like his big brother. In the meantime, their parents got Paul a pair of kids skates and let him and Pat spend just about as much time as they wanted with Mr. Davies over at Bennet's backyard rink. Mrs. Davies was pregnant with Peter at that time so it was a good excuse to get the boys out of her hair and burning off some energy.

Paul was almost as slow at learning to skate as his brother had been, but between Pat and Mr. Davies' eager and patient instruction he got it figured out. Paul had a shot that could rattle the boards though. From the first time he stepped out on the ice the kid had the ability to hit the puck hard enough to make everyone below a ten-year old duck out of the way. And sure enough, Paul joined the minor hockey program as soon as he was able to, too.

The two started ending up on the same team when Pat was 9 and Paul was 7, when they both were on the same U10 team together. This happened twice but only lasted for a year each time before Pat aged out and into the next division. Paul was a star forward on every team, even in his rookie years. His shot only improved over time, and as his skating lessons progressed he got faster too.

Pat was a workhorse defenseman who didn't have any outstanding skills but worked hard and had enough body mass to give the other team a hard time. When the two were on the team together, Pat acted as Paul's personal bodyguard throwing himself completely at anyone who came near his younger brother. In those years, Paul was able to put up incredible numbers as his speed and shot were able to be used freely without being pestered by the other team.

The two were on the same U16 team for the last time when Pat turned 16 and aged out. Paul, 15, had one year left with the team when his brother was done. Pat hadn't made the cut in the junior draft and that effectively meant his career was over. Paul on the other hand, was a solid prospect and in his draft year. There were rumors that the Saskatoon Blades and the Moose Jaw Warriors of the CHL/WHL had their eye on him for the entry draft at the end of that season. Paul joked that he'd rather quit playing than go to Moose Jaw, but that was just an act to avoid giving on that he was really excited about any draft possibilities.

Pat made getting his brother into the draft his main focus after aging out himself. He went to almost all of Paul's games and they would work together after on skills. Pat started taking videos of Paul's games on his phone and he and Paul would watch the videos and look for areas Paul needed to work on. It got to the point where Penny's parents started to get worried about Pat being *too* involved in Paul's hockey life, especially after he turned 16 and offered to start driving Paul to his games once he got his license. But it did make life easier on the family, and it didn't seem to be hurting anyone, so Pat's parents left their concerns unspoken and just appreciated the fact that their sons were so close.

They didn't need to concern themselves too long however, for Pat soon started to get focused on his own life again after successfully applying for early admission and earning a hockey scholarship to the University of Regina. Pat might not have made the draft for Major Juniors, but apparently his play and academic transcript were sufficient to earn him a place with the UofR Cougars. His parents were both thrilled, and Pat himself was very happy even if he did feel a little bit like it was a consolation prize.

This set the stage for "the incident". Penny's family would only ever describe it as such. Her parents refused to give Penny or Peter any of the details of what went down. Pat had *never* told her what had happened, and it was only after his second surgery on his arm and under the influence of some strong painkillers that Paul let the story slip.

The incident occurred in Paul's first game back after Christmas when he was still 15 and playing for the U16 squad. Pat had brought him to the game and there was nothing special about that particular game. Paul had been having a solid game, already with 2 goals and his team was on a lengthy 5 on 3 power play with Paul firing away at center.

The hit came late, late enough to earn the other team's defender a 10-minute major and game misconduct. Paul had been lining up a redirect on a point shot that was fluttering towards the net at waist level. The defender that had been covering Paul apparently decided to completely ignore his covered player and try to play the puck. In a move as dumb as it was dangerous, the defender made a baseball bat swing with his own stick, trying to bat the puck out of midair and apparently earn a home run at the same time. Both he and Paul missed the puck, which the goalie managed to deflect up and out of play, but Paul would never see the result of the play.

The defender's stick missed the puck and followed through directly into Paul's forearm. There was a sickening *crack* sound even louder than the sound of the puck impacting the goalie's pad at the same time. The defender's stick broke in two places and the blade and center of the shaft flew apart, leaving the defender holding a comically tiny handle with no stick attached to it.

Paul screamed and collapsed to the ice. He rolled onto his back and cradled the injured arm, though that just seemed to make the pain worse. He writhed in utter agony, "ugly crying" as Paul self-described the moment.. The trainer and one of his assistant coaches rushed off the bench and assessed him while the on-ice officials conferenced and ultimately gave the other player the misconduct penalty.

Pat had rushed to the glass and was pressing his face worriedly against the clear pane. He had broken an arm playing the game several seasons back, though through his own misadventure and not the actions of anyone else. From the glass at ice level Pat could easily see that it wasn't a good scene. The trainer had Paul's helmet and gloves off and was shaking her head gravely at the bench. She made the gesture for the team to alert the rink staff they needed to get an ambulance to come bring the player out of the building immediately. Pat's stomach dropped to his toes and he felt like the arena started to spin around him.

Pat hurried out of the spectator area and around to where the dressing rooms were. He got there as Paul was being helped out of the chute and towards the locker room. He hurried forward to help, taking over from the assistant coach holding Paul's shoulder on the uninjured side.

"Is he ok?" He asked the trainer anxiously.

"He can't keep playing in this game," the trainer answered flatly. "He needs to be seen by a doctor for a proper assessment. There should already be an ambulance on the way."

Together they managed to get Paul onto a bench in the locker room and get his skates off and shoes on. The trainer gave him some painkillers to swallow. He had stopped howling but was still crying and regularly wincing whenever he shifted his weight and moved his arm. He had mostly caught his breath though, and at least seemed to be ok other than his arm. The trainer wrapped an ice pack around his arm and then used a bandage to affix arm and ice in place across his chest. She then instructed both Pat and Paul that they were going to go meet the ambulance.

Pat got up and opened the door, holding it while Paul and the trainer walked through. She held the elbow of his good arm and guided him, but he was able to move his feet and walk on his own now. Pat followed them out and for the first time saw the other player skulking around the hallway. It was the member of the opposing team who'd been given the misconduct and been responsible for Paul's injury. They were going to have to walk past him to exit the corridor and get out to the ambulance.

He was walking towards the trio now. "Look, I wanted to say I'm sorry." He muttered. "I didn't mean to injure you."

Paul gritted his teeth and nodded at the other player as they walked past. But the player reached out and grabbed Paul's shoulder... the shoulder of his injured arm... and started to say, "I really mean it," but a howl of pain from Paul cut him off at the first syllable.

The trainer tugged Paul away from the other player and hurried him out the hallway, glaring behind them.

Pat grabbed the boy by his jersey with both hands and slammed him backwards into the wall of the hallway.

"We get it." Pat growled. "You're sorry. No shit. You make a dumbass move and his season could be over, you deserve a lot more than a misconduct." He released the boy and stepped back, taking a breath.

Except the other player then shoved Pat, hard. "Think I don't know that?" There were tears in his eyes. "It was an *accident*." He pounded a fist in frustration against Pat's chest.

Pat has only ever said that he doesn't remember the next few moments, and Paul had been led out of the hallway and hadn't witnessed what came next. The other boy's version of events was that Pat "went totally Donkey Kong apeshit" on him. Pat had grabbed the kid's jersey and pulled it over his unhelmeted head, and then landed several blows against the kid's face while his jersey was over his head. The other boy claims he didn't have a chance to fight back, but Pat ended up with a split lip and black eye that took nearly two weeks to heal.

When the paramedics arrived, they were just loading the player with the broken arm into the back of the ambulance when two other boys about the same age appeared. One wasn't wearing a jersey and was bleeding from the lip and had an eye swollen to the point he couldn't open it anymore. The other was in a jersey that would never be white again, gushing blood from his nose and mouth and holding at least four teeth in his fist although he could've been missing more than that even. The paramedics shared a look with the trainer who looked as clueless and dumbfounded as they were at the bonus arrivals. In the end, the trio traveled as a group to the hospital, leaving the trainer behind and keeping one paramedic in the back to act as a chaperone.

The fallout from the incident was messy. Most of it Penny was oblivious to, although she knew that there were important hockey meetings both brothers and Mr. and Mrs. Davies had to go to over the next few weeks. In the end, what Penny did know was that Paul had suffered a double compound fracture of his arm. Initially there'd been some hope that a 6-8 week recovery might let him rejoin the team for the playoffs or at least be healthy by draft time. But his arm did not heal well and he needed two surgeries in the end to re-set the bones and put pins and rods in place to help with the remodeling. He was in recovery for the better part of 8 months. After that, he had also aged out of U16 and missed his draft window. He also had a strong medical recommendation to avoid contact sports for the rest of his life, given how long his body had taken to heal from this round of injuries. Hockey career over.

Pat got it both easier and harder. Pat's eye and lip healed in a couple of weeks and he wasn't very laid up while they did. The other kid's parents had pushed for charges against Pat because Pat wasn't an active player when the situation occurred. The other kid had permanently lost two teeth and also had to miss several of the remaining games of the season. The minor hockey league tried to wash their hands of any involvement, but ultimately stepped in and put forward a deal everyone could live with. Penny didn't know the specifics, but Pat didn't end up going to Juvie, instead he just had to talk to an anger management counselor once a week for a few months. The league, however, also reported the incident to the University sports authority including their recommendation for a lifetime ban from post secondary leagues for Pat. The University hockey authority didn't enforce their recommendation, but the UofR did pull Pat's scholarship offer. Hockey career also over.

Mrs. Davies would regularly point to this event as an "I told you this would happen" moment in every argument for the next decade. Both of her boys no longer able to play because of the stupid violent culture of the game. Quietly, she would express relief that they were no longer in the system and could focus on "real prospects for their lives" now, although she didn't hesitate to bring up the incident any time she needed to win an argument with another member of the Davies clan.

Mr. Davies was more torn. On the one hand Pat had clearly been out of line, but he'd stepped up to defend his kid brother who'd already been injured. His biggest concern was that Pat had never been able to provide a clear retelling of the event, in his own defense or otherwise, which left Mr. Davies with a nagging feeling that something more might've happened than what the other boy and his family claimed. Nonetheless, both boys were done their hockey lives. Peter didn't have the affinity for the game that his elder brothers did and was already talking about not going back in the fall. Only Penny, still happily in the relative safety of the Ringette world, remained. Her desire to play was clear, but it was going to be that much harder for his wife to get on board with Penny ever picking up a hockey stick after what happened to her brothers.

Nevertheless, Mr. Davies and his boys still strap on their skates every Sunday while Mrs. Davies prepares the Sunday night feast for the family, and they go play pickup at Mr. Bennett's rink a few doors down. There's nothing at stake, no drafts or scouts or rankings to worry about, just three boys of different ages with ice, a puck, and a stick holding them together.

4. Pond Hockey

Two doors down from Penny lived Mr. Bennet. Mr. Bennet had been in the neighborhood since before Penny's family had moved in. When they had first moved, Mr. Bennet still had his two sons living with him, who were a few years older than Pat and Paul. Nowadays both boys are off at school and Mr. Bennet lives alone. He is a quiet widower who is equally famous for his lifelong presidency of the neighborhood Block Watch program and for the backyard hockey rink he builds every year.

Mr. Bennet's backyard rink was a thing of local legend. *Everyone* knew about the time his son's Junior team had been locked out of their arena and ended up playing the opposing team in his back yard. Everyone knew that the league officials used samples of Mr. Bennet's ice to test the quality of the community rink against. And of course, everyone knows the infamous story of how Mr. Bennet converted his John Deer riding mower into a home sized Zamboni which he rides daily all winter keeping the rink's surface perfect for kids in the neighborhood to play pickup on.

Mr. Bennet's rink was a thing you had to be impressed with. Complete with half-height boards, painted blue lines and a center faceoff circle, and with hand-drilled net peg holes, Mr. Bennet's rink was the place for kids in the neighborhood. And Mr. Bennet, for his part, couldn't he happier with that arrangement. As common as the sight of kids playing shinny in the back yard was Mr. Bennet leaning over the boards, watching the game with a steaming thermos of coffee in his hands and his worn "Quebec Nordiques" toque on.

Penny figured she had spent as many hours over the years learning the game on Mr. Bennet's rink as she had in actual arenas. It was where she first started to understand the etiquette and rules of the game not written down in the rulebook. Mr. Bennet's rink followed a strict hierarchy for protecting players. With everyone from 16-year old AA leaguers to 6 year old Timbits kids still learning to skate, and mostly all playing at the same time, you had to learn how to play while watching out for the little guy. The older, bigger players would defer to playing defense or goal when there were younger kids there. You wouldn't check someone smaller than you unless they started in on you first. Everyone took turns digging pucks out of the snow or out of the alley, and you never told someone they couldn't play if they showed up with skates, a helmet and a stick.

With no referees, battles on Mr. Bennet's ice were free of the incumbrance of rules and stoppages that slowed down arena games. The game established a flow and life that meant you could get more ice time over the course of an hour as an entire game at the arena. The game also followed a natural law that put every player in the role of an official and enforcer.

Penny remembered with painful embarrassment the time she'd hip checked Kevin Miller, a full 2 years her junior even if he was a boy and built like a farmer. He'd gone over the boards and into the snow pack of Mr. Bennet's yard. Penny hadn't fully appreciated what had just happened and was carrying on with the play, but instantly all the other players stopped and split off – some coming at her shouting and the others hurrying over to check on Kevin.

Penny got a stern lecture from one of Paul's teammates who'd been on the ice that day. She had a responsibility for the safety of everyone, on her team and not, whenever she stepped on the ice. Penny, red faced and hot with shame, had skated over to where Kevin had just been pulled back over the boards. He was assuring the other skaters around him that he was ok, though Penny could see he was breathing hard and sniffling back any more tears than were already streaming down his cheeks. Penny went up to apologize, but Kevin locked eyes with her and glared. "This isn't over." He told her before she could start.

A few minutes later, Penny picked up a pass from one of her teammates. She had turned her head to watch where the pass was coming from, and as soon as she felt the puck hit the tape on her stick, she looked back forward… just in time to see the arm coming at her. She looked away and took the blow to the side of her helmet, but the clothesline hit was enough to knock her flat on her back and completely wind her. She gasped, greedily gulping in air while her brain caught up with what happened. Then Kevin's face appeared above her, inches away from her own. For a terrifying moment Penny thought he was going to kiss her while she was helpless, but then he said "now we're even", before wiping the icy palm of his glove over her face in the universal sign of disrespect between hockey players.

Mr. Bennet's ice had been host to hundreds – thousands probably – of these lessons over the years. Not just for Penny either. She was just one of the many skaters to have crossed his ice

Whenever kids, or later adults, who have skated on Bennet's ice get together off the ice, the most lively discussions center around what has been the "most epic" game ever played on Bennet's rink. It was an impossible task to decide, considering the nearly 20 years of skater's of all ages that had used Bennet's rink, but that didn't make the debates any less lively, or less entertaining.

Penny knew that for her, it was an easy question. And there was no debate. Halloween when she was fourteen. It hadn't been anything anyone had *organized*, nothing on Bennet's rink had ever been formal enough for that word to apply. Far as anyone could remember, someone gave up early on their trick or treat route and had grabbed their their skate bag with and stopped by to practice some shots. Someone else heard the puck and the sound of skates on ice and decided to join and well, by the time Penny got there the rink was going full tilt with enough costumed skaters to be running two full teams with benched players tagging on and off every few minutes.

The teams had loosely aligned to the costumes. One side was clearly the "scary" costumes. Notable contributors were a couple zombies, a vampire, werewolf, two young kids in matching Frankenstein costumes and masks, and the goalie… on point in a Jason Vorhees mask, though machete traded for a more useful goalie stick. The other side were the fun or sexy group. Nurses, firefighters, police, Ninja turtles and even a throwback to the 80's classic Rainbow Brite. Penny had been dressed as a witch although the flowing black dress could have been any number of things since she lost the distinctive had in favor of her helmet.

Like all the most memorable games, the score wasn't something Penny could remember, and it didn't matter. What mattered were the memories. Penny remembered with particular enjoyment the moment when Rainbow Brite and a teenage boy dressed in a "sexy nurse" costume got a breakaway from the Frankenstein twins and had put one top shelf over Voorhees' shoulder. As the players had started celebrating there was a roar of applause and whistles and all the players had stopped to look over at the commotion. They found that Bennet's yard was filled with the parents of the players, some in costume, some not, but all cheering and whistling for their kid with enthusiasm they never got to show at their games.

When the players finally called it a game and began to leave the ice, it began to snow slightly and the reunion of child and parent took on a decidedly festive feel to it. Most people who were there that night didn't get home until will past eleven. Mr. Bennet had fired up his hot chocolate maker and started passing drinks around in little Styrofoam coffee cups, complete with the necessary mini marshmallows. An entire generation of neighborhood players gathered with their families, sipping hot chocolate in the snow, laughing and talking about the game they loved. That was what Penny would always consider the best game on Mr. Bennet's rink.

5. Goon

Penny's gloved hand tightened around her stick. She stole another quick glance at the clock. Three minutes gone already in the first period. Becks and her first D line had been pinned in the Beavs' zone while Bricks faced shot after shot from the 'Snakes, who had managed to fit in two line changes already. Another quick glance at the score clock told Penny that Bricks had managed 8 saves already. She gripped her stick tighter and gritted her teeth. Penny could tell that Becks and the first line were exhausted. They'd stopped moving their feet and were relying on wide, lazy sweeps of their sticks to try and deflect the puck out of the zone or out of play long enough to get their first line change in.

Another shot and Bricks came up with a lightning-fast glove save to shut down the scoring chance. She Immediately huddled down into a protective ball in front of the goal after catching the puck, leaving no question she was looking for a stoppage. The ref blew the play dead, and there was a solid ka-chunk sound as both teams' bench doors were pulled open for a line change.

Penny was first on the ice from the second line. She skated towards Becks who was slowly making her way to the bench, breathing hard. Suddenly in a blur of white and orange, Becks was on her back and Fleur, who'd been skating off behind her, tripped over Becks' fallen form and went down awkwardly next to her. There was a roar of anger from behind her and Penny's brain caught up with what had happened. Regina Rattlesnakes player 14, the big girl who played point on their second D line, had skated through the ranks of exiting Beavs and shouldered Becks to the ice as she'd skated past.

The referee, who had been collecting the puck from Bricks, turned back to see what had happened, but too late. By the time she took in the scene both Beavs players were getting back to their feet and the offending player 14 was hopping onto her bench.

Penny clenched her jaw tighter and skated over to her spot next to her net, glaring over at the offending player on the Snakes bench while she waited for the rest of the players to get in position for the faceoff. That had been a dirty move. Two of her teammates could easily have been injured in there. And 14's consequences had been…what? It looked like the worst she was facing was some pats on the back and laughs at the Beavs' expense.

No. The word resonated through Penny's mind and body like an electrical current. No. That wouldn't do. Penny thought back to all the scrimmages on Mr. Bennet's rink and she knew what the natural law of the game demanded after a play like that. Through the blood pounding in her ears, she almost missed the puck coming free towards her after the faceoff. Penny hit it on instinct, much harder than she meant to, and the puck sailed down the ice clear of her zone and along the far boards. One of the Snakes players skated out to retrieve it and the ref whistled the Icing call. Penny cringed and gave an apologetic look across to her linemate, who shrugged in response. *It happens.* Penny could almost hear Shiv saying in her mind.

The next faceoff led to a drawn-out battle along the boards. Penny had a stick on the puck and wedged her body between it and a pair of Snakes who jostled her relentlessly and jabbed at the puck with their sticks. Penny could see Shiv a few feet away – unmarked by any opponents – but couldn't get her stick loose to make the pass.

"MOVE." The nearest linesman shouted. Meaning the puck.

Frustration welled up in Penny as one of the Snakes slashed her stick out of her hands. Penny felt a red haze descend over her. She planted her feet as close to the puck as she could to protect it while she bent down to retrieve her stick… except she didn't. Instead, from the half crouch she launched herself upwards, straightening as she did, towards the two Snakes that had been pressuring her.

Penny felt the top of her helmet collide solidly with the front cage of one of the other girls and she was rewarded by a shriek of surprise as Penny's hands came up a second later and shoved the girl – hard. Penny also came down hard, landing on the heels of her skates and falling over backwards, though she was pleased to see that *both* Snakes players had gone down together in a messy heap of gear. The puck now lay in an empty no-man's land between the two sets of fallen players, and Shiv was already getting her stick overtop her fallen linemate to grab it and start a rush up the ice.

Penny got to her feet and watched her team race up the ice on an unexpected 4 on 3. It was the Beavs' first offense of the game. Shiv got the puck up quickly to Jess H., who carried it over the center line and sent a fast cross ice pass over to Jess M. Jess M. made a nice move around the Snakes defender on her side of the ice and with one player from each team tangled up at the blue line that left the Beavs with a 3 on 1.

Jess M. passed it back to Jess H. who carried it behind the net and then popped a quick pass out to the slot in front of the Snakes' goal. Jenn was waiting and connected solidly on the one-timer, sending the puck hurtling towards the Snakes' goal. Their goalie managed to get an arm up and deflected the shot out of play with her stick-side blocker. The whistle went.

Penny heard the ka-chunk of the bench doors opening and saw her line was being summoned for a change. She hurried off the ice and onto the bench.

"Pens!" She heard someone shout her nickname. Penny leaned forward over the edge of the boards to see who was yelling at her. Jess H was trying to get her attention. "Nice play! They never saw you coming!"

Penny smiled, but it didn't last long. There was a loud, rattling crunch from the ice and Penny looked over to see the Snakes' 14 picking up the puck from a crumpled teammate who was down on the ice and whose number Penny couldn't see. A moment later there was a whistle, and the referee was skating over to 14 for a conference. The call was body checking, and 14 was sent off to the penalty box for 2 minutes of "quiet contemplation". Penny smiled at hockey karma catching up with the big player.

That left Penny's team on the power play and Penny wasn't on either power play line that game. She positioned herself on the bench so she could open the D-side door when her teammates were changing lines. Her team managed to put up four shots on the power play, but the game remained tied 0-0 when Penny's next shift started.

She lined up for a faceoff to the left of the Snakes' net, taking the point position. She found herself paired up against the permanent scowl of the Snakes' number 14. Beneath the harshly arched eyebrows and steel grey eyes, 14 wore the world's biggest shit-eating grin. And she was grinning at Penny. Penny, for her part, couldn't shake the thought that 14 looked like the Joker from the Batman cartoons Peter still binge-watched sometimes.

The puck dropped. The scramble ensued. The puck squirted over to Penny's side of the ice and she found herself against the boards battling 14 for the puck. For all the other player had a size and weight advantage, it was obvious she was the less skilled of the two with her stick. Penny managed to dig the puck from her possession fairly easily and sent it across to Shiv to cycle back into play.

14 didn't like that very much. "Think you're hot shit don't you?" 14 spat across at Penny as she skated back into the play, making sure to bump shoulders – well more correctly – bump her triceps across Penny's shoulders because of the height difference – as she skated past. Penny felt the impact and stumbled on her skates from the sheer weight of the impact.

Penny got two more quick touches that shift, as the puck came to the point and she held the zone before passing it back into play, but mostly the play was over on Shiv's side and behind the net. A shot went off one of the Snakes' defender's stick and out of play and Penny was back on the bench for the rest of the period.

In the locker room, Penny listened briefly while their coach congratulated the team on holding the game to a tie as if this was some great achievement. They were told to shake off the no-calls that had happened and to keep respecting the refs and focus on playing "their game". Penny turned off at that point and when the coach was done put her headphones in and teed the next song up on her game-day playlist. The upbeat intro to Pink's "So What?" blared to life in her ears and she leaned back against the wall of the changeroom, closing her eyes for 4 minutes and letting the music wash over her. The final "ba-da ba-da-buh-bah" had barely concluded when the room around her livened as players got to their feet and readied to go back to the bench. Penny took out the headphones, stowed them in her pack, and followed the line out.

The second period started on a different tempo. The Snakes had clearly gotten a more useful message during the break than to keep playing their game, because they hit the ice with a purpose. They put up 2 quick goals and drew a delay of game penalty off Becks as a bad clearing attempt went over the glass before leaving the zone.

With Becks in the box, that promoted Penny to the first PK line. She hit the ice determined to use the opportunity to show that she could compete alongside the first liners. It did not go well. She fanned on her first attempt to clear a loose puck , instead turning it over to the Snakes' center who had a quality scoring chance Bricks had to handle. Penny skated over and patted Bricks on the head in thanks and apology.

After the faceoff, she was skating for a loose puck and caught an edge, sending herself spinning out into a heap on the ground. From there she had a fantastic view of the Rattlesnake player she'd been racing grab the puck along the boards and slide it into the net on a wraparound for the Snakes' third goal of the period.

Penny slammed her stick against the ice as she got to her feet. Her line was summoned off and she skated to the bench. The coach leaned over when she was back in the lineup and suggested that she take a seat behind the line and cool down for a minute. Penny did as she was instructed but rage welled up in her as she stepped back from the line of her teammates and sat down on the bench. She hung her head and rested her helmet on the end of her stick.

Penny looked up expectantly at the coach for the rest of the period but wasn't given the green light to get back in the lineup. Cool off apparently meant cool her heels for that shit performance on the PK. The Snakes put two more away before the end of the period, and Penny felt increasingly frustrated at her helplessness. When the buzzer rang, she shoved herself to her feet and was the first one down the chute and into the dressing room. She angrily hit the wall with her stick and threw herself down on the locker room bench. Penny unclipped her helmet and slammed it onto the ground in front of her, stuffing her gloves into it too.

The next one through the door was one of her coaches. Penny glared at her. For the first time since she'd been benched, the coach looked back with a coldly emotionless gaze.

"Are you ready to leave that little display in the second period and move on?" Coach Mom 2 demanded. Before Penny could respond the locker room door swung open and a couple of players were about to enter. "Wait there." Coach mom 2 demanded. The girls looked at each other in surprise but shut the door amidst a wave of whispers and giggles.

"Yes coach." Penny replied.

"Good. Those mistakes were sloppy and you're a better player than that. You're not here to impress us, you're here to contribute by doing your job on the ice. No more. No less. Any questions?" Her gaze

"Yes coach, I mean, no coach." Penny looked down.

"Good. Because we need you on your game in the third." The coach looked away from Penny. The door swung open again as a new group of girls tried to enter, "Yes yes come in." She said.

Penny realized she was crying and quickly wiped the tears from her eyes. Shiv came and sat beside her but didn't say anything. Penny fumbled her headphones into her ears and took herself out of the moment. Soleil's "Rise Up" followed by Destiny Child's "Survivor" helped Penny center herself. As the intermission wound down and the team headed back to the ice, she repeated the chorus of "Rise Up" to herself.

"Ri-ise up now. If you don't ev-er fall, you don't change at all. Rise up now."

Penny slid off the edge of the board and onto the ice. Her legs pumped hard and she dug her blades deeply into the ice as she joined her team on the rush. The on-the-fly d-line change had been well timed and the Beavs had caught the other team on a bad change. Penny got to the blue line just in time to pick up a rebound from the first shot. She saw her center looping around the back of the net, and the two wingers in tight coverage around the boards trying to get better position.

She passed the puck over to Shiv, who had just reached the blueline herself. Shiv skated in a circle, pulling the defender off one of the wingers and passed the puck back to Penny. Penny passed across to Jess H., and Jess picked up the pass just before a defender intercepted it. Jess H. turned quickly, protecting the puck, and dumped it blindly backwards towards the point. Jenn at Center had just gotten back into position and grabbed the puck, she deked twice before burying it behind the goalie's shoulder for the Beavs' first goal of the game.

The red light went on and the buzzer blared. The Beav players on the ice erupted in jubilation and skated together, hugging and patting each other on the back and helmet. As the group split apart Jenn threw her head back and roared (not screamed, roared) in triumph at finally having put a point on the board this match.

Penny's line was left on the ice to continue their shift after the goal, but the Snakes made a full change and Penny was once again across from 14 and that Joker-ish grinning scowl. Jess H. cleanly won the face-off and passed it back to Penny. Penny picked up the puck and saw the lumbering form of Snakes' 14 barreling towards her. She clearly had no intention of playing the puck and was aiming to "take the body" on Penny rather than try and make a play.

That was when Penny decided to ignore everything Coach had told her in the intermission. Penny spun and passed the puck *backwards*, sending it into her own zone for Bricks to pick up and play. Then, she pushed off with her foot, taking her body towards the boards, and ducked.

The move had originally been one of self-preservation. She'd hoped that the hit from 14 would avoid her head or other important body parts. Instead, the height difference caused 14 to collide with Penny's turtled body just above 14's knee pads. 14, already off-stride from the surprise back-pass and indecision whether to keep going or break off and chase the puck, went fully off-balance and fell… no… not fell… *flipped* forward overtop of Penny and went into the boards with a crunch.

Penny didn't see it but she heard the impact and felt the weight of the other player going over her and then sliding off. Penny stood up and looked back to see 14 face-down on the ice. Penny just stared for a moment. She was mutely aware of the competing jeers and cheers from the two benches at what had just happened. Penny bent down and put a hand on 14's jersey, about to ask how she was doing.

14 suddenly brought her elbow up into Penny's face cage and Penny stumbled backwards. 14 was getting to her feet, blood trickling from a cut on the bridge of her nose. She glared at Penny as a bull would glare at a matador. Penny backed away slowly, giving her space, but 14 was on her feet and coming towards her now. From the corner of her eyes Penny could see the referee whistling at the player and skating towards them, but too far away to help with what came next.

14 drew threw her gloves off and pulled a meaty fist back as far as her helmet. Penny shut her eyes and dodged to the other direction. The force behind the punch must have been intense because it threw 14 fully off her skates. She missed Penny entirely and her body followed her fist in a downward arc all the way to the ground. Penny took a breath but the referee was now on top of 14 and struggling to get her off the ice. The two linespeople arrived a second later and the three of them tried to subdue 14.

Penny's bench was shouting at her, so she skated over to the safety of her team while the officials swarmed the still-combative Rattlesnake player. Shiv skated up next to her. "Holy shit I can't believe you just took that on." Shiv said – pointing to 14 who was now being led off the ice, her game done for the day.

"I didn----" Penny started but got cut off.

"You're a fucking goon, girl!" Becks shouted from the bench. "Did you see her go down *twice*?"

"No I---"

"Goon, goon, goon!" The bench was chanting, picking up on Becks' lead. "Goon! Goon! Goon!"

Penny's cheeks burned. She was hardly the world's toughest player, and was in no way whatsoever a goon, but after her 2nd period she was glad to be part of the team getting back into the game.

Penny's line changed during the stoppage and the Beavs scored twice during the extended 5-minute power play that followed 14's ejection from the game. Penny got back on the ice for two move shifts after the power play, but the game had changed pace again. Both teams were clearly tired and playing lots of long passes, dumping the puck once they gained neutral zone possession and making quick changes.

Penny only got a few touches doing clearing passes from her own zone, but the Snakes didn't seem to have it in them to send anyone after the puck into the Beavs' zone at this point. Penny was fired up but the rest of her team seemed to have spent their adrenaline during the 5 minute major and lost their wind. This was the time when she remembered her coach telling her not to show off but just play a solid game. And she did.

Time expired with a final score of 5-3 for the Rattlesnakes. It wasn't a particularly important game in the season, neither the first nor last loss for the Beavs and it hadn't decided anything in the standings. It had been an awakening for Penny though, seeing how fired up her team had been after she had stood up to number 14 and how the game had changed afterwards. The nickname had stuck with her after that. Shiv and Goon were now the 2nd D-line for the Beavs. And Penny decided it was a nickname she was going to live up to. Even if she wasn't ready to do so just yet...

6. Locker Room Pranks

Penny and Shiv jockeyed for position atop the toilet seat in the single bathroom stall that was attached to the Beavs' dressing room. They made a racket that only two teenage girls being *extremely quiet* could make. Thankfully when they heard Becks and Fleur enter the room the two of them were talking loudly and didn't notice the muted commotion coming from the bathroom.

The conversation stopped abruptly a second later.

"What. The. Actual. Fuck." Becks employed her well-rounded vocabulary.

"I am going to kill them." Fleur breathed.

The girls burst out of the bathroom stall and started laughing uncontrollably. "GOT YOU!" Penny and Shiv laughed and ran out of the dressing room before the other two could process they were there.

Becks and Fleur looked at each other and then at their spots on the locker room bench. The team was just coming back from a pre-skate warmup and the two girls' skates, gloves, and helmets were sitting on the bench full of shaving cream. Laughter erupted from the rest of the team as they came into the locker room.

This event was just the latest in an epic prank war that had gone back to the very start of the season. Becks and Fleur had started it. At the team's first formal practice they had sent the rookies to bring all the practice equipment out to the bench, and while they were gone, put clear packing tape on the bottom of all of the rookies' skates. To a girl, the rooks hit the ice and collapsed like sacks of potatoes. One on top of the other. Further adding to the hilarity, of the moment were the failed attempts to get back up, and girls grabbing onto the boards for dear life while their legs windmilled uselessly underneath them. The phone videos were hilarious. Someone posted one to the team's social media where they'd sped up the players' video and put it to a version of "yakety sax".

Most of the rookies had taken it as a basic hazing. Shiv and Penny, used to having older brothers and knowing that letting something like this go was just an invitation for more, accepted the challenge that had been thrown down.

At the team's next home game, Becks and Fleur who had orchestrated the prank got the first clue of what was coming their way. Every time the announcer mentioned either player, they were referred to, respectively, as Barfs and Floor. It didn't take long for the two red-faced, hot-and-sweaty from the game, and steaming angry to boot, girls to get a description from the rink announcer who had put him up to the joke. When they found out that a pair of rookies were stepping to them, they knew it was time to dial things up a notch.

Shiv and Penny had a pretty good idea that there was going to be more coming. They had a heightened sense of vigilance for the next few practices that bordered on paranoia as they expected anything and everything to happen. Both were surprised when several practices passed and nothing did. Their next home game came around and they checked their bags for things that shouldn't be there and made sure to pee one at a time, and always stayed with at least one other player so as not to get caught alone. And yet, still they were able to gear up and get out for their pre-game warmup skate without any issues. Then it started.

Penny noticed it first. A warm, pleasant tingling sensation in her fingertips and palms. Then a similar sensation started in her knees, and elbows. It started to get warmer, and warmer, and then pin pricks of cold started stabbing her. She looked over nervously at Shiv, who was shaking her left hand as if she'd just been hit with the puck. They locked eyes, and immediately they both knew.

"Cheese and fries this burns!" Shiv said as she skated past Penny.

"The knees are the worst!" Penny cringed back when she was next near Shiv.

After the warmup the players lined up on the benches getting ready for the first period. Becks came up behind the two girls and put a gloved hand heavily on both of their shoulders. "Hey! Did ya hear?" She grinned. "This first period is being brought to you by Icy Hot Muscle Pain and Relief!" She pushed off the two girls, almost pushing Penny over the boards in the process and did an up-down high five with Fleur. The two veterans laughed and shouted, "Have a good game rookies!" and took to the ice.

The Icy Hot incident demanded retribution. It came on their next road trip. Becks and Fleur had been roomed together, so it was pretty inevitable something was going to happen. Shiv tracked down a local 24-hour pizza delivery restaurant and Penny got her mom to share her credit card so they could order a pizza. At four am in the morning, the Pizza delivery man delivered the anchovy, onion, pickle and no-cheese pizza to the most tired and confused young women he had ever come across in his life. The two made such a disturbance denying that they had ordered a pizza, that they woke the teammates on either side of them, and the hotel night manager had to accept the awful-smelling package on their behalf. It wasn't until the bus ride home that it occurred to the pair that this was part of the prank war.

Thing escalated quickly from there. Penny found a fake tarantula in her glove and had hid crying in the bathroom for over half an hour while she calmed down from the fright.

Fleur found her deodorant stick a few days later had been replaced with a stick of butter. Though not before giving both pits a good lather of salted full fat bread spread.

Shiv came to practice to find her missing helmet, which she had been looking for all week and been terribly stressed thinking she'd lost, encased in a jello mold in the middle of the locker room.

And then had come the shaving cream.

Any one of the girls individually would have admitted the whole thing was stupid and they were ready to stop. Any one of them would gladly have admitted things had gone too far by that point. But doing so in front of everyone else involved? Having to lose face this late in the game? That wasn't an option anymore.

To this day, nobody in the club knows which pair of players is responsible for what happened next. Shiv and Penny had done the last prank that the whole team had witnessed, so it made sense that it was Becks and Fleur's turn. But really it could have been either party. The only thing anyone knew for sure was that nobody claimed responsibility for it, and it was the end of the prank war for good.

It was early February and bitterly cold. The Beavs' 5:30am practice had been a low energy affair. It was late in the season and the Beavs' last place finish had been secured three games previous, so the players and coaches knew there was little on the line to keep working towards. The Coaches set up the drills and the players skated, but neither party had the same intensity as they had earlier in the season. They skated. They practiced. They scrimmaged. They wrapped up and hit the dressing room.

The coach came fuming into the dressing room a few minutes later.

"Whose idea was this?" She demanded. A roomful of perplexed gazes looked back at her. She sat down on the edge of the bench nearest the door. She sat next to Bricks. "Help me with this." She stuck her unlaced skate out in front of her. Bricks knel and pulled on the blade. It didn't budge. Bricks grunted and repositioned and pulled harder. The coach winced in pain and told her to stop.

"Stuck." Bricks observed, needlessly.

"Glued." Coach growled, needlessly.

A hush fell across the room.

"Can we slide your foot out of your skates?" Bricks suggested.

The coach gave her a wan look. "A whole season and the lot of you don't know I skate barefoot?" She looked around. "Or maybe some of you did, and that's the point."

It was now dawning on the room exactly what was going on. "Nailpolish remover, that works on superglue right?" Li offered.

"Maybe. Do any of you have any?" The coach asked hopefully. She looked around at the room and had a sinking feeling realizing this was probably the only group of 20 teenage girls she could ask who wouldn't. The players awkwardly made a show of checking their bags and backpacks but nobody had anything with acetone.

"Coach," Bricks asked gently, still trying to get the skates loose. "Do you have any allergies?"

"No, why?" Bricks pointed down to the bare skin of her calf that was visible above her skate. It was red and swollen and had ballooned to fully fill the top of the boot where there had been a decent amount of free wiggle room a few minutes before.

"Dammit." The coach cursed. "Ok, one of you call 9-1-1."

The next fifteen minutes happened quickly. The team carried the coach in her skates out to the lobby of the rink and set her on a bench near the door. In a flurry of flashing lights and uniforms a pair of EMTs and some firefighters unloaded from emergency vehicles in the parking lot and came inside. They hooked the coach up to wires and sensors and fussed over her increasingly swollen calves. After some discussion, the EMTs came back with a pair of fabric scissors and they began to carefully cut away the skate fabric from around her foot. They gave her medication for allergies and swelling. Eventually they got enough of the skates released so that they could slide Coach's foot out still attached to the sole of the skate's boot.

The EMTs got a good look at her feet now and had a quiet conference. Penny was observing the interaction and thought they looked like the refs when they were discussing a serious penalty. The firefighters were sent out and they came back with a gurney. The EMTs loaded the coach up and wheeled her out, inner boots of her skates still on, and loaded her in the back of the ambulance.

The team's parents received an email later that night. It told them that the coach had been treated at hospital and released, including getting the super glue dissolved off her feet. She had shown an allergy to the superglue and that was under control. However the coach wanted everyone (and their parents) to know that anyone involved in any pranks before the end of the season would be off the team.

The prank war came to a hard stop after that. The Beavs played the last few games of the season and finished out their last place standing for Penny's first year with the team. The coach who'd been pranked wrapped up her time with the team the next week, handing off the remaining duties to the remaining coach mom. To this day, none of the players from that year's team have admitted to the super glue prank, and no explanation has been offered for how the coach got targeted. Penny is the only one who noticed that she and the coach wore the same brand and style of skate, just a couple of sizes apart.

7. First Ejection

Penny's second season with the Beavs started with a breath of fresh air. The dual parent coaches who had coached the team the previous season, and whose laissez-faire approach to the team's competitiveness Penny never really bought into, had ceded the reigns to a Beavs' alumni who had moved back to town over the summer. The new woman, a recent university graduate who had played for the women's squad at Carleton University, understood the game much better than her predecessors and brought with her big ambitions for the team.

Coach had introduced herself with the greatest new coach speech Penny had ever heard. "I'm Coach. Don't bother learning my name you'll only ever refer to me as Coach. I don't care that you're young women. I don't care that you're teenagers. You're hockey players and in Canada that means the same thing regardless of your age or gender. I have one rule on my team: everyone works, nobody quits. Come here to work, and we will get along just fine." Penny liked the new Coach immediately.

The new season brought with it a new and more demanding practice schedule. Coach had managed to score them two practice ice times a week instead of just one. The team had lost some of the graduating 3rd years from the previous season, but they'd actually had more recruits than roster spots for the first time in the team's history and had put together a full roster for this season.

Penny found herself promoted to the first D-line that second season and had a lot more ice time. She was also playing against the Beavs' opponent's top lines and that made the games a lot more interesting. In particular, games against the Moose Jaw Maidens were some of the most interesting. Thanks in no small part to Courtney Schmidt, number 6 for the Maidens. Schmidt was a third year player with a reputation in the league. And in the South Saskatchewan Minor Hockey League, you didn't earn yourself a reputation as the nicest, fastest, or smartest player. No, Courtney had a reputation as the meanest girl in the league. For whatever reason drives players to do so, Courtney focused most of her meanness on Li, one of the first line forwards Penny was usually on the ice with.

Courtney was as smart as she was cruel. Devious even, Penny often thought. Courtney had good game senses and seemed to have a ESP for when the refs weren't looking so she give someone an extra jab here or little slip of her stick across someone's wrists there. She also knew when to get under your skin, and when to shut up. In close games, Courtney was mum. But if her team was winning or losing and they needed to get under their opponent's skin, Courtney was a chatterbox who needled the opposition so much they could've left the ice in new sweaters.

Courtney's focus on Li seemed to pick up on the young girl's self-awareness of her Chinese appearance and the fact that she never had anyone cheering her on at her games.

In their second matchup against the Maidens, Courtney had been lined up against Li waiting for a faceoff. "Hey, slant-eyes," she hissed, "no parents again? What are they off adopting themselves another replacement villager?" Li gritted her teeth and leaned into Courtney, putting too much of her body weight on the big girl's frame. When the puck dropped, it came towards them and Li tried to shove forward through Courtney. Courtney was three steps ahead and had shifted her weight to the *side*, so most of Li's force went directed at empty air. Li tumbled to the ice on all fours and the puck skidded under her straight to Courtney's stick. "Go back to math club." Courtney laughed as she passed the puck to a teammate for a shot on goal.

The two were back up against each other for the next face off a few moments later. "You play like shit." Courtney observed. "Makes sense now why nobody's here to watch you. You probably *dishonor* them."

The face off was dug loose by the Beavs' center and Li tried to skate up along the boards to follow the play. "Nope." Courtney laughed, pushing her larger body against the boards and blocking Li's entrance to the neutral zone. Li spun around trying to go up the center of the ice but found Courtney's body in the way again. "Not this way either." The big girl goaded. Li was tangled up in her stick and skates and tried to force her way past. Suddenly Courtney just fell over and screamed, crying out as if in pain. "Ow!" She cried. "Come on!" Li stood over her incredulously, stick stuck under Courtney's body but loose from Li's hands. The referee skated back from the blue line and called a tripping penalty against Li.

Li started to protest but the referee cut her off. Instead Li grabbed her stick and fumed her way into the box, slamming the door behind her. Courtney rolled once or twice more for effect, grabbing her shin. "That's intent to injure!" She called up to the ref before making a show of laboring her way to her feet and limping off to the bench.

Penny had observed this whole interaction from a few feet behind Li. She was shocked, and angry for her friend. Nowhere else aside from a hockey rink, or maybe the anonymous comments section of an online forum, could you get away with being that offensive and someone not standing up and putting a stop to it. And on it went. One period. Then two. Li was tormented every time the pair were on the ice. Li's own play was suffering greatly, with easy passes being missed and her totally shutting down when it came to communicating with her linesmates. Li became more and more of an island on the ice, lost at sea and getting further and further away from the game she was in.

When the second intermission buzzer went, Li told Coach that she thought she had injured her wrist and needed to sit out the third. Her eyes stung with tears as she did, and even though the trainer couldn't find any indication of a problem, Li sat out the third in the locker room.

Jenn was assigned to Li's spot on the first line. When they first got onto the ice together, Penny tapped her shin guard with her stick. "Hey," Penny said. "Look don't get into the faceoff circle against 6. I'll take your spot." Jenn looked at her weird, but shrugged and nodded. That first chance came about a minute and a half in.

At a blue-line faceoff at the edge of the Maiden's end of the ice, Penny lined up across from Courtney. "Guess your chink friend couldn't handle this heat." Courtney gloated.

"Injury." Penny said through clenched teeth.

"Yeah." Courtney scoffed. "Injured ego I bet." The puck dropped and skittered free to the far side of the ice. Courtney looked, was about to take off, and suddenly Penny's hand shoved down on the top of her helmet with force. Courtney, still squatting with her body leaned forward from the face off, easily went off balance and went hard to the ice. The ref's back was to them and she barely looked back when she heard Courtney go down. She paid it no notice and carried on.

"Oops." Penny waved. "Sorry, I hope you didn't injure your ego." She skated off after the play while number 6 struggled back to her feet.

Their lines changed before the two met again that shift and it was nine minutes left in the third before both were on the ice together again.

"That was a cute little move." Courtney had just skated up against Penny's body in the corner of the boards. They dug for a puck tied up in Penny's skates.

"Glad you liked it." Penny said back. "Lay off my teammate."

Courtney jammed the blade of her stick into the back of Penny's calf, the part where the shin pad didn't protect. Penny cringed but stayed upright. "I'll lay into anyone on your team I want." Courtney said.

Penny got a skate on the puck and managed to kick it backwards and away from the boards. Courtney spun loose and chased after it. In a move Penny knew she would regret even as she did it, she spun her body in the opposite direction, and let her stick flay wildly around in an arc with the momentum. Her stick connected with Courtney's midsection and Penny hauled it back towards her body as hard as she could. The blade hooked between Courtney's torso and arm and pulled the big girl down off her feet. Her body hadn't even finished sliding when the referee's whistle blew and Penny was sent to the penalty box for the hook. Courtney furiously cursed after her. From within the penalty box, Penny flipped her the bird.

The Maidens scored late on the power play. Penny went back to the bench and had to listen to Coach tear her a new one. Penny stood as close to at military attention through the verbal lashing as she could, though she hardly processed any of what coach was saying. On the opposite side of the clear glass between the two benches, Courtney had her face up against the glass and was pulling at the skin at the side of her eyes so that her eyelids squinted together. Penny glared back as Coach told her to take a seat on the bench. Penny sat down in a huff, and number 6 made a crying motion with her hands and then pointed at her and laughed. Penny actually felt better at that point, at least they were making fun of her now. That she had no problem with. They weren't picking on Li anymore.

The game ended in a decisive victory for the Maidens. The Beavs piled off the bench and skated slowly to their end of the ice, patting Bricks on the helmet in appreciation for what had been a tough game to be in goal. They lined up and clapped hands with the Maidens players, muttering "good game" as they went. When Penny got to Courtney, the bigger girl grabbed her hand in a handshake and leaned in. "Good game, just uh, don't let your cat out near that teammate of yours eh? Pro tip."

Penny launched her body at Courtney, and this time the antagonist wasn't ready. She fell over backwards with Penny straddling atop her. Penny's gloves flew off over her head and Courtney let out a gargled but obnoxious laugh. Penny pulled her arm back, ready to punch the girl.

Two sets of strong arms were suddenly grabbing her and pulling her off and back to her feet.

"That's ENOUGH!" She heard and looked over to see an official grabbing her right arm. "Get of the ice NOW." Penny glared down at Courtney, who had sat up and was still laughing. The rest of the players had taken several steps back and were milling about awkwardly. One of the officials led Penny back to the gate to her bench and Penny's coach shook her head as Penny walked past her and straight down the tunnel to the change rooms.

Penny was sitting next to Li when Coach came into the room, still wearing everything but her skates. The rest of the team hung back in the hallway, waiting for permission to follow. "Davies. You're with me. Now." Coach led Penny out of her team's change room, waved the rest of the team in, and then led Penny down the hall until they found a change room without any team names taped to the door. They entered and Coach threw on the light. Now it was just the two of them.

"Davies, I'm going to talk and you're going to listen. Understood?"

"Yes, but---"

"Can it. This isn't a call-and-response show. You probably think you're on the side of angels, doling out justice for your wronged teammate and punishing the villains who hurt her."

"I—" Coaches eyes *flared* and she sucked breath in through her teeth, silencing Penny with the look.

"Two things happened out there today. A player on the other team played her game exactly the way she is supposed to, she got under the skin of not one but TWO of our players, and put nearly half of our starters on the bench for most of the third period. The second is that our players failed their team and *let* that happen. Now I can see the racist faces and gestures and I can only guess how inappropriate she was being on the ice, but there's a process that us coaches and officials go through to deal with that. Unfortunately, instead of punishing *their* player, I'm now going to be dealing with the league for the next week sorting out how long you're going to be suspended for. I hope it's just 2 games for dropping your gloves, but it could be longer since you had your little tantrum after the game was over. Now you're going to get into that locker room and apologize to your team, grab your shit, and get to the lobby. I don't care

46

what the league says, your suspension from *this team* starts right – the hell – now."

Penny realized she was crying but she nodded. She hurried off to collect her items. She sniffed heavily and took a long, shaking breath before she could force out, "I'm sorry everyone, especially Li, for letting you down today." She grabbed her bag, stuffed her loose items into it and walked to the lobby. Thankfully Pat had already pulled their family's van up to the little pickup loop outside and Penny was able to leave right away.

"What's wrong?" Pat asked when she got in, seeing the state of her.

Penny shook her head, not ready to answer.

They drove in silence more than half of the way home. Even the radio was left off. Finally, Penny managed to get her sobs mostly under control and was able to breathe again.

"I screwed up Pat, and I need help. Your help." She told him. Pat was stopped at a red light and looked over at her.

"Of course, anything you need." He said.

"I need you to teach me how to fight." Penny said flatly.

Pat regarded her sternly for a moment, but then his disapproval melted into the biggest, proudest big brotherly smile Penny had ever seen him wear. But before he could formally answer the blare of a horn behind them snapped him back to the road and he noticed they were sitting at a green light. He waved apologies to the other driver and got himself back under control driving.

They were pulling into their driveway when Pat came back around to respond to her request. "I'm going to make you the toughest little enforcer in your girls league." He promised. "Starting right now. Keep your kit on. We have work to do."

8. Sparring Lessons

Penny's second season with the South Saskatchewan Minor Hockey League's female U15 team, the Maple Creek Hungry Beavers, or 'Beavs' as her team called themselves, had started out on a rocky footing. Penny had been full of hope and excitement with a new coach coming to the team, one who had played the game herself and brought a vision for the team that was bigger than just keep scraping the bottom of the league. But Penny had screwed up, badly, and been goaded by another player into losing her temper and taking that girl down after play ended. Penny had been suspended from the league for two games, and Coach wasn't letting her attend practices or do anything else with her team until she had served her full suspension. The league didn't *require* that last part, that was just Coach piling on to make sure Penny *got – the – message.* Which she did. Sort of.

In Penny's mind, she hadn't been wrong to go after Moose Jaw Maidens' number 6, a big girl named Courtney, because Courtney had gone after Penny's teammate Li in a wildly inappropriate manner herself first. Li wasn't a strong enough player – physically or mentally – to stand up for herself, and so Penny had stepped up. That she had done so was something Penny was proud of. But *how* she'd gone about it – letting Courtney get under *her* skin and making it about punishing the other girl instead of looking out for Li, or herself, those were mistakes Penny was determined not to make again.

She'd asked her brothers to use the suspension time to help her with an area of the game completely foreign to Penny: fighting. The rules in minor female were very clear that body checking and fighting were not allowed. Those physical aspects of the boys' game were against the rules in Penny's league. But Penny had seen enough in her first season and early in this second to have made the conclusion that some players just needed to be taught a lesson about what was appropriate in the game and what wasn't. Courtney was just one example. Penny had nearly come to blows with another player near the end of her first season, a big third year from the Regina Rattlesnakes. In the end the player had gone off balance and taken herself out before she could touch Penny, though from a third party's perspective it apparently looked like Penny had dodged a punch and then laid the older girl out flat on her ass. That incident had earned Penny her team nickname, Goon, even though she still denied having earned it.

Pat and Paul, Penny's older brothers who had retired from hockey and acted as Penny's mentors and chauffeurs now, fully understood. "Too many players think they can just say whatever the hell they want when they're on the ice," Pat had observed at Penny's first 'sparring lesson', "Things get said on the ice that you'd never hear someone dare utter out in the *real world* because they'd get their ass kicked."

"And not to mention the ones either too careless or too clueless who endanger other players. Like that guy I played a few years back who "accidentally" took my team's goalie out three times in the same game. After the third our tough guy beat him up pretty good. Took him out of the game because the other guy needed to go get stitches at the end of the battle, but at least the goalie was safe the rest of the game too."

"You get it." Penny nodded. "With these girls, so many of them just don't know what to do about a player like that. They don't even consider they-hit-us-so-we-should-hit-back as a possibility! But with some players that's the only way to get them to get the message, and to stop."

"Ok so we all get that part." Paul agreed. "Now let's get into the parts you don't."

Penny got into a "ready" stance. She had her helmet and jersey on, but was just wearing workout pants and socks below. They were in the Davies' unfinished basement which they'd agreed would serve as her dojo for these sparring lessons.

"Whoa there, Rock." Pat laughed. "Put 'em down we're not there yet."

"We're gonna start with how to get someone's jersey over their head?" Penny asked.

"No. There's some things you need to understand about this part of the game before we proceed." Paul bobbed his head excitedly in support.

"So first, you *never* just lay into someone." Pat said firmly. "Blindsiding or sucker punching some hapless opponent is just as bad as whatever caused you to go after them in the first place, and that's how players get hurt. Never. Fight. An unwilling. Opponent. Understood?"

"Yes." Penny replied, holding back the urge to add "sir" in response to Pat's suddenly drill-sergeant like demeanor.

"Second, do everything you can to warn the refs. They will try to talk you out of it, that's their job, but if two of you are intent on going a few rounds most refs will let it happen. IF you let them know. If not, they're as likely to break the two of you up before you get anywhere as they are to just toss you both from the game then and there."

"Ok." Penny was starting to understand why they were doing a classroom session first.

"Third, keep in mind your goal is to *hurt* the other player, not *injure* them. That's an easy one to forget in the heat of the moment, but you're not battling someone to the death. You don't want to go after their eyes or their ears or anything that will cause long term damage. You want them to feel your commitment to protecting their team, not end up in the hospital."

"Wait, but Paul weren't you *just* saying some guy ended up in the hospital and that meant your team's goalie was safe? Isn't that a good outcome?"

"No." Paul said flatly. "That same outcome could've been achieved just by ending the fight and the other guy getting the message. It's not a good outcome for anyone if someone ends up in the ER."

Penny made a mental note of that.

"Finally, look for even battles or ones that give you an advantage." Pat concluded.

"What do you mean?" Penny asked.

"Ok so from what I've seen, you're suddenly toying with being a firstline defender and a pretty decent one at that. And you're in a league where one or both of you drop your gloves and you're out for two games. Minimum. That's worth it sometimes, but if there's some third line rookie shooting her mouth off and you want to shut her up, don't do it by picking a fight. Your enemy losing a third line hothead versus your team losing a first line you isn't a fair trade. Your team is worse off for the loss of you in the end. So you need to be very strategic and pick opponents that will strategically benefit your team."

"Huh. I'd never though of it like that." Penny admitted. Because she hadn't. She'd thought of it in black and white terms of right and wrong, not really that there was a larger team strategy to dropping the gloves with someone that made it such a *deliberate* decision. "Got it."

"Good." Paul said. Then shifted gears. "Penny, have you ever actually been *in* a fight, even at Bennet's rink?"

"No." Penny said.

"That's what I thought." Paul shook his head. "Pat, what do you think of that?"

Before Penny could even process what was happening her brother had pulled her towards him and knocked her helmet off with a hand that she suddenly realized was a lot bigger and meatier than she'd ever noticed before. She cringed and tried to bring her arm in front of her uncovered face but that just made it easier for the larger, stronger boy to reach back and grab her jersey and pull it over her head.

The blows that followed were deliberately weak, Penny could tell. Pat was basically just giving her light stage slaps through the fabric of her jersey against her face and the back of her head. They stung, but they didn't do any damage. As he intended, she was sure. After four or five solid hits he released her and she struggled her jersey back down to where it belonged. She let out a string of curses and shoved both boys on a shoulder while they stood laughing.

"Now you have." Paul chuckled. The action caused his tall, lanky frame to shake like a tree in the wind.

Penny adjusted her equipment and glared at them both, red-faced. "Look, be pissed but that was part of the lesson. Doesn't matter who you're up against, in any fight you could just as easily end up the sucker getting whooped as you could the one doing the whooping. And whoever wins is going to have one very angry person with them."

Penny had regained her composure. "Yeah, ok I get it." She said. "Now, show me how you did that jersey trick."

"No." Pat responded. "Later. The most important move you'll learn is the helmet pull."

Paul nodded agreement. "In your little girls' league they make you all wear those full face cages. Til that's out of the way you're just going to be shredding your knuckles against their grill."

"Ok." Penny agreed, seeing the sense in that. "So, is there a specific way to knock the helmet off?"

Both boys laughed at her. "No." Pat said. "You don't *knock* the helmet off. You *pull* it off." He quickly but lightly smacked Penny in the belly, below where her chest protector ended. "Start with a belly shot, that'll force them to double over and try to cover that spot." Penny had done the same when he'd tapped her belly. "Now that they're bent over, grab their lid with both hands and PULL hard towards you."

"Won't that hurt?" Penny asked?

The boys laughed again. "You're committing to beat someone in the face until they give up or the refs pull you apart, but you're worried about their helmet coming off hurting a bit?" Paul laid out the irony of her statement.

"Oh. Right." Penny acknowledged.

"Are you sure you have this in you?" Pat asked directly.

Penny steeled herself. "Yes." She thought back to Courtney and the verbal abuse Li had put up with. There was someone who deserved to learn a lesson and nobody else was going to step up and be the teacher. "I have this in me and then some."

Paul laughed heartily. "Ok, we'll make sure we add *better trash talk* to your lesson plan." Penny shoved his shoulder again.

"Now, helmet." Pat brought her back to the moment.

The next few weeks of her suspension blended together in Penny's mind. It seemed like a sports movie montage of her "working the bag" at the local community center in the morning, then practicing specific moves with her brothers in the garage in the afternoons. Penny pulling the helmet off over and over, from different positions, then following up with a fist to the back of the head. Penny struggling to master pulling the back of her opponent's jersey over their head, limited by the length of her arms. Penny throwing down stick and glove over and over getting used to the feeling of getting free of them all in one fluid motion. Body punch, body punch, punch to the face. And through it all the pounding baseline of punk and metal songs like Drowning Pool's "Let the Bodies Hit the Floor" fueling her on.

As the days passed she got better. Her first few sessions were lots of getting love taps to the face from her older brothers as she slowly and awkwardly tried to land blows on them. Then she would start to score a few of her own. And finally, as her suspension wound down, her training sessions ramped up in intensity and balance and she and her brothers would be locked in full, even sparring matches.

Three days before her suspension ended, she won her first mock battle against Pat. The day before the suspension ended, she won her first one against Paul. That night, to celebrate they went to Boston Pizza and had pizza for dinner. It was a special commemorative moment. As Penny's dad had instilled in every one of the children through their athletic careers, "pizza is only for winners", and the family would only ever be allowed to order pizza if one of the children had won a game with their team that week. This time, Pat and Paul were acknowledging Penny's progress and that she had completed her training.

The only thing she needed now, was a real opponent. And thankfully, the South Saskatchewan Minor Hockey League was going to provide one very soon.

9. First Fight

Penny Davies, second-year first line defender for the Saskatchewan Minor Hockey League's Hungry Beavers team, had finished her suspension. Or more correctly, she was done her suspension in the eyes of the league, but as she stood alone in front of the team's new coach, Penny wasn't sure she was back on her team yet.

"Davies, you care a lot about this team and the girls on it, don't you?" Coach asked. Penny nodded. "I've been assuming it's that, and not some latent homicidal instinct I need to be calling a counselor about that led to your suspension."

"I was just looking out for Li." Penny told her.

"That's what I figured." Coach nodded. "Which means we have a problem."

Penny's heart sank.

"I played a whole career in female hockey." Coach stated flatly. "And so I *know* there's no shortage of players who deserve getting their heads knocked straight." Penny nodded in agreement. "But I also know *most* of them just have big mouths and just want to get under your skin. Not many of them will outright hurt someone." Penny chewed her cheek thoughtfully.

"When I was playing at Carleton there was a girl on my team who had our backs. A lot like you, actually. Not the biggest girl but *tough*. She was smart too. She could tell the players that were annoying from the ones who might hurt someone, and she kept herself in check except for when faced with a real threat. Her *being there* kept us safe and able to play our game. That was great. But you know the worst part of having her on our team?"

Penny shook her head.

"Whenever she had to drop the gloves to send a message to someone, even if it was rarely, it meant she was gone for a game or two. And *those* games were the worst for us because those were when our opponents would make up for lost time. So having her as a teammate was fantastic *when she was there*, but very difficult *when she wasn't*."

"Like I wasn't the last few games." Penny agreed.

"Exactly." Coach said. "Now you don't have the game sense yet to tell the difference between annoying and dangerous players, your little display three games ago showed me that. So you don't get to make those choices anymore."

"But what if…"

"I wasn't finished." Coach cut her off, annoyed. "So I will. I'm going to assume that you're willing to go all the way *when it's needed* to protect your teammates. Am I right?"

"If you mean, am I willing to fight someone? Yes." Penny nodded.

"Ok. I'm not going to tell you that's never going to happen, but if it comes up, I needed to know that. What we're going to do is develop a signal. You have a **hard red light** that means no stupid shit unless you see me give you the signal, understand? If you get into it with anyone, even if *they started it* before I give you the green light, you're off the squad. Can you live with that?"

"And what happens when I get 'the signal'?" Penny asked.

"Do what you need in order to protect your teammates. And yourself." Coach explained. "Got it?"

"Yes." Penny replied.

"Good. Then welcome back Davies. Your squad's missed you." She extended her hand to Penny, who grasped it and shook it. Coach held onto her hand from the handshake and pulled Penny closer, leaning her face in towards the girl. "But let me be absolutely clear – any more extra curriculars outside of the 60 minutes of play time and you're done, not just on this team but in this league, understood? Your family name ain't the best in the biz as I've been educated over the past few weeks, you gotta be doing this better and cleaner than everyone else." The last sentence sounded like it came from some movie Penny had never seen.

Penny gulped and nodded vigorously. Coach released her. And with that, Penny was back.

Penny's return earned her something of celebrity status within her team. Two weeks had done little to temper their enthusiasm over the circumstances that had landed Penny on suspension in the first place.

"I wish the officials would have let you take her out!" Shiv said, referring to the rapid intervention of the referees who had stopped Penny from beating Courtney Schmidt of the Moose Jaw Maidens after tackling her in the post-game handshake line.

"You could've taken her." Li agreed. It'd been Courtney's offensive, racist remarks about Li that had set Penny off in the first place.

Penny's humble and repentant view of the event, particularly following the discussion with Coach upon returning, put her at odds with the excitement of her teammates. Penny had spent her whole suspension stewing over the league's decision and their failure to look out for Li. Now, Penny just felt like a dumb kid who'd acted out without knowing any better. Today she felt smarter than she did two weeks ago. But she couldn't exactly explain that to her teammates, not the least of which because most of *them* hadn't learned the same lesson and couldn't understand until they had. So Penny played along as best she could without actually condoning her own actions.

It seemed to everyone in the locker room that there was some cosmic hockey karma happening, because the Beavs' first game after Penny's return was a home game against the same Moose Jaw Maidens. It was one of the toughest in Penny's career.

Hitting the ice Penny saw that the opposing coach had lined Courtney up against her line. She rolled her eyes. *Great* she said inside her head.

"Look who's back. Little goonie girl." Courtney said, pressing Penny against the boards while they struggled for a puck.

"Just go back to the farm you came from." Penny said back. She won the puck loose and turned to pass it back to a teammate, but felt a hard blow to her back and she was suddenly face-down on the ice. "Dammit!" Penny shouted in pain and frustration. A whistle went and a referee skated over to send Courtney to the penalty box for the cross-check.

"See you again *real soon!*" Courtney called cheerily as the penalty door slammed shut on her. Penny glared but then looked over at her coach. Coach was looking at her and held up a palm. *Patience.* Penny could almost hear her saying. Then Coach pointed to the score clock where "6 – 2:00" had just shown up under the "Visitors" column. Penny looked back at Coach and nodded.

Penny's team scored on the power plan and Courtney seemed to double down her efforts to get under Penny's skin when they next met on the ice. "Think I'm getting you." Courtney said. "You only give a shit about that foreign fucker, right? You won't stand up for yourself, you're too weak for that." Penny ignored her. "Hey! I'm talking to you!" Courtney shouted angrily after Penny while they skated to catch a loose puck. Still, Penny focused on controlling the puck that had come her way. Courtney then shouted an obscenity at Penny that you're not even allowed to say in a minor hockey rink and earned herself another penalty for unsportsmanlike conduct this time.

Penny's line was pulled off to let the first power play line take over. Coach rested a hand on Penny's helmet. "Great work." She said. "You earned us that first goal and look who 6 is focused on. Your teammates are in the clear." Penny smiled. That was true. "Keep it up." Coach patted her helmet and started yelling at someone on the power play to get into better position.

As they entered the third with the Beavs' sporting a 4-1 lead, Courtney seemed to be coming unraveled. No matter what she said or how many times she shoved and shouldered and speared at Penny, she couldn't get the younger girl to confront her. And the more frustrated Courtney got, the more centered Penny became.

Breathless and red-faced, Courtney skated up to Penny at a faceoff, leaning her heavy frame against the younger girl. "Got some lessons in Buddhism from your Chinese friend during your suspension?" She asked. Penny still ignored her. The faceoff ended and Penny's team skated the puck out of the neutral zone and into the far end. Meanwhile Courtney knocked Penny down from the back and then gave her an extra shove while Penny was on the ground. Penny tried to get to her feet but Courtney knocked her down again. Penny looked initially for a ref, but they were all at the other end of the ice where the play was happening. Penny balled her free hand into a fist and pushed herself up on it onto all fours. She looked over at the bench, hoping for the signal… but Coach was holding her hand up again.

Penny let out an "Argh" of frustration.

She was shoved to the ground a third time and Courtney breathed into the ear of her helmet, "We done yet?"

"Oh, I've got all day." Penny laughed. In that moment, her frustration melted and she could feel just how angry she was making the other girl by doing nothing at all. Laughing, she rolled a little and managed to get to her feet.

"You want to go yet?" Courtney asked when Penny had gotten to her feet, squaring off against her.

"What? Out with you?" Penny laughed, circling her. There had been a whistle a moment ago and play had stopped. Everyone in the Maidens' end of the ice was looking over at them and an official, finally cluing into what was going on, started skating towards them. Penny was facing them, Courtney had her back to them. "Just let me alone!" Penny responded very loudly, and dropped her stick on the ice.

Courtney, as Penny hoped, mistook the motion and in a split second threw her gloves and stick down and came up in a fighter's ready stance. Her big, meaty hands ready to grasp at Penny except the smaller girl was already taking a step back and out of reach. "No!" Penny yelled as the official reached Courtney and grabbed one of her arms. Courtney's eyes widened as she realized what was going on.

"No. NO! She suckered me. You little piss-ant!" She shouted at Penny. "Chicken-shit!" But a second official had arrived and they were hauling Courtney off the ice in the direction of her bench. "This isn't over! It isn't over you hear me?"

"It is for you." Penny called back softly.

Penny ended up benched for the rest of the game while her team enjoyed a lengthy power play from the major penalty and misconduct that Courtney had earned by dropping her gloves. They put two more goals up before the game was over. At one point, Li came and sat next to Penny on the bench. "That was incredible." She told Penny. "You beat her at her own game."

"Wasn't easy." Penny said.

"Probably not." Li agreed, "But you went total Sun Tzu on her."

"Huh?" Penny asked.

"If your opponent is temperamental, seek to irritate her."

"What is that, some Zen saying?" Penny asked.

"Don't be racist." Li said, giving her a playful shove. "Sun Tzu was Chinese, not Japanese, and it was on some IKEA artwork next to their kitschy bamboo plants for white college boys."

Penny laughed. "Sorry." She said.

Going into that game, Penny was sure that this was going to be her first major battle with another player. And in a way, she was right. Instead of being disappointed at not getting to fight her nemesis though, she felt freed and redeemed for her suspension and for winning the mental game against her. That somehow made the victory better, and made Penny feel like she'd leveled up as a player at the same time.

In fact, after her little locker room tete-a-tete with Coach, it was most of the rest of the season before she was given "the signal", and in that instance it was under much different circumstances.

The Beavs were chasing a playoff berth coming down the home stretch of the season, and aside from their rival teams for the playoff spots, they had a few throwaway games against teams long out of consideration for the post season. One of them was the Swift Current Swifties. So called because the team couldn't afford new jerseys with a team logo, so wore the same generic "Swift Current" ones they'd had for the better part of a decade; but their coaches let the girls choose their own team name each year since it didn't matter for the jerseys anyway. That year Taylor Swift had just dropped her first remake album and all the girls on the team were going mad over it; thus – the Swifties.

The game against the Swifties was a blowout, completely meaningless to the standings and generally a low energy affair between a capable, competitive team and a recreational one. Except for Swifties number eleven, ironically, named Taylor.

Taylor was in her final year in the league and had been a member of the Regina Rattlesnakes for her first two seasons before her family moved to Swift Current and "ruined her life." Her league reputation was someone who was only angrier at her family than she was at every other player on the ice, her own team included. Taylor called her teammates "the Shitties" and made no effort to hide her disdain for being on the team after spending her first two years at the top of the league.

Penny had largely moved on from thoughts of fighting other players by that game. Word had gotten round the league that she was a cool as a cucumber hardass and they were best to steer clear of her. Except Taylor wanted to leave her mark, on the league and on Penny.

Taylor's first shift she had a "high stick" while doing close coverage of Fleur in front of her net, which despite being "accidental" was still swung with enough force to break the stick on contact. When she was on the ice with Penny next, she found Penny and asked flat out, "Did your French amiga give you my message?"

Penny's blood went cold. "If you want to take a run at me just do it."

"No, no." Taylor growled. "I'm not gonna be suckered in like you did to that chick on the Maidens. If you want to stop me, you're going to have to come for me. Up to you how much blood it takes to get there." She skated away and a few moments later laid a heavy open ice check on Li, knocking her to the ice and winding her. Li was close to the bench so managed to crawl her way off the ice.

Taylor had added Becks and Jess M. to her list of victims by the end of the period. Nobody was out of the game but the whole team was feeling her presence. Locker room discussions focused on what a bitch she was and what exactly her problem was.

"I am." Penny said when Becks asked the question. "She wants me to fight her." The room went silent. "She told me." Penny added.

"So take her down a peg." Fleur said, holding a bag of ice against the back of her head. Penny glanced over at Coach, who gave the familiar palm up signal telling her to hold her ground. Penny gave Coach a slight nod of acknowledgement.

"I actually think it's best if I ride the bench." Penny said, her voice catching in her throat. "If I'm not playing, she has no reason to goad me by hurting anyone else."

Coach let out a slow, low whistle. The silence in the room turned its focus on her.

"I want you in here." Coach finally said. "If you're out there on the bench, she can still put the hurt on the team to lure you out. It's worked before." She let the last comment hang in the air. The silence shifted to Penny.

"Yeah. I agree." Penny nodded. "Be safe everyone."

As the team filed out and back to the ice everyone patted her on the head.

Penny knew something was wrong. Periods ran 40 minutes, give or take 5. It had been nearly an hour since her team had gone into the second.

She finally heard the buzzer and the demeanor of her team as they came in a few moments later confirmed it. A few threw their helmets on the floor, Becks broke a stick against the wall. Many swore as they walked into the room.

Penny sat silently, waiting for someone to fill her in. Coach hurried in after everyone with a sense of urgency Penny hadn't seen in her before.

"Look, I know you're all angry and we're all worried, but as soon as we hear anything back about Jenn I'll let you know." Penny suddenly realized neither Jenn nor the team's trainer were in the room.

"How did she not get ejected?" Shiv demanded. "It's a fucking shit show from that ref!"

"They can't call…" Coach began.

"What they can't see." The entire room intoned defeatedly.

"What happened? What didn't they see?" Penny used the brief break to ask.

"That defender of theirs that wants a go at you just about took Jenn's foot off." Shiv snapped. "Stepped on her ankle with her skate. Blood was everywhere."

Penny felt sick.

In the silence, they heard another voice. "Hey GOON! DID YOU GET MY MESSAGE?" Taylor's voice boomed through the hallway outside the changing room. The assembled squad in the locker room looked in disbelief around at each other. A few scrambled to their feet and tried to rush the door, but Coach made a gentle sidestep and leaned against the door challenging them to bustle past her. That ended any thoughts of immediate retaliation.

The call came again. Penny looked at Coach. Coach looked at Penny.

Coach raised her hand, and Penny's blood rose in her ears expecting the usual raised palm gesture. Instead, Coach clenched her hand tightly into a fist. That was the signal.

"Here's the plan." Coach started.

Penny heard the echo of Joe Esposito's "You're the Best Around" fading from her ears as she led her team out onto the bench. Before the opening faceoff Coach got one of the officials' attention and had a quick but unhappy exchange with them. It ended with the official skating off with an "ok ok". Coach looked over to Penny and nodded.

Penny flexed her hands open and shut over and over, feeling the muscles tighten and relax as she did. It appeared however, that cooler heads had prevailed, as they looked over to the opposite bench and saw number 11 was sitting behind her teammates on the bench, head down and resting on her stick. She didn't even seem to have noticed that Penny was back in the lineup.

Penny saw the game was a 7-0 affair now that the third period was starting. Coach started the second lineup to start against the Swifties' first line. Penny could tell at some point her team had been given the message not to pile on because they were mostly holding the Swifties in a neutral zone trap and dumping the puck back in the zone for them to chase. It made for a dull game but neither team seemed up for much more. Penny had two shifts in the first ten minutes and that was it. Coach was obviously letting the other lines get some ice time under their belts now that things had cooled down.

Penny got her third shift just after the ten minute mark. She'd picked up on the dump in game and was doing her best to hold the puck against the far boards and not let any out passes get past her. She shoveled the puck back into the Swifties' end and their defenders skated for it while their forwards made a changeup. That's when the commotion started.

Everyone on the ice looked over at the cries of surprise from the Swifties' bench. Eleven was on her feet and was holding back one of the forwards that was about to get on the ice. Instead, Taylor pushed past the entering forward and skated onto the ice. Her coach shouted something after her but she wasn't listening. She skated directly towards Penny.

Penny noticed that players on both teams were lining up on the blue lines as if it was the start of the game. That left her and Taylor alone in the middle of the neutral zone, circling the center ice circle like it was the center of a boxing ring.

Try to be best, cuz you're only a girl, and a girl's got to learn to take it.

Penny dropped her stick and it clattered to the ice. Her gloves followed with muffled thuds. She took a deep breath in through her nose.

Try to believe when the going gets tough that you gotta hang tough to make it.

Taylor's stick and gloves hit the ice. In the silence of the arena the sound echoed ominously.

History repeats itself, try and you'll succeed.

The two girls came together at center ice. Their hands were both up at the ready. Taylor was a few inches taller than Penny, but Penny had a sturdier build and was steadier on her skates.

Never doubt that you're the one and you can have your dream.

Taylor lunged forward first, body following a heavy fist aimed at Penny's gut. Penny sidestepped the blow easily, using her better footing to her advantage.

You're the best around.

Taylor stumbled out of her lunge and Penny was waiting. She ripped the bigger girl's helmet off with enough force to pop the chin strap loose of its peg.

Nothing's gonna ever take you down.

Penny tossed Taylor's helmet aside. The girl's brunette hair made a wide wave of brown as she flipped her head around to look at Penny.

You're the best around.

Penny's fist collided with her cheek. Taylor's head snapped to the side and her hair flipped around in a wide arc.

And nothing's gonna ever keep you down.

Taylor brought her head and her whole body with it around in Penny's direction. Attached to her body was a fist that was aiming for Penny's head.

You're the best around.

Penny let the punch connect with her cage, bracing her neck for the blow. There was a ring of metal and Penny felt warm drops of blood spray her cheeks as the fist connected and tore skin off Taylor's knuckles.

Nothing's gonna ever keep you dowwwwwwn.

With Taylor's body turned from the blow, it exposed her back, and Penny grabbed the bottom of her jersey and pulled it up and over the top of Taylor's head. Penny unleashed a flurry of blows through the opening in the jersey.

Taylor flailed for a few more moments, trying to get her arms free but in the end lost her footing and went down.

Penny stepped back, feeling blood pumping heavily through her ears. The girl on the ground in front of her fought to free herself from her own jersey, leaving little drag marks of blood where her bloody knuckles contacted the ice. When she finally got the jersey off it looked like she was about to get to her feet again but now the officials came between them and guided them both off. Both teams were cheering the outcome, and it seemed like the Swifties were cheering for Penny too.

Penny exited the bench and went down the tunnel to her dressing room. As she passed Coach on the bench, Coach gave her a brimming grin and thumbs up.

Penny took her skates and socks off and let her bare feet cool in the open air. She wiggled her toes and then tried to match the motion with her fingers. Her left hand was already swelling up and the knuckles were bruised. Penny went to look for ice and caught an image of herself in the bathroom mirror with little trickles of blood on her cheeks. She ran water in the tap and splashed it over her face until she got it off.

Then the team came in and there was an eruption of cheers and her teammates swarmed around her. Penny was hoisted off the ground and hugged by a mob of humans all at once. Coach hung at the back of the mob, but when Penny caught her eye Coach nodded and repeated the closed fist signal to Penny. Penny managed to get a hand free to return the signal and nod back. The two understood each other.

All in all she thought, as she sat in Pat's truck getting a ride home after the game and holding an ice pack over her knuckles, if she was ever going to do that again she needed to prepare for the celebration a lot more than the fight.

10. First NHL Game

Growing up in southern Saskatchewan, the only professional sport that Penny's family had followed had been the Saskatchewan Roughriders of the Canadian Football League. Fall and winter might have been for hockey, but summer was for football. And Penny's dad bled as green and white as they came. A lifelong season ticket holder for the Riders and a proud member of Rider's Nation, Mr. Davies would take turns bringing a member of his family on the trip into Regina with him for a game. Some of Penny's earliest memories were those long days of driving and football, hot dogs, watermelon hats, and warm pretzels. If it was a really late game, Mr. Davies would rent a hotel on the outskirts of Regina and he and his companion for the weekend would get to stay overnight and stay up watching movies on the hotel's movie channel until they fell asleep. At least, that was what Penny had always done on those nights.

As Penny's hockey career continued, her interest in the Riders and the CFL dropped off. She would still go to the games with her dad and watch the away games on tv. Doing so was still a requirement for continuing to live in the Davies house and carry the Davies name. But more and more Penny wanted to see a real NHL game. It didn't even matter which teams were playing. Saskatchewan didn't have a professional team in the NHL, so like many of her neighbors Penny was stuck choosing between the Calgary Flames, Edmonton Oilers, or the Winnipeg Jets, all of which were over 800km away (in opposite directions) if she wanted to pick a "local" favorite. Penny had an affinity for any Canadian team, but beyond that none of them had any stronger claim to her affections than any other.

Her parents had struggled to handle her request. The expense and challenges of traveling to a game in the middle of their already active schedules with 3 boys and one Penny in the middle of th school year while NHL play was underway seemed like insurmountable barriers. Penny had understood this, or at least heard the same explanations for why it wasn't possible enough times to have stopped asking. Shortly after she stopped, the Winter Classic was announced. And that changed everything.

In the mid 2010's the National Hockey League resurrected the Heritage Classic game. The Heritage Classic is an annual game played outdoors at one arena in Eastern Canada and one arena in Western Canada. Whenever possible, these games are held at venues in host cities that are not normally home to an NHL team. In 2019, the Western Canada Heritage Classic was to be held at Mosaic Stadium in Regina, the same stadium that the Roughriders play at. The same stadium Davies senior had been taking Penny to watch football at for her entire life.

Penny heard about the Classic from her coach one morning at practice, and the second she was released from the dressing room she raced out to her car to ask her dad to get tickets. She'd had to ask three times, having to calm down in between each retelling, before Davies senior could comprehend what she was asking. But once he finally understood it was agreed he would do whatever he could to make sure Penny could go.

Mr. Davies set out on his quest to fulfill that commitment with the same zeal as if he was joining King Arthur on a quest for the holy grail. He researched everything he could about the event. When and where it was being held. What teams were playing. When would tickets be released. He found out tickets were being offered to the two competing teams' season ticket holders first, then "remaining tickets" would be made public a few weeks later. Mr. Davies phoned everyone he knew in Winnipeg and Calgary. He connected with family he'd not spoken to in years. He found old school friends on social media and asked if they were season ticket holders. He even entered every single local radio call-in contest he could to get the tickets before the public release but in the end he was unsuccessful.

Mr. Davies spent the next week until the public tickets were released in mortal dread. He knew this was something he *needed* to do for his daughter. Things were already changing in their relationship as she was getting older and more parts of her life were getting closed off from him. Pat was already more involved in her hockey life than he was, and of course, Mrs. Davies and her teammates were the only ones involved in the ever-expanding *female* parts of his daughter's life. All that to say however, Mr. Davies still had a daughter that seemed to love and respect him and had not been failed by him. Not yet anyway. And he was afraid that this was going to be the first time he wouldn't come through for her.

So on the morning the tickets became available to the public, Mr. Davies took the morning off from work. He set himself up in his garage away from the rest of the family, and poured himself a coffee with Baileys. Or more accurately, a Baileys with coffee. Something told him by the end of this morning he'd need it.

At the moment his phone clicked over to 10am Mr. Davies hit "send" on the phone number he'd looked up earlier that morning. He was so ready for a busy signal and the need to redial, he hung up as soon as the other end started ringing. Dammit! He thought to himself and dialed the number again. Once again it rang. This time he waited. "Thank you for calling. Our menu options have changed. Please listen to all options before making your selection." Came the automated voice from the other end. "For new ticket sales, please press 1".

Mr. Davies pressed 1 on his phone. He hoped there were lots of other people out there who would actually listen to the instructions and wait to hear all the options first. He'd be ahead of them at least. A few moments later a sleepy and surprisingly un-frantic voice clicked on the other end of the line. "Hello?" It asked.

"Hello." Said Mr. Davies. Dead air responded. "Is this the ticket company?"

"Yes sir." The voice yawned. "If you are having issues with your online order, please hang up and call back to our technical support number."

"I don't have an online order." Mr. Davies told him.

"Oh, do you need someone to help you setup an account to create an order?" The voice droned on.

"No, I just want to buy tickets." Mr. Davies replied. There was a long pause.

"Like, over the phone?" The voice on the phone sounded as if Mr. Davies was asking to take a walk on Mars.

"Yes, *like*, over the phone." Mr. Davies said mocking the tone. "Two tickets to the Heritage Classic in Regina."

"Um, just a minute. I need to check something." Another long pause. "Oh, yes ok I can still do that." Came the reply, not a small amount of surprise evident. There was typing on a keyboard on the other end and Mr. Davies heard the voice mutter, "Man you see something new every day."

And so, thanks to the advanced technology of the telephone, Mr. Davies scored himself and Penny a pair of tickets to the game. Meanwhile, a news story erupted about the online ticket system crashing and thousands of people sitting in infinite queues for available tickets or losing access to the ones they had already purchased. Mr. Davies listened from the blissful position of someone with *his* tickets safely available at Will-Call.

Mr. Davies told Penny about the tickets after her next game. Her team had lost again but he wanted her to have something happy to hold onto. Penny had given him such a tight hug of thanks that he could feel the breath being forced out of him. When she finally released him, she bounded off into her own space in their house, laughing like a little girl and calling thank you behind her.

Penny counted down the days, and it became part of their daily ritual to mark a big red X on the calendar as they counted off the months, then weeks, and finally days before the game. Every night before supper the red marker would come out and the game would inch one day closer, becoming that much more real each time.

It finally arrived on a crisp late October day. The Davies' had spent the Friday night before the game getting their home ready for Halloween. They had carved pumpkins and put them out on the porch, blown up the big inflatable Frankenstein and staked it into the yard, and went through the annual odyssey of finding and making operable Mr. Davies' Halloween Candy bowl with the motion activated hand that tried to grab your hand when you were reaching for candy.

He and Penny left for Regina just before lunch the day of the game. The slow, flat highway trek saw a mix of snow and rain as the weather outside bounced around the freezing mark. There was nothing to impede their progress though, and Penny and Mr. Davies passed the time chatting about Penny's increasing presence on her team as one of the squad's tough, physical defenders.

"I didn't realize women's hockey allowed enforcers." Mr. Davies was saying.

"Oh geeze, I'm hardly an enforcer." Penny laughed back. "How can you be an enforcer in a league that doesn't allow fighting or checking?"

"Isn't that what your team calls you though?" Mr. Davies pressed. "I was sure I heard Shiv calling you "Goon" the other day."

Penny laughed again. "Yeah, that's my nickname on the team now. I didn't pick it. They call me that because I sort of not really meaning to stood up to a big bully in one of our games. She ended up getting herself thrown out and I got a nickname out of it."

"Ah." Mr. Davies replied, clearly not appeased by the answer. "Even if there isn't hitting or fighting, you need to be careful out there. You don't need to look much farther than your brothers to see where getting your nose into the wrong business can get you in the game."

Penny rolled her eyes at that comment. Always back to Pat and Paul and their misadventures. "Dad, I'm being careful." Penny promised. "I know my limits. Sometimes I just have to stand up for some of these girls though, you know? Some of them don't know what the game is about like I – like *we* do in our family, and if someone isn't watching their backs they're going to get hurt."

"Well, it's you getting hurt I worry about." Mr. Davies concluded, but let the subject drop. They spent the rest of the trip chatting about the current Roughriders' season and the challenges the team was facing as their playoffs were coming up in a few weeks.

It was just after entering Regina that the problems started. Mr. Davies cell phone battery died and along with it the navigation to the stadium. Penny quickly realized the charging cable he'd been plugged into for the drive wasn't working anymore, so they had to make a detour to three separate gas stations to find one that sold the right car charger. Penny offered repeatedly to let him use her phone, but Mr. Davies wanted his own back in case they got separated.

When they were coming out of the gas station they had purchased the charger from, they were just in time to see a couple of kids in an old station wagon clip their truck's fender trying to park. On its own the accident would probably have been fine, but the panicked driver locked eyes with Mr. Davies and kept going forward instead of stopping. This had the effect of further denting, and then shearing off completely the big metal fender from the back of Mr. Davies truck, which the station wagon promptly ran over before finally stopping.

Between the exchange of information, getting the police out for the mandatory police report, and Mr. Davies doing enough reattaching his fender, a slow and easy afternoon in the city had been eaten up entirely.

Penny and her dad continued their travels as it was starting to get dark – nearly 5pm. They made it to the stadium parking lot two hours before the initial puck drop was to take place. It was lightly snowing with a harsh edge to the wind. It reminded Penny of "rink weather" – a long running joke between hockey players about the perennial conditions they played in skating a mere few feet over a frozen slab of ice. The two Davies generations sat in the back of the truck eating a picnic meal with warm canned chili Mr. Davies cooked on a small camp stove. They watched the fans wearing all flavor of jerseys – most of Canadian teams of course – filtering into the stadium. Penny smiled noticing that over half the people were wearing Roughrider jerseys anyway, just like her dad had chosen to do. Soon they heard the scraping of skates on ice carried on the wind when the warmup skate started. They talked of all the memorable games they had seen at this place over the years, and players current and past that they had cheered for. None in a hockey jersey before today. Finally, about half an hour before puck drop they grabbed their blankets and made their way to the ticket booth, picked up their tickets, and went inside to find their seats.

They were high up in the stands and their seats looked down into the visitor's end corner. The rink was surrounded by an artificial snowpack, but it was only a few feet wide. The rink itself only filled about half the playing field and the empty space and football markings where it had been set up made it look as if the rink was a child's toy that had been left in the middle of the lawn, even though it was about to be host to a professional sporting event.

The lights dimmed and the players hit the ice amidst a flurry of spotlights and the classic jock jam version of "Panama" blaring. The starting lineups were announced and the players lined up, while at center ice a pair of young men entered the ice to sing the national anthem. The stadium stood and removed their toques and put down their beers to sing "O Canada". As the song ended there was a pair of fiery eruptions from the Flames' end of the ice as flame cannons sent plumes of fire upwards. Even from their seats Penny and her dad could feel the heat and both were caught off guard by the intensity of the surprise.

"The Flames take their name seriously." Her dad joked, laughing off the shock. Penny just nodded agreement. The opening faceoff had started and the players were now fighting for the puck at center ice.

Penny watched intently as the teams spent the first five minutes in a hurried end-to-end game that saw them changing ends impossibly fast but not getting much offense going for either team. There was finally an icing and the players skated to their benches.

"Why are they doing that?" Penny asked. "Shouldn't they just be back on the faceoff?"

"I don't know." Her dad said. "Maybe the refs are looking at a penalty?"

From behind her a gruff voice muffled by a heavy scarf piped up, "It's a TV timeout. The players might as well get some water while the average Joe at home watches the beer and truck ads."

"They stop the game for *that*?" Penny asked incredibly. She'd never really thought about how commercials in live sports might work before, but that made sense. She'd seen this in Riders games but the interruptions felt more normal in football because of all the play stoppages in the game to begin with.

"'Cor!" The gruff voice laughed. "That's what all this is! Just the window dressing to sell beer and F-150s!"

The players were getting back onto the ice to resume play. Penny couldn't believe that her minor female league wouldn't stop for a player break like that in a million years, but here at the highest level of professional play in the country, the entire game came to a halt just to "be back after these messages". Wow! She thought.

The play continued back and forth until the next break, after which Winnipeg finally got a strong offensive push going and managed to hold Calgary in their own end for a couple shifts in a row. The Flames goalie had to make a big save which Penny found herself "oooooh"ing to along with the rest of the crowd, and Sean Monahan sent the rebound flying with a frantic backhand. Unfortunately for him it went flying over the glass, earning him a delay of game penalty.

Penny edged forward in her seat. There was a sudden hush across the 33,000 fans in the stadium as the tension built. The referee dropped the puck for the first faceoff in the Calgary end. A quick shot from the point! Wide! It was picked up along the boards and the Jets got a good cycle going. To the faceoff circle, to the point, a cross ice pass, to the slot, but no shot, and back again to the point. Winnipeg held the zone for nearly the entire two minutes and Penny caught herself holding her breath more than once. Her hands gripped the sides of the cold, hard plastic seat below her and she bounced her legs nervously. But for all the excitement nothing happened. The penalty ended, and the teams ended the first period in a 0-0 tie.

A band called the Sheepdogs started playing from the opposite endzone from Penny and her dad and the snow picked up during the intermission.

The Zamboni executed its mesmerizing ice ballet and disappeared, leaving the glistening ice to freeze under the falling snow behind it.

Penny's dad went to the concourse for a restroom break and came back as the band was finishing. He handed Penny a hot chocolate in a small disposable Styrofoam cup. She didn't drink it at first but sat holding it with both hands between her thighs, welcoming the warmth it gave off.

"Thanks dad." She said out of the blue.

"It's fine," he said, "the line wasn't that long."

"No I didn't mean the chocolate – I mean – thank you for that too. But um I mean for doing this. I know you said getting the tickets were no big deal but to me…" Her gaze swept over the giant crowd and the rink with the players just returning to their benches. "…this IS a big deal. Thank you."

For the entire drive back and years to come, Mr. Davies would say that at that point a very large snowflake landed on his eyes and melted down his cheek. Penny will know however that it is one of the few times she had seen her father shed a tear.

The second period picked up with an amped up tempo over the first. The teams started with quick line changes and got their "energy lines" on the ice. That got the hitting going in the game and there were some big hits. Penny shouted out more than once in surprise at the sheer force of the impacts even as far back as she was.

Calgary picked up a pair of penalties in the first half of the period, and gave Winnipeg dangerous back-to-back power plays. Once again the Jets swarmed but failed to convert. Penny joined a chorus of boos from the crowd as their second back-to-back power play ended. She could only imagine what Coach would be saying to her bench if they had gone 0 for 3 on the power plays.

Momentum swung the other direction shortly thereafter. Winnipeg lost a man to a hooking call and Calgary put one in to take the first lead of the game on the powerplay. Once again flames erupted from the pyrotechnics at the Calgary end of the field and regardless what team you were cheering for, a smile came to the face of every person in the stadium when the wall of heat reached where they were sitting. As the penalty expired, Winnipeg got hit with another penalty that resulted in a lengthy coach's challenge and video review. Penny and the rest of the stadium waited in the cold wind and sleet while the referees huddled around the 55-yard line of Mosaic stadium and waited themselves for the ruling from Toronto.

The conference finally ended and the call on the ice was upheld. Winnipeg went to another PK which Calgary spent failing to do much more than play dump and chase as they struggled to gain the zone without the Winnipeg D-line icing the puck. Penny clapped harder each time the puck slid back out of the Winnipeg zone and down the ice, cheering in proud camaraderie with the skill the defense was showing in killing this power play.

At the second intermission, Penny joined her dad on the concourse and put her "sharp elbows" as Shiv called them to use fighting through the crowd to the restrooms. Not that the effort mattered much when there was a ten minute lineup to use a stall.

The third period started right as she was sitting back down. Her dad was finishing off a conversation with the gentleman in the row behind them who had explained the TV timeouts. Penny thought it sounded like they were sharing thoughts on the Riders' post-season chances.

The third started in a flurry (both literal and figurative as the snow picked up.) Calgary started on the power play after a boarding call on Winnipeg at the end of the 2nd. Calgary pushed hard and got several shots off while also holding the zone for most of their 2-minute advantage. Winnipeg was back on their heels and only their goalie seemed to be on his game, keeping everything out until the clock expired.

Fresh legs spent, Calgary gave up a sloppy transition after the power play ended and a bad line change exacerbated their problems. Just before the 5-minute mark in the 3rd, Winnipeg tied the game. Fatigue and frustration caught up with Calgary and their Captain, Mark Giordano, took a bad hooking call a few seconds after the play resumed.

Penny was on the edge of her seat again as Winnipeg went back on the powerplay. A quick back-pass from the faceoff and a shot from the point – saved! Held for a faceoff. Back into play Winnipeg cycled it to the board, across, then back through center ice trying to find an open man in the slot. Calgary gained possession and tried to skate it out but that led to a turnover and Winnipeg had an odd man rush back from the neutral zone. A pass in front – the shot – saved and held again!

Penny took a breath. The pace was incredible, she couldn't believe how fast the skaters were making their plays and transitioning from one direction of play to the other. The next faceoff went to the boards and there was a bone rattling crash as Calgary went full body on the Winnipeg forward who went to retrieve it. Both men went down and were immediately back up to their knees, sticks jamming away to get the puck loose.

The power play ended and there was an icing call immediately after Winnipeg's fifth player got off the ice. That led to a TV time out and players and spectators alike had a chance to catch their breath. Play resumed but slower and more deliberate as both teams tightened up their defensive play to avoid giving up a late game goal to their opponent.

The third ended, tied one-one and sudden death 3-on-3 ensued. Calgary got a penalty almost as soon as the period started, but managed to hold off Winnipeg's 4-on-3 for the whole advantage. However they had a bad change right after the penalty expired and let Winnipeg get a 1 on 1 breakaway. The Flames goalie went down into his butterfly a split second too late and Winnipeg won the game in OT.

Penny was with the rest of the stadium on her feet and cheering at the finish.

In the moment, Penny wouldn't stop and think about what it meant or that going to her first NHL game would do for her in the future. She was just happy that her team had won and done so in a very exciting way. She was swept away on the tide of emotion rippling through the stadium and sharing the experience with thousands of other like minded lovers of the game. Later, when she was nodding off in the car on the way back home, she would find herself taking a moment to think about that moment. She thought about how hard her dad had worked to get them the tickets, and wondered how many more games they would be able to see together like this. She had never much appreciated the Riders games he took her to as more than a daddy-daughter activity, but she was suddenly very thankful for them and for the ones they would have together in the future. She smiled and tried to think of what the feeling had been when she'd jumped to her feet to celebrate and the rest of the stadium had done the same. Excited? Yes, but it wasn't the excitement that she felt the most she realized. Being excited with that many other people at once, about a hockey game played outside in the cold and snow in late October, she had felt *Canadian*. Felt like this was a place that she belonged and was a part of as much as it was a part of her. It was a feeling that she thought back to whenever she got on the ice to warm up after that. And many years in the future it would be the night she talked about when she gave her dad's eulogy in front of her own daughters. He had, after all, on a snowy night in October, been the one who'd shown her what it meant to be part of the country she lived in and in time, played for with their name on her jersey. But those days were still ahead of her, those many moments of deeper meaning not yet lived. For now, Penny rested her head against the window and listened to the wind whipping past the car and drifted off to sleep.

11. Hockey Gear for Girls

In Penny's house growing up the biggest event of the summer was Wilson's Old Fashioned Hockey Shop's annual gear sale. For four days following the August long weekend, Wilson would put his new gear for the next season on sale. This was a tradition Rashid continued after buying the store from retiring Wilson a few years back, and if anything the sale had grown.

It wasn't just that Wilson's had the largest selection of hockey equipment in the town and your next option was the Canadian Tire sports section just up the highway. It wasn't just that Wilson's was a local institution and when you were part of a close community like the Maple Creek hockey parents, you supported the institutions that supported you. No, the popularity had endured because Wilson's annual gear sale had become *the* hockey social event of the off-season.

Wilson's store was packed for the four days. Parents had to wait for a chance to go through with their kids and select their gear. This meant that there was a big crowd every day of hockey parents and hockey kids waiting in the parking lot with not much to do but talk to one another. Well, at first there hadn't been much to do. Carol's bakery from across the road had been the first to capitalize on Wilson's sale and started setting up a pancake breakfast station in the corner of his parking lot to feed the crowd and issue out much needed coffee. Over the years more businesses had pitched in and now the wait to get into Wilson's was more of an event than the shopping sprees happening inside. There were face painters and roller skates for the kids. Leroy who ran the music and announced for hockey games would bring his Pontiac Vibe and leave the windows open with the 2017 NHL Stadium Anthems jock jams mix playing on repeat. And even Mr. Perlich and his wife would ride their antique Ford pickup into town with a pair of their goat kids and let them walk around for the little ones to pet.

None of this was organized of course. There was no festival committee and neither Wilson, nor Rashid after him, had ever invited or had to approve any of these businesses to come operate in their parking lot. The community collectively saw that a big group of people together in the same place and time every year had potential and the New Gear Day festivities just popped up like overnight dandelions.

One of the biggest hits every year though was the corner of the lot where the parents gathered who had equipment to trade. Wilson's had a used equipment section of course, where returned or consignment skates or pads could get resold to the next generation of players. But during the sale buying and pricing and inventory control was too much so before he retired Wilson had made a rule that there would be no exchanges for old equipment during the sale. The only hard and fast rule that the kindly AA men's league retiree had ever had in his business.

So instead, a widely approved "grey market" popped up in the corner of the lot. Parents with kids aging out of gear would bring their equipment and parents with kids growing into a new size would bring their kids along to try their luck. There was never a guarantee, of course, that you'd find something in your kids' size or that someone would need exactly what you were offering, but if a pair of people could find a match, it was a win for you both. The kids of course, hoped for anything but. Getting lucky in the grey market corner meant you were getting someone else's used equipment instead of brand new only-ever-yours gear inside. A much more sensible mindset when you weren't the one paying the bill.

If you were a lucky kid and made it into the store without finding everything you needed used, then it was like Christmas. During the sale week, Wilson's was crammed to the rafters with every new hockey gadget, doodad, cardboard cutout, and piece of NHL apparel the shelves could fit. Every kid had that *one* new thing they knew they absolutely needed for the upcoming season. A specific helmet, or stick, or type of skates that was guaranteed to make them a better player than they were last season. The thing at the top of their wish list that all their teammates would envy. And Wilson's always seemed to deliver, too. It was rare that Rashid didn't have that *one* height and flex of stick in a special display off to the side somewhere, and even rarer that you went away empty-handed after he told you he would "check the back, but don't hold your breath."

No celebration Penny had experienced elsewhere had ever lived up to those days visiting Wilson's. Her brothers would reunite with their former teammates, often seeing them for the first time since the start of the summer. Her parents would run into other parents they knew, often not seen in just as long. Combining the festive air of reunion with the festival atmosphere of the vendors and the event itself, and capped off with the promise of a shopping spree for a piece of hockey equipment you had been dreaming of all summer, and Wilson's new gear sale days were the best of the year.

As exciting and festive as the experience had been though, Penny had endured her share of disappointments as well. Like a kid that doesn't get what they want from Santa, or the cousin at the end of the kids table who misses out on the rice pudding because they were the last in line, Wilson's annual hockey sale could disappoint too.

The disappointments were never Rashid's fault.. Like those enterprising women going back to the Monstrous Regiment whose trailblazing forays into male-dominated fields left them woefully lacking in equipment fitting to their needs, Penny would venture forth to find *her* needs sort-of-kind-of met. At best. Finding skates for example, in women's sizes meant you could get recreational skates or figure skates. If you wanted women's hockey skates, you had to drive into Regina and even then you usually had to get them special ordered. Penny and her teammates were mostly stuck with the second-hand lineup of boys skates, which always ended up being a bit too wide and with more wiggle room in the toe than they should. And they smelled like boy feet to boot!

A helmet was a helmet, though the rules for the female league required full cages. Most of the boys were already into half-visors by the time they were the age Penny could join the female league, so full cage helmets appropriate for her age group were rare. Penny's team had taken to buying back the helmets from previous players who had aged out, but the quality and sizes varied widely. And you hoped the girl that had it before you didn't use some weird, exotic conditioner that made you gag every time you put the helmet on. Except they usually did. That made helmets a problem too.

And then there were the pads. God give me strength, Penny thought, the pads. Whoever's idea it was to force young women just on the cusp of getting their first period to confront an older middle eastern man like Rashid and with a straight face ask him if he had pads in the right size for a teenage girl and explain to him, for the third time, why the latest set of pads he'd pulled out of the back was still *too tight across the chest*, those moments were a special kind of torture.

And all the while, the line of teenage boys waiting impatiently for their turn just gave the scene the worst possible audience. You can imagine what they did when Penny asked for a "chest protector" or "stiffer stick shaft." If Penny had a low opinion of hockey boys before going in each year, the trips to Wilson's always seemed to reinforce for her the image of immaturity and general douchery of the males her age.

Future seasons would get easier, but the shortage of appropriate gear and prodding from the boys never really got better. Instead, Penny found that innovating solutions to limitations of equipment for her needs and trying out "equipment hacks for girls" she found online were great fun. Penny became a master at modding her equipment to be just right for her. Like so many women before her, if the path that had been walked before didn't fit for her, she would learn to make a new one.

Despite the challenges, Penny did find Wilson's annual sale one of the best parts of the season. It was one of the few times that players from all the different ages and leagues came together. Just as any good festival should, it provided a chance to run into old and new faces and get acquainted all over again. Penny's equipment hacks meant that she developed a following among the moms and younger players that gathered in the parking lot. Whoever was lucky enough to get her hand-me-downs won the girls' equipment lottery, and the moms would watch attentively as Penny showed them how to do the same to their kids' equipment. Those were moments Penny loved.

One year when Penny was 15 Rashid actually offered Penny a job for the event. He was getting tired of getting caught in between the town's small female hockey player community and the limitations his suppliers and general business economics imposed on his ability to meet their needs. So he hired Penny to meet up with the girl players in the parking lot before they even got into the store, come back with lists of what they needed, and run the samples and options out to them. Penny relished the job, though the *best* part was the envious glares all the boys gave her and the girl players that they were getting this special concierge service while they had to wait around in line. The job didn't pay well, but Penny would have done it for free just to have the chance to see those looks of envy all sale long.

Penny will, in time, use her experiences with procuring women's hockey gear as the basis of her University entrance essay as an "example of a time she overcame adversity." The challenge of finding gear suited for women would plague Penny long after she grew out of the minors and eventually left Maple Creek. In her higher levels of play, she still found herself spending evenings or weekends off working on new mods she would research to make things fit and work that much better *for her*.

12. Goon Goalie

Everyone knew that Bricks was going to Mexico. Twelve days, all inclusive. She had been talking about it since Penny's 2nd season with the Beavs had started, and there hadn't been a single practice or game where it hadn't made its way into the conversation. Reviewing the game calendar – did the team know that the ancient Mayans had developed the most advanced calendar of their time and used it to predict everything from weather to natural disasters hundreds of years after their civilization fell. Did the team know that many believed the first precursor to soccer was played in the great temples of the early Central Americans?

It was safe to say that the entire squad was relieved when she finally went on the trip, if only so that they could stop hearing about it. The entire squad that was, except number 38, Emma Francis, who played backup goaltender. Emma sat on the bench through the season wearing goalie pads and took a few shots during warmup *just in case*. Twelve games into the season, Bricks left and Emma hadn't seen a single minute of ice time. Emma was in her first season, a rookie, and had offered to be the backup goaltender because it meant she had to play as little as possible. Her skills in training camp hadn't been bad, not exceptional but certainly passable for a new recruit with no previous hockey experience, but her confidence had never emerged about being on the team. Enrolled by her father to try and get her out of the shell of her bedroom and its equal mountains of books and stuffed animals, Emma was about as home on the ice as a polar bear in Arizona.

But like everyone else, Emma had known Bricks' vacation was coming and knew that meant she was going to have to step up eventually. And in fairness, she did. For Exactly twelve minutes and sixteen seconds of the first game after Bricks left.

It had been a rookie mistake, even Emma knew that. The puck had come down on a long shot from the far end and she was sure it was going to be an icing call. It had gone wide of the net and Emma had seen members of the opposing team going for a change and one of the Beavs skating back for it. She *hadn't* seen the forechecking forward, fresh off a line change, jump into the play ahead of her teammate and clearly going to win the race to the puck. Emma was expecting a whistle any second when she skated out of her net and over to the puck, against the back boards almost eight feet from the net and the safety of her crease. She beat the forechecker by a full second, but the incoming forward came in shoulder first and collided hard with Emma.

Both girls went down on the ice but the forward was up quickly – being the only one of the two aware of and ready for the impending collision – as well as the only one of the two without any injuries. The forward slid the puck easily into the net before the other players got there and the goal light went on.

While the other team skated their celebration and did the fly-by their bench, the Beavs' trainer came out on the ice where Emma was moaning and grabbing her leg. It didn't take long to assess that she was properly injured and needed more than an ice pack or pat on the shoulder to get back into play. It took a few minutes to get her off the ice and to the dressing room where she could be treated before the ambulance arrived. Those few minutes gave the players on the bench time to discuss just what the hell to do now.

With their first stringer in Mexico and their second stringer down, the Beavs were at the bottom of their depth chart in net. If someone didn't step up, they would have to forfeit.

The ref skated over and had a conference with the Beav's coach before skating over to talk to the other team. "Shiv," Penny whispered while they were talking, "You were great in goal on our other team." Shiv gave her a look and shook her head. "No really, you could bail us out."

"I can't." Shiv said more firmly than Penny expected. "My mom said I could play hockey but not play in goal. If I do she'll pull me from the team."

"Oh." Penny's face flushed, looking behind the bench and spotting Shiv's mom in the stands a few rows from the top, arms sternly crossed. "Sorry, I didn't mean to push."

"Okay everyone we have a problem." Coach said loudly, sounding like it wasn't the first time she'd said it. "Emma's out and the ref is giving us 5 minutes to get a replacement geared up and in net before we forfeit. Do we want that, or do we want a chance to get back in this for Emma?"

The murmuring on the bench was hardly the resounding battle cry Coach had hoped for. She looked coolly at each player and locked eyes with as many as she could. She fixed her gaze on Penny and Penny looked at Shiv, Shiv's mom, and before she knew what she was saying Penny put her hand up and said she'd do it.

Her teammates and Coach looked at her with relief, and Penny went to the locker room to put Emma's pads on.

Penny emerged from the dressing room and back out onto the bench. The unfamiliar equipment wasn't exactly her size and shifted awkwardly as she moved. She carried the oversized goalie stick over her shoulder like a sword to keep it from whacking her in the shins each time she walked.

Penny got onto the ice and skated over to her net. The ref came up and checked if she was set and ready to resume play. Penny shrugged at the question. "As I'll ever be." She sighed. Penny pulled the goalie cage down over her head, glancing back quickly at Emma's water bottle still atop the netting, and got into her best approximation of the goalie "ready" squat position with her stick on the ice in front of her and her glove hand up at the ready.

The faceoff was to Penny's right side at her end of the ice, and the other team's center easily won the puck from Fleur. It fluttered back to the point and the big waiting let loose a slap shot. The shot blew clean through the screen of players between Penny and the shooterin what seemed like far too little time. Penny heard, then felt, the solid **thud** as the puck impacted her chest protector. Then everyone was skating at her. Penny looked down, breaking her surprise and searching for the puck. It was near her feet in the scratched blue paint of the crease.

Muscle memory kicked in and Penny tried to swing the heavy goalie stick in a sweeping motion to move the puck off to the corner, but it was far too heavy and her grip was wrong for that maneuver. In desperation, Penny fell to her knees and threw her body atop the loose puck. Whack, whack, WHACK, thud… Penny felt several blows on her back, arms and helmet as the players reach her and fought to get the puck loose. Then there was a harsh tweet of the referee's whistle and it was over. Penny huddled there a second, catching her breath from how fast everything had just happened. She barely noticed the first time the ref asked if she was ok to resume play. The second time Penny unfolded her body, handed the ref the puck, and steeled herself.

The next faceoff Fleur won and Becks managed to pick the puck up and skate it out to center ice before dumping it into the other end. Penny watched both teams changeup their skaters and the Beavs managed to hold the zone for a solid minute of offensive zone possession. Penny watched the other team's goalie handling the shots from the Beavs, wondering at how she seemed to have her glove in position before Penny's teammates even took their shots.

The puck came free to center ice and the teams changed again, which led to an attack by the other team. Shiv's d-line was slow getting back and Penny found herself facing a 2-on-1 with the opposing team coming straight at her. Her sole defender tried to poke check it away from the puck carrier but missed and had planted her feet in the process, letting the two opponents face Penny unopposed.

Penny watched as they passed the puck from left to right. Penny stepped to the right, pushing her body as tight up against the post of her net as she could and holding her left glove hand in front of as much of the empty space to her other side as she could. She watched the winger's eyes as they got closer, and saw a flicker for a second while the other player looked to her side. Penny didn't wait. She pushed off to cover the other side of the net. The puck left the incoming winger's stick heading to her offensive partner. Penny caught the edge of her skate and fell sideways, the world taking on a strange angle as she fell. The winger receiving the pass had her stick back ready to bury the one-timer. Time slowed. Penny's heartbeats did too. Beat. The puck reached the feet of the left winger. Beat. There was a CRACK and the slap shot connected. Beat. The puck was in the air, heading to the empty space Penny had left. Beat. Penny felt the cold hard surface of the ice receive her body and pain in her shoulder as it was the first part to make contact. Beat. The puck collided squarely with the stick-side blocker that was following Penny's body to the ground.

The puck shot straight up but away from the net. Penny tried to follow it but in the goalie mask and lying on her side she couldn't do so. She scrambled to her feet but not before the incoming player whose shot she had just blocked stopped hard right in front of Penny and showered her with a tiny storm of ice shavings. Penny blinked the melting snow from her eyes and re-centered herself. The play was now against the boards to the left of her. It looked like Shiv was digging into one of the opposing players hard, and sure enough the other player lost her footing and went down, leaving Shiv free to skate the puck out. Penny let out a long breath she had been holding and let fresh air fill her body.

She faced four more shots that period and managed not to let any in. She didn't feel as if she'd made any saves, but she'd gotten her body between the puck and the net and so far that had been enough. She followed her team to the dressing room for the first intermission feeling generally ok with how things were going.

During the intermission Penny quieted her mind by putting in her headphones and tuning out the teammates trying to chatter at her and give her pointers. After the game there'd be time for that. And besides, how much help would any advice really be for her first time ever playing a new position needing as much preparation as goaltender? No, dumb luck and a general lack of skill by the other team were about the only things she had going for her and whatever hand-me-down nuggets of wisdom her teammates had in the middle of this game weren't going to change the outcome. So in went the headphones. Penny knew exactly what song she needed to hear right now, and it wasn't one she had on her game day playlist. She pulled up an online streaming service instead and a few moments later the funky intro to the Commodore's "She's a brick house" filled her ears. Penny grinned broadly at the aptness of the song. She had time to repeat it once before the intermission ended, and Penny swaggered back down the tunnel and onto the ice strutting her stick and blocker out in front of her in time as she sang in her head, "Oh yeah, I'm a brick – house – oh yeah."

Channeling her inner brick wall and more prepared now, Penny skated out onto the ice and lined up at the goal. And immediately noticed her mistake. The other team was taking to the ice now and their starting line were lining up... directly in front of Penny facing the other way! Penny realized what was going on just as the opposing goalie tapped her on the shoulder and pointed insistently to the empty net at the other end of the ice. The teams had switched ends at the intermission and Penny, not used to leading the team onto the ice, had been so caught up in her own head that she'd skated to the net she covered in the first period! Flushing crimson she skated as quickly as she could in her pads to where she was supposed to be.

She might have broken down at that point. She might have been ready to walk off the ice in embarrassment. But as she crossed center she heard Shiv jeering at her from her own bench – "Cherry Picker!" She heard Shiv shouting, and others on the bench joined in. It was such a ridiculous, situationally inappropriate thing to say Penny had to laugh. And she did the rest of the way to her net. If there was one thing her team was good for, it was a shot in the arm right when she needed it most. Penny got into her position. The puck dropped. And the second period was underway.

Her first two shots were soft ones. One was barely a shot but just a hard dump-in from the neutral zone that she passed off after her team changed lines, the next was a fanned-on one-timer that she dropped to her knees and covered with her glove for a play stoppage. The other team got a penalty off the face-off and Penny had a long pause before she saw more action.

The play clock was down to fourteen minutes when the players found their way back to Penny's end of the ice. Her team was doing a good job of bottling the other team up at the blue line. They weren't doing much in the way of offense, but Penny could tell that her team were really stepping up their defensive game to keep as much of the play away from her as possible.

Their opponents were getting increasingly frustrated and desperate in their efforts to break into the zone. At the eleven-minute mark their center got some open ice and skated fast into the Beavs' zone, taking a long lead pass in the process. Penny saw the lineswoman raise her zebra-striped arm for the offside, but the opposing center didn't see it. The ref blew the play dead as the center was reaching the slot. Instead of stopping, the center sent a hard wrister directly into the emblem on Penny's jersey… then continued to skate straight on into Penny, knocking her to the ice. Penny crumpled in a heap atop the center while the referee blew a trio of tweets on her whistle.

"Get off me you fat cow." The center growled from beneath Penny.

Pain shot through Penny's shin from the collision. "Shut the hell up." She snarled back. "This was your fault." She struggled to get her feet under her and the other body pushed out of her net.

The center got to her own feet and shoved Penny in the shoulder. "Too bad you're back on your feet." She sneered. "I was hoping I'd get to take out two of you today."

In that moment Penny realized she was facing the same player who'd taken Emma out of the game in the first. And now she'd blatantly ignored the ref and offside and tried to do the same to Penny. Penny glared back and pushed her. The center stumbled over backwards and fell back on the ice. The ref blew the whistle again and arrived at the net. She forced her way between Penny and the other player, holding them apart as the center got back to her feet. If she'd been a cartoon you could have seen steam billowing from her ears.

"That's enough!" The ref shouted. "Roughing penalties for both teams. Get out of here." The center and Penny started to skate off the ice, but the ref grabbed Penny on the shoulder. "Whoa! Where are you going?" The ref asked Penny.

"To the… penalty box?" Penny answer asked.

"Goaltender penalties are served by another team member on the ice. Stay where you are your coach will pick someone."

Jess M. got to sit in the box while the play went four-on-four. Because of the offside before the call the officials decided the face-off should be at center ice. The neutral zone is where most of the penalty time was spent. Neither team seemed to be able to get the upper hand and get a solid offensive push into the other end. Penny was fine with that. She was still breathing hard trying to shake the adrenaline from the encounter with the opposing center. Finally, one of the opposing defenders lost an edge at their own blue line and that opened things up for her team to get a quality scoring chance. Fleur skated the puck in up the boards and got a clean pass back to Li who buried it deep into the other goalie's glove. Fleur and Li skated fast around the back of the net as the goalie dropped the puck and sent it down the ice for icing.

Except the penalty box doors were swinging open. Jess had jumped out the second they'd let her out and she was already halfway to the bench. The opposing center had dawdled her way out of the box which put her in perfect position to grab the pass from her goalie with all the other players still back on the other end of the ice. She skated the puck relentlessly towards Penny, no one even close to her. She deked once, twice, and lined up her shot. Penny skated back and back again, raising her glove hand and filling the net with as much of her body as she could. The center shot to Penny's stick side, and Penny tried to get her stick in front of it but once again got caught up on the weight of the stick and her arm moved impossibly slowly... too slowly... and the puck skittered across the ice and into the net. A buzzer went off and Penny saw the red goal light reflecting off the boards. The center did a victory lap around Penny's end of the ice and just before joining up with her teammates to celebrate, she looked straight at Penny and blew a kiss.

Penny's blood boiled.

The Beavs rallied through the latter half of the second and tied the game up at 2. Penny faced six more shots that period but managed to luck her way through them to avoid giving up any more goals. She was still angry, though a bit less so now, when she and the team went to the dressing room for the intermission. Penny's coach waited for her on the bench so they could walk to the dressing room together.

"You're doing a solid job." Coach told her. "Your whole team sees the extra mile you're going covering for Emma."

"Yeah, well, I should have had that save." Penny grumbled. "This damn thing is useless." She flapped the goalie stick around limply in front of her. "Is there somewhere in the rules that says I *have* to use this stupid thing?"

"Technically no," coach replied, "you can use whatever stick you want, but what else would you use? It's not like we can run you over to Wilson's for new gear in the middle of the game."

Penny suddenly perked up. "Oh, that's not what I had in mind at all." And grinned.

"Wait, what? What are you doing?" The coach asked, but Penny was already bounding ahead of her into the locker room.

Penny came onto the ice to start the third feeling like a new person. The outro of Bachman-Turner Overdrive's "you ain't seen nothing yet" was ringing in her ears and her team were patting her on the helmet and shoulders in the tunnel heading to the ice. Penny skated to her net – the same one she'd *accidentally* gone to the previous period but this time it was where she was supposed to be. Penny tossed her water bottle beside Emma's on top of the net and adjusted her mask. Then she squatted down and gave each post a solid smack with her stick. *Her* stick this time, and *her* gloves. The unfamiliar glove and blocker lay abandoned back in the locker room and Penny had on her defender's gloves and she was carrying her own personal stick. B-b-baby you ain't seen nothin' yet she sang in her head as the ref blew the whistle.

The opening faceoff squirted out of the neutral zone and came straight to Penny. She handled it easily and with her proper stick in hand, was able to confidently flip it back out of the zone and Jess H. picked it up at the blue line to skate it into the other end. Her team got a solid thirty seconds in the other end before getting off a shot that the opposing goalie held to force a play stoppage.

Her team won the faceoff in the other zone and she saw Shiv snap a quick wrister at the net. The red light went on – Shiv had scored! The Beavs were up 3-2. Her team hugged in the other end of the ice and Shiv led the player flyby past the bench. Penny skated out of her net and got a fistbump and big smile from each of the players as they cycled back into position to restart play.

The tempo of the game picked up now, and play went back and forth between the ends. Each team got a good rush going, managed to get a shot off, then would break off and chase the other team back towards their own end trying to avoid getting scored on themselves. Penny faced down a fast-moving two-on-one but knocked the puck safely away. Not long after, another rush and there was a hard shot from the point. Penny got her body in the way and felt the puck rebound off her leg pad. The other team was there to jump on the rebound and Penny faced another shot point blank. That one went straight up and bounced off the grill of Penny's mask with a *CLANG*. Penny managed not to lose sight of the puck and as it came down she hit it with her stick like a baseball bat when it reached chest height and sent it caroming off down the ice.

Pad, shoulder, chest, stick, Penny was finding her groove and handling each new shot with increasing confidence. Without the encumbrance of the heavy goalie stick her body moved like normal again and she was able to get between the puck and the net much more easily.

The center that had taken out Emma and knocked Penny over had her first shift midway through the third period. She led a rush into Penny's end, breaking a check from Shiv to get free ice in front of Penny. She took a shot that Penny managed to get her stick on and sent it sailing out of play. The center skated past Penny's goal, grinning evilly at her as she did.

Play resumed following a faceoff in Penny's end and her team struggled. The opponents were moving the puck with quick short passes, moving it in a tightening box between the points. Penny's defenders were getting drawn further and further from the net trying to block the passes or get their body on the other players in their zone. One of the wingers picked up the puck, dodged a collision with Li, and made it to the slot all alone. Penny got ready, the player lined up for a slap shot, her stick came down... but instead of slapping it hard the winger sent a soft pass to Penny's left. Where it was knocked into the wide open side of Penny's net by the waiting center, who had perfectly timed a wraparound and popped out from beside the net to knock it in.

Penny dug the puck out of her net in frustration and passed it towards the nearest official. The other team were in the middle of their celebrations. "Hey, GOON," Penny realized someone was calling her. Shiv and Jenn were standing a few feet away. "It's no big deal. Groove with us – this song's our jam!"

Penny let her senses defocus and realized that the arena speakers were pounding out a garbled version of "Low". Penny laughed and joined in as the three girls stood beside their net and danced up and down while the other team celebrated. The bench shortly joined in and the celebrations on the other end of the ice stopped to stare in confusion at what exactly was going on. When the song faded out the three girls on the ice came together and touched their helmets before breaking apart, laughing.

The Beavs held the game to a tie until the last three minutes. With just under three minutes left Jess M. got hooked and Penny's team got a power play. Just as the 5 on 4 was starting, Penny heard the coach shouting her name. "PENNY!" Penny looked over and the coach was wildly gesturing with her hand for Penny to come towards her. It took a second for Penny to understand, then with a quick glance up the ice she took off from the net.

"WAIT" the whole bench seemed to yell it just as Penny was getting to the blue line, and Penny looked to see a wild clear pass coming out to the middle of the ice and directly towards her. Penny stopped abruptly and brought her stick back, giving the puck a hard hit and sent it right back where it came from. Then she stepped into the open bench door and the world erupted around her.

"WHAT! No way! Impossible! I've never seen that before!" Around her, teammates were shouting and clapping. Penny turned around and saw that the goal light was on and her team was skating to the bench laughing.

"What just happened?" Penny asked.

"You just SCORED, idiot." Shiv shouted at her.

"But, I didn't even take a shot!" Penny said not believing it.

"You sent that bitch bar-DOWN from halfway across the ice!" Someone said, Penny couldn't tell who in the chaos.

"Better get back out there." Coach cut through the noise. Penny's head was still reeling but she turned around and got back on the ice and skated to her net. The penalized player was back now and it was back to even strength. Penny faced two more shots before the game ended but that late goal seemed to have deflated the other team and the final shots were soft, slow shots from the outside and not very dangerous. When the buzzer went her team cleared the bench in seconds and Penny found herself buried under a pile of gear and bodies as her team swarmed over her.

Finally the dogpile came apart and her team lined up to shake hands with the other team. Penny's final surprise of a seemingly unreal five minutes came when she grabbed the hand of the opposing center who had taken out Emma. Instead of shaking Penny's hand, the center reached out and embraced Penny in a huge bear hug. Penny was completely caught off guard. "That was absolutely incredible. I'm glad I got to see you play today." The center said to her, giving her a broad smile completely devoid of malice or the vileness Penny had seen in the game. "I hope we can play on the same team some day." And she let Penny go and was onto the next player to shake hands.

Goon Girl: The Minors

13. Blocked Shots

Penny squeezed shut her eyes in pain while the trainer unwrapped the ice pack from her arm. The blood started rushing back to the injured area and Penny could already feel the throbbing where the puck had struck her.

It had been late in the third period and her team was up by 1. The other team had pulled their goalie and a delay of game penalty on her defensive partner meant her team was down a body. Six on four with forty one seconds left. Big game time as Paul would have said at that point.

The PK center had lost the faceoff, and the other team had dropped a slot pass back to the point. Penny had seen the forward at the point lined up for the one timer, and on instinct had just let her body drop. She heard the slap of the forward's stick against the ice. Then there was a thunderclap of sticks slamming against the boards from the direction of the benches.

For a moment Penny thought the shot had gone in and the other team had tied the game. She hadn't seemed to *feel* anything. Had the puck gone right over her? Been deflected? Then Penny registered that her three linemates were being chased up the ice by all six of the opposing team's players. There was the strangled goose honk of the goal horn and she saw the red light at the far end go on.

Penny rolled onto her stomach and did a push-up to get onto her knees. Or rather, she rolled onto her stomach and her brain told her arms to do the push-up. What actually happened was one arm did as it was told and the other simply… didn't… and she ended up pushing herself back over onto her back.

Her teammates were skating in victory formation to fist bump the goalie after the empty-netter that put them up by two. Shiv was pounding the glass in the penalty box expressing her own emotions at the change of fortunes. Fleur slowed as they neared the goalie, and skated over to where Penny was on the ice.

"That was a boss bitch move." She laughed. "Need help getting up?"

Penny nodded. She tried to point at her arm at her side, still not listening to her brain's encouragement to move. Instead, she dropped her stick and reached her other hand up. Fleur grabbed it and tugged Penny to her feet. There was another round of applause from the crowd and thunder of sticks on the bench. Penny grabbed her limp arm with her good one, pulling it close to her body, and began to slowly skate back to the bench.

The team's trainer had opened the bench door and helped Penny to a sitting positionand thrust an ice pack at Penny to press against the area. As she rolled up Penny's jersey to look at the limp arm, the first wave of pain hit Penny. She sucked in a fast breath, except each beat of her heart seemed to send another angry wave of fire shooting from her shoulder down into her fingers. The trainer had her sleeve up and was looking at the injury.

"Just soft tissue." She assured Penny. As if this news made the pain any better. "You just keep icing it."

So they did, and that had been half an hour ago. Her team had won. Penny had swayed to the locker room while the team celebrated and shook hands. She'd leaned back against the wall in the corner while her team went through their end of game rituals. She'd tried to laugh when Shiv offered to punch her other arm to give her a "matching pair" of bruises, an offer Penny declined.

After the ice came off, her arm was a mess of black, blue, and yellow bruising. But the pain was the usual pain now and carried the promise of a persistent ache for the next several days. Her fingers no longer burned, just tingled with the pins and needles of full circulation returning, and if she concentrated, Penny could lift the arm and wiggle those fingers.

Penny's trainer assured her and the coach she'd be fine to play in next weekend's game. Her coach was relieved and thankful to hear that news. After all, making plays like that blocked shot she just had, the team would need her.

14. Injury

Penny's second season with the South Saskatchewan Minor Hockey League's Maple Creek Hungry Beavers, or just 'the Beavs' as Penny and the team called themselves, was a complete turnaround from her first season. Entering February and the last month of regular season play, the Beavs had improved from last in the league the previous season to 2 points behind the Moose Jaw Maidens for the final playoff spot this year. With three games remaining, the Beavs were looking at their first chance at making the playoffs in over a decade.

Coach had been riding the team hard since they got back from the Christmas break. Merciless conditioning sessions at every practice and bonus practices each week outside at Mr. Bennet's rink in the frigid early February temperatures. Each player was also given homework, yes, hockey homework! They were given position specific skills to work on at home each day between practices. Nobody dared complain. Coach said at least a dozen times eachpractice that if they weren't the most surprising underdogs in the playoffs, the Beavs would be the best conditioned knockout at the end of the season.

Their schedule started with an easy win against the Dog River River Dogs, and then a much more challenging game against the Saskatoon Ice Toons the Beavs were forced to settle for a tie in. The Maidens won one and lost one. The two teams were destined to face each other in the final game of the regular season, with that final playoff spot on the line. Tensions were high going into that final game, and as it drew near Penny found herself snapping at her brothers more than she meant to and having a harder time sleeping than normal. It wasn't just that it was a big game coming up and Penny wanted her team to advance. No, it was the fact they were going up against the Maidens and she *really* didn't want to lose this season to *them*.

Penny's league nemesis that season had been the Maidens' number six. Courtney. Courtney was a big farm girl from just outside Moose Jaw whose personal depth was the only thing shallower than the gene pool she crawled out of. Courtney who had been so racist to Li that Li had left a game early. Courtney who had gotten Penny suspended for 2 games. Courtney who Penny had been forbidden by her coach to fight at threat of being thrown off the team for good. There was a four letter C word Penny thought summed Courtney up pretty well, but knew she'd have to wash her brain out with soap if she actually used it.

But whether it was the team's future hanging in the balance, the game being against the Maidens, or having to face Courtney a final time this season, the stress had gotten under Penny's skin and itched at her constantly like a fiberglass sliver.

When the game finally arrived, Penny felt sluggish and irritable on the ice. All through warmup skate she felt like her hands were stuffed inside lead gloves and her feet encased in cement. Someone watching from the sidelines probably wouldn't have noticed a difference, but Penny could feel she was already off her game before it even started. What was worse, Coach had her on the second line instead of her usual spot on the first line so she would run into first-line Courtney as little as possible. Rubbing salt in the wound, every time Courtney skated near the bench she would call Penny out with some jeer or another.

Penny did her best to focus through the first period and "rise above" it and not let Courtney force her into playing any game but Penny's own. Penny felt like she was doing a reasonable job. As coach had instructed, Penny was on quick line changes and found her way back to the bench if Courtney's line was put out while Penny was on the ice. This seemed to really frustrate the big girl by the end of the first period, so Penny felt that the strategy was working. Her own play was far from her best ever, and Penny found she had her hands full just doing the fundamentals of skating, passing, and getting into the right position to defend against the Maidens' rushes. More than once she caught edges she was sure she wouldn't have done any number of other games that season. One time she had such a bad blowout behind the net that she got ice shavings up the inside of her helmet, and had to take it off back on the bench and clean it out!

As if the universe needed to put an exclamation point on how difficult a game she was having, it was the toughest game of the Beav's season too. They made it through the first holding the Maidens to a 0-0 tie, but just barely. The posts made as many saves for the Beavs as Bricks did, which was more than a few. The Beavs had given as good as they got and had several quality scoring chances down in the Maiden's end, but neither team went to the dressing room at the end of the first feeling satisfied with how the period had ended.

Penny plopped down on the bench and attempted to put her headphones in and reset. However, in keeping with the general karmic theme of the day, the ear on the side of Penny's head that got snow up the helmet wasn't sitting right. Penny tried to scratch the ear with her pinky but it seemed to be full of water. She called the trainer over and asked her to take a look at it. The trainer used the excuse to whip out her clip-on penlight that she never got to use, and took a look.

"Oh yah, no worries. You just got some debris in here. I can clean that out no problem." The trainer assured Penny. Penny began to object, feeling like swabbing her own damn ear was something she could probably handle on her own, but stopped because the trainer already had the cotton swab out and nearly to Penny's eye height. "Just hold still, this'll just take a second and won't hurt a bit."

She lied. A second later a stabbing pain shot through Penny's head like an electric bolt and Penny doubled over, grabbing angrily at her ear. Around her everyone stopped what they were doing. Penny didn't realize she was crying out in agony but her shriek was filling the locker room.

"Oh god." The trainer said looking at the blood on the cotton swab. She got off the bench she'd been sitting on beside Penny and knelt in front of her.

Penny was still clutching her ear and squeezing her eyes shut in pain. The trainer put her hands on Penny's knees.

"PENNY!" She shouted. Penny half-heard her. She heard her like the trainer was a voice in a dream, or underwater. It was there but something about it was distorted, and unclear. Penny forced herself to take a deep breath and look up. Concern was etched over the trainer's face, along with the entire dressing room. Everything was silent, and Penny had an immediate, gut-wrenching realization. Whatever had happened had just made her deaf! Her mind reeled and she pulled her hand away from her ear to find a small blotch of blood there. Her head was bleeding! She was bleeding out of her ear and she was deaf – she must have a concussion, or worse… then she realized that the trainer was speaking and Penny could, in fact, still hear her though in that muted half-clear way. "Pen-ny, can you stiiiill he-ear meee?"

Penny forced a nod.

"Are you in paaaaain?"

Another nod.

"You are going to be Oh – Kay." The trainer assured her. "We pro-ba-bly punc-tured your ear druumm with some debris. We neeeed to get you to a hosssspital to get assssessssed by a dock-tor."

Penny nodded. She realized she could still speak, and her voice came out a full scale louder than she meant. "I DON'T HAVE A CONCUSSION?" She yelled.

"No." The trainer assured her. Penny's brain was adjusting to only hearing out of one ear already. She handed Penny a gauze pad, wiping the blood off Penny's hand and then pressing the pad against her ear. She then guided Penny's hand to reach up and hold the gauze in place. "Pressure." The trainer instructed directly. "You don't need an ambulance but you do need to go in case they need to irrigate the ear. Do you have a ride here?"

Penny started to nod then her stomach sank again. "WHAT ABOUT THE GAME?" She shouted at the room. Awkward laughter rippled through the other girls.

"Goon just broke her damn ear and wants to get back into the action." Becks laughed. "Good ol' goon."

"I'm afraid your game is over." Coach stated flatly. Penny was about to rebuke but Coach shut her down with a raise of her hand. "Not up for discussion. We're gonna play our asses off so you can rejoin us for the playoffs, but player safety is top priority for every one of us." Penny nodded and didn't argue. Coach started rallying the rest of the girls while the trainer got Penny sorted. They tracked Pat and Paul down in the stands and explained the situation. Both brothers were concerned but understood what was being asked of them. Emma, the Beav's backup goaltender, had packed Penny's gear while they'd been gone and met them with it in the lobby. Penny got the bulkier stuff off then let Pat help her out to their van. And then they were gone.

Penny's parents met her at the hospital and they spent the better part of the day doing tests and exams and seeing a revolving door of doctors and nurses through the ER. In the end they concluded that yes, Penny's ear drum was perforated, but no, she wouldn't need surgery or any procedures to repair the damage. It would heal on its own. In six-to-eight weeks. Penny hadn't been willing to process that and had demanded if she could go back to playing. Due to the risk of further damage that could lead to permanent hearing loss or infection, as well as the risks associated with vertigo and equilibrium issues while she was healing, that was a hard no from the doctor. Like it or not, they were adamant that

Penny's second season with the Beavs was done. And Penny definitely did NOT like it.

She was home that evening before she was finally able to dig her phone out of the pocket of her street clothes from the gear bag Emma had hastily packed for her and find out what had happened with the game. "No shit." She breathed reading a text thread with hear team. Aside from lots of well wishes and inquiries about her condition were about a dozen messages all telling her that the Beavs had pulled off a 3-4 overtime win. They'd knocked out the Maidens and were going to the playoffs! Penny's heart leapt for about 3 seconds before she realized that the team was about to embark upon its first playoff run in nearly a decade, without Penny. She dropped her phone on her bed, let her body follow, and sobbed until she fell asleep.

The next few weeks passed in a blur. Penny adjusted to the hearing issues. Her mom was the most difficult part of adjusting to her injury. Mrs. Davies, ever fearful that "something like this" was going to happen to Penny while playing, hovered like a nervous hen and coddled Penny to the point of madness. Penny gave up after the first three days on correcting her mom that the injury hadn't even happened when she was playing, but had just been a fluke accident off the ice like Darren Turcotte and Rick Lessard. She realized she probably shouldn't have referenced other *hockey players* injured off the ice by ear swabs, but regardless the argument had been pointless. Penny's injury was the culmination of two years' worth of fears and worst nightmare scenarios for Mrs. Davies and there was nobody who was going to stop her from forcing as much bedrest, chicken soup, and "mom's TLC" on Penny as humanly possible.

For Penny's part, she just wanted to get out of the house. She was thankful for school days. Penny had been an adequate student for most of her academic career, but now found herself looking forward to school for the first time in years. It was there that she got to see some of her teammates and get updates on their preparations for the playoffs. It was also her one and only allowable break from the prison of coziness that her mother had converted her home bedroom into.

Her teammates did their best to raise Penny's spirits. They complained about the doubling down on rigorous conditioning and hockey homework Coach was imposing ahead of their upcoming playoff game. They told Penny with rolling eyes about how the Maiden's coach had launched an official complaint and request for review of the Beavs' winning OT goal that ended the Maidens' season, and the league's response that the coach had to be on something because they knew damn well the league didn't make (let alone keep) video recordings of their games. What was there to review but the eyewitness accounts on the ice, and the most impartial of which were the refs who had made the call in the first place. So in the end the complaint went exactly where it belonged: nowhere. They also told Penny that Courtney, the big girl who'd tormented Li and Penny throughout the season, had asked about her when she didn't return to the bench after that first intermission. She'd been told Penny had been injured.

"You should've seen her face." Fleur laughed in the telling. "It was like someone told her that her puppy had just gotten cancer. I know you two were at each other all season, but I think you might have a secret friend." Fleur insinuated *friend* to mean clearly more than that.

Penny just rolled her eyes. "Yeah, I bet. She probably cried all the way home."

"She did cry." Fleur said seriously. "In the handshake lineup. It was her last game in the league. Whether you were there or not, she's done now."

"Right." Penny chewed on that. Thinking of big-girl-with-the-big-mouth Courtney now having to go back to being the small fish in the pond in the U18 league, IF she was even able to get a spot on one of the provincial teams. As happy as she was to be done with her, Penny felt bad for her too.

Those brief moments where she felt like she was still on the team helped Penny survive the first week. It was very weird not having to get up at 5 am every other morning to go to practice, and Penny's body started to catch up on sleep she'd been apparently craving all season. With her mom around all the time at home, Penny was also able to apply ample pressure that Penny should be allowed to go spectate at her team's first playoff home game the following weekend. The playoffs were only the best of three, with two rounds making up the entire playoff run – a 3-game semi-final and 3-game final round, so chances were Penny would only get to go to one game anyway. Mrs. Davies acquiesced on the fourth day of pressure, *provided* Penny stay in the normal spectator area and not on the bench, in the tunnels, or down at ice level where – as Mrs. Davies put it – "those Amazon savages you play with can break through the glass and finish the job". Penny agreed she would sit with the parents and other families, safely up and away from play and protected by the mandatory netting that hung from the ceiling and prevented loose pucks from reaching unsuspecting fans. Penny almost pointed out that trips, falls, choking, and other routine accidents accounted for more injuries at hockey games than anything down on the ice did. Almost. But in the end she held her tongue and Mrs. Davies agreed that she could go.

Watching the team from the stands was even harder than Penny had imagined. She'd gotten there early and shared some eager waves through the glass at her teammates before play started, but now there were both figurative and literal walls between her and team. She could tell the team was playing their best. As the game proceeded and they went down by one, two, and then three goals going into the third, she could hear the desperation in their voices as the players shouted to one another on and off the ice. Penny clenched her seat's arm rests angrily as the final five minutes wound down and the other team was awarded a lengthy two-player advantage off a pair of (to Penny's eyes anyway) soft penalties late in the period. The game ended with her team facing a solid defeat. Penny gritted her teeth hard at the frustration and anger of being unable to have helped them. Numerous times she'd seen loose pucks that she was *sure* she could have cleared, and at least one of the goals had come from an opponent left unchecked in the zone, something she would never have allowed to happen.

Penny found her way to the dressing room after the game, but saw the door was propped open and everyone inside were hanging their heads or stowing their gear in silence. Penny knew better than to come in as a third party to that. She instead found Pat and had him drive her home.

The Beavs' season ended on the road the next day. Penny wasn't able to attend as the game had been in another city and the travel logistics simply hadn't worked out. She followed the progress as best she could via the team chat, but knew there was a lot being left out. Online at least, and maybe partially for Penny's benefit even, her teammates were looking on the bright side and taking their first-round playoff elimination as a big victory and an indicator of better seasons ahead. They were proud of themselves and having made it as far as they did. Penny was sure that if she had been there though, she'd have faced down a lot of teary eyes and disappointment. She certainly felt both of those things, multiplied by the fact she hadn't even been able to participate.

So ended Penny's second season with the Beavs. As the saying goes, not with a bang but a whimper. Penny faced a long and challenging road to recovery from the fluke injury. It was nearly three months before she was fully back to herself and a doctor was able to confirm that she had recovered completely. Penny often looks back and wonders how the season might have ended differently if she had been there. Would she have made a difference? In her mind Penny has played out a hundred times both scenarios, where she is the difference maker that takes the team through the first round and all the way to the championship; as well as completely ineffectual and she is just there to share in the team's failure.

In the end, she knows it doesn't matter what might have happened. Things ended how they did and she needed to live with it. Spring and summer stretched long and lonely ahead before she could get back on the ice the next fall for her third and final year with the Beavs. All Penny could do was heal and be ready.

15. First Girlfriend

Penny's third year with the South Saskatchewan Minor Hockey league's Maple Creek Beavs she was paired up with a new defensive partner in Jenn. It was tough to say who was more surprised by the matchup, since Jenn had spent the previous two seasons centering the forward line with the pair of Jessicas. As this third season started the Jessicas had graduated out of the Beavs' age category and that left Jenn orphaned on her line. She had mentioned to Coach that she might want to shake things up a bit this season and try something new, meaning she would be open to playing winger or picking up a different role on the PK line. What it had earned her was a spot on the first D-Line with Penny.

Penny had known *of* Jenn for two seasons now, though the two had never really had much in common. Jenn had mostly moved in her trio of forwards who had acted like "the cool girls" clique in the locker room. A clique Penny had no interest in joining and had been assured on numerous occasions she was **not** a part of. Now that they were on the same line and skating together every practice and game, Penny was getting to know her, and what she was getting to know what they she did not like Jenn.

It probably didn't help things that Jenn very clearly viewed the move to the first D-line as a "demotion" from her prior seasons as a center. Her sulky and generally sour demeanor towards Penny and the coach made absolutely sure there was no way anyone could mistake her for *wanting* to be there. Penny, on the other hand, had always viewed her role on the D line with a quiet humility, feeling like the defenders were the unsung heroes of the team whose job was to have everyone else's backs. It quietly offended Penny that Jenn was so negative on joining her, wondering if Jenn had looked at her and Becks with the same derision in previous seasons but had just kept it to herself. Penny found her views were so at odds with Jenn's flashy shock-and-awe approach to the game that the two struggled to find even the smallest things in common.

Jenn also had a mile-a-minute mouth that had gotten her into trouble more than once at forward. Penny had sat out more than a few penalty roughing minutes over the last 2 years after getting in between Jenn and whoever she had just shot her mouth off at. Jenn, in addition to having been a forward and not someone you wanted to lose to a penalty or a black eye, was exactly five foot nothing. She was solidly built but her size never seemed to fit with her personality. Jenn was also half native, and lived with her family on the Nekaneet Cree reserve just southeast of Maple Creek. She was so defensive about that that she had full on clocked one of the other rookies in Jenn and Penny's first season when the other girl had made the mistake of asking if Jenn was Chinese or Japanese.

The pair seemed on a collision course for disaster as the third season got underway. Everyone around them could tell it too, although Coach seemed determined to keep the pair together. That at least sort of made sense. Coach had brought a "leave your personal shit at the door" approach her first day in the role and had never left that mindset behind. Penny and Jenn's issues with each other would just be something they would have to get over and get on with playing. Or they wouldn't be playing. The two girls knew that too of course. But *knowing* you need to make a change and actually *doing* something to change have always been radically different things.

Their tensions reached a boiling point in the fifth game of the season. The Beavs had been hot starting the season, winning three in a row after their first game. For the first time ever they were at the top of the league's standings and felt like they had momentum to keep that going at least a little longer. Everyone's tempo was at the max trying to avoid being the player that broke the streak. As the second period ended, rookie defender Jada got a lazy tripping call and that was going to start their team on the PK to kick off the third. Penny was one of the last players off the ice and caught an exchange between Jenn and Jada in the hallway.

"It doesn't matter you didn't *mean* it." Jenn was saying. "You can't do stupid shit like that. It screws all of us over."

"Look I'm sorry." Jada replied. Penny had been mentoring Jada, one of the club's first years, and had also been frustrated she'd made the very *rookie* mistake. Penny was glad the girl understood her mistake and was apologizing.

"Don't be *sorry*. Be *better*." Jenn growled.

That was when Penny stepped in. "I think she gets the message." Penny suggested.

"Just stay out of this." Jenn sighed, but Jada was already using the interruption to hurry off to the safety of the dressing room.

"We can't just go off on the rookies when things don't go our way." Penny refuted. "That's not who we are."

"It's sure who the team was when I joined." Jenn seethed. "You too. You should remember. When we were rookies the seniors buried us in scut and blamed us for every loss. And they weren't anywhere near as talented a group as this one is. This rookie group is a bunch of whiny babies and they'll only get better if we ride them hard."

Penny knew she was right, but also wrong at the same time. "Look, Jenn, you and I had shit rides as rooks and we both know it. But it didn't make us *better*, it just made some of us *bitter*. Wouldn't you have had a better first season if you'd had this group of seniors instead of the one we had?"

Jenn looked like she was about to snap something back but instead she sighed heavily and looked down at the floor. "Better if we had *some* of the seniors we have now, that's for sure." Jenn admitted. Penny was momentarily shocked. It was the closest thing to a compliment Jenn had ever given her and she wasn't sure how to respond. After a silence that just kept getting more awkward as it dragged on, Jenn finally looked up. "Let's just go." She said and started walking to the dressing room. Penny followed.

Things thawed a little between the two after that. Jenn continued to be short and direct whenever she was talking with Penny one on one, but on the whole the air of antagonism around her seemed to melt away. On Penny's side she managed to adopt a sense of frustrated indifference and accept there was little she could do to change the other girl's attitude and she wasn't going to invest any further effort in trying. They were teammates. Linemates. But they'd never be friends, and that was ok.

Despite this new normal of mutual, begrudging acceptance, Penny still spent a lot of her time thinking about and complaining about Jenn. Especially to Shiv.

"Like, I get it, I'm not going to be friends with everyone on the team, but what is her actual deal?" Penny asked Shiv as they waited together for a ride one morning following practice.

"You know I never liked her." Shiv repeated her mantra. After so many times having the same conversation with her friend, she was out of new ways to agree with her and had gotten into a routine of repeating the same sentiments over and over.

"It's not that I *don't* like her," Penny continued automatically, giving the same response she always did, "it's just I don't get why she doesn't like *me*. Like what have I ever done to her?"

Shiv had blown her breath against the glass and was trying to finish drawing a large butt in the condensation before it evaporated.

Penny continued. "Of all the seniors she's the one I don't get. We've all been together for nearly three years now."

"Almost." Shiv nodded, admiring her handiwork.

"Don't you think we'd be over this shit by now? Whatever it is?"

"Maybe." Shiv shrugged.

"Like, if she'd ever, even once, actually say 'hey Pen, I don't like you cuz you're dumb and your bodywash smells so bad it makes me puke' like that I could live with you know? Because then I'd *know*. And maybe I change my bodywash to make the problem better or maybe I don't but at least I'd know I could *do* something."

"Or maybe she is waiting for you to ask." Shiv offered, not the first time sharing this blindingly obvious insight.

"I just don't want to make things worse." Penny sighed. "We're sort of not in a bad spot right now. If I can just keep ignoring it, then this season will be done and I probably don't have to deal with her again."

"Uh-huh." Shiv agreed, being careful *not* to say, "because you're doing *such a good job* of ignoring it.". Her mom pulled up and she left as quickly as she could without actually running out of the door and away from the awkwardness of the conversation.

The team's first road trip of the season was the next weekend, and it was tough to tell which girl was more shocked or disappointed to find out that Penny and Jenn were going to share a double room together. In their first united effort of the season, they both protested the room assignment to Coach but the argument lasted all of five seconds before Coach informed them that the room assignments were final and that was that. The two looked at each other in quiet resignation and got ready for practice.

The hotel they were put up in was a small one, with even smaller rooms. No pool or restaurant like the Jamboree hotels, this was the sort of place you'd only stay if twenty of you needed to stay at the same place on a shoestring budget, or maybe if you were on the run from the law and needed somewhere to "lie low" for a few days.

Penny and Jenn hauled their gear into their room and laid claim to their respective beds. Neither needed to actually draw a line down the middle of the room to make it clear that they each had their own space and the other wasn't welcome in it. A few minutes after they had gotten in, there was a knock at the door. Penny went over and found Shiv standing there.

"Coach needs your room keys." Shiv groaned, flashing her own. "Something wrong with the reservation, she'll get it sorted and bring them back."

"Oh, uh, ok." Penny said and grabbed the little plastic cards from the bathroom counter where they'd been. She handed them to Shiv. Suddenly Shiv pulled the door closed and there was a rustle of movement outside the door, it sounded like there were more people though Penny hadn't seen anyone else.

"Alright can you hear me?" Shiv shouted through the door.

"Yes." Penny replied.

"Good, Jenn get your ass over here we need to speak to you too." Jenn was already off the bed and on her way over to see what was going on. "We're not letting you out or giving your keys back until you two sort out your shit. We're ALL sick of it." Shiv said. There was a murmur of agreement from an unknown (but large) group of voices outside.

Penny's first reaction was to try and yank the door open, but that didn't work. They'd either jammed the handle or someone was holding it because all she could do was jiggle the handle, it wouldn't turn far enough to open the door.

"We're stuck." Penny told Jenn. Jenn gave her a panicked look and shouldered Penny out of the way, trying the handle herself and earning herself the same result. "See?" Penny asked.

Jenn's panic level seemed to ramp up a notch. "How do we get out?" She gulped.

Penny rolled her eyes. "Just sit down. They'll get bored after a few minutes of us not beating the living shit out of each other and move on."

"No we won't!" Came a laughing reply through the door. Penny flipped the door off and went to sit on her bed. She took her headphones out of their case, popped them in her ears and flopped down on the bed's pillows. She tugged her phone free from her pants pocket and set her playlist to shuffle and closed her eyes.

She hadn't been sleeping but had been deep in the checked-out music zone when she felt a tapping on her arm. Penny opened her eyes to see Jenn standing next to her. She took her headphones out.

"Maybe we should talk about… you know… our mutual shit or whatever." Jenn was strangely not meeting Penny's eyes.

Penny sat up. "Ok." She agreed. Jenn sat down on the other bed and waited while Penny packed up her headphones.

They sat in silence for over a minute.

"Well?" Penny asked expectantly after the silence became too much.

"Well what?" Jenn replied. "You start."

"Well what's your issue?" Penny demanded.

"*My* issue?" Jenn scoffed.

"Ever since you got moved to the D-line you've made it obvious you don't want to be here. I'm sorry it isn't *up to your standards* but it's pretty hard to have a linemate who doesn't want to be there."

"Wait, what?" Jenn asked in honest confusion. "I have no problem being on Defense. I actually enjoy it."

Penny looked at her as if Jenn had just said the moon was made of cheese.

"No, seriously. It's been a great change." Jenn said earnestly. "My problem is being on a line with you."

That landed on Penny like a ton of bricks. "What the hell?" She blurted. "Me? What's your problem with me?"

"It's a lot of pressure!" Jenn told her. "You've been doing this for 3 years. You're our best defender…" There was a coughing at the door that Penny could only assume was Shiv. Clearly they still had an audience. "Our *best defender*," Jenn repeated more loudly, "And I mean you're a bit of a legend. I've been on the team the same amount of time you have and you're *Goon* and I'm still *just Jenn*. If someone ever wrote a book about the team it wouldn't be about Jenn, that's for sure."

Penny sat too honestly shocked to respond. She was trying to process her own cold shoulder response to Jenn given this new information.

Thankfully Jenn kept going and saved Penny from having to come up with a response. "It's a lot of pressure! Yeah we've been on the team the same amount of time but I've never played this position before. Coach and the team and *you* just seem to assume that I was good at forward so I'll be good at defense and expect me to be at the same level as you. But I'm just learning this position and I've got no help or mentorship. You spend so much time and patience helping the rookies but you've never stopped to give *me* feedback on a shift or done any special drills with *me* to help me. You just assume I should be on your level and Jesus girl it's a high level to match!"

Penny thought about Jenn taking the strip off the rookie in the hallway and realized it hadn't been about the young woman's mistake at all, rather Jenn's frustration at the unbalanced treatment.

Jenn had tears in her eyes now. "And of course, it wasn't Shiv or anyone else I got paired with but *you*." There was something in how she said that last syllable that caused her to start crying.

"What about me? Wouldn't it be the same if you were on a line with anyone else?"

"No you idiot." Jenn blurted. The suddenness of it and the frustration confused Penny even more.

"I don't understa—" Penny was saying in her best reconciliatory tone when Jenn suddenly pushed herself across the small aisle between the beds and kissed Penny. Penny's eyes flared open in complete shock. Her brain started to work again and she could feel Jenn's hot, wet tears against her own cheeks. Sensed her soft lips and tasted the strawberry lip chap Jenn wore. And her body relaxed. Jenn started to pull away in embarrassment, and Penny's brain wasn't focused on anything else in that moment except that she wanted more. She grabbed Jenn's arms and pulled her back to her, kissing her back now and letting the two of them begin the ritual of figuring out kissing when neither had had a real kiss before.

The moment lasted, and lingered. When at last they pulled apart they looked at each other with completely new eyes. The animosity and angst that had hung between the two for weeks had evaporated in the heat of the exchange. They sat across from each other again, mostly looking at anything but each other and breaking out into nervous fits of laughter when their awkward, furtive glances met.

Finally Jenn started to say something. "I'm sorry, I don't know if you're, I mean, I don't know if that was ok…"

Penny let herself laugh off some of the awkwardness she was feeling. "I never really thought about it. But I guess I am. At least, with you."

Jenn blushed. "Do you want to…?"

"Hell yes." Penny responded and this time she pushed herself towards the smaller girl and pinned her down on the opposite bed while they let their mouths work in other ways.

After enjoying each other's company for a few minutes, the two girls bolted upright as they heard the beep of a key card in the door and the door being pushed open.

Shiv led a group of their teammates into the room. "Things got really quiet and we were worried one of you killed the other one." She said. Then stopped. She looked at Jenn, hair out of place, sparkly ruby chapstick smeared across her upper and lower lips, shirt strap slid half down her arm; and then at Penny, hair also a mess, face also covered in glittery strawberry lip chap, and completely unable to meet her friend's gaze. "oh. My. GOD." Shiv gasped and pointed at the two. "You're…" she pointed at Penny with one arm, "and you're…" she pointed at Jenn with the other, "Ohhhhhhhh."

The girls behind her were a few seconds slower than Shiv on the uptake, but they caught up just in time to say "Ohhhhh" at the same time as Shiv as they got what was happening.

"We'll just leave you two love birds to it then." Shiv laughed and ushered the other girls out before any awkward questions could start. The door swung back open a second after it shut. "And uh, I'll just leave these here for you when you're ready." Shiv tossed the cards on the ground by the door and shut it behind her.

"That went, well?" Jenn asked.

"Who cares." Penny said, knocking the other girl back onto the mattress and picking up where they left off.

After the road trip, the two girls worked much better together. Penny spent as much extra time helping Jenn with her defensive skills as she could, although the time was mostly just an excuse to see her as opposed to helping her game get better. The tension between the two was gone, which helped the team. The news of their reconciliation interruptus spread through the team quickly, and while their teammates had different views on the two of them, any comments were limited to the "ooooohs" you'd expect from 14-year old girls when someone gets a boyfriend or girlfriend for the first time.

In future years Penny would have to reconcile her gender identity and struggle to decide which pronouns best described her. She would have her share of girlfriends and boyfriends and learn what each gave to her and what she needed most from relationships. She'd bear the slings and arrows of the bigoted, and have to defend her feelings to people who couldn't understand any view except their own.

But those days were ahead of her yet. Now, in her third year of the Beavs and coming up on her 15th birthday, Penny only cared that Jenn was someone she hadn't gone looking for, but had found her and opened her eyes to a world she'd never spent much time thinking about before. For now, every kiss, touch, term of endearment and stolen glance were a new and electric experience that made her feel warm and loved and open to loving someone else in the same way.

Goon Girl: The Minors

16. The Jamboree

The South Saskatchewan Minor Hockey League's Female Hockey Jamboree has for years been widely considered **the** event in the Saskatchewan female hockey calendar. For five days in March, all hockey playing girls in Saskatchewan converge on Regina or Saskatoon for a tournament that spans every age and skill range of female hockey in the province.

Because of the scope of the event, more players participate than in the provincial tournament or any of the league finals. For many players it is the only event in the year where they get to interact with players from other ages and leagues. For these reasons, it is often the most expected date in the provincial hockey calendar. For Penny Davies, this was true as well.

When Penny received the schedule for her third year with the Maple Creek Beavers, she didn't even bother looking at the regular season games. She flipped right to the Jamboree and circled the date on her Team Canada calendar hanging on her wall. She then carefully counted backwards, labeling each date leading up to the Jamboree until she got to today. In fine tip sharpie she wrote "86" in the corner of today and then quickly put an "X" through today. Today down. 85 days left to go.

Penny texted her mom at work and gave her the dates of the tournament. "You need to take these days off work." Penny messaged. "My life depends on it." Another mom might have been startled receiving that statement out of the blue. Another mom might have called Penny right back to check if she was ok and then lectured her about not scaring the life out of their mother in the middle of the work day. Mrs. Davies however, well acquainted with her daughter and knowing this could only be the jamboree days, simply responded "We'll make it work." Penny replied with a heart emoji and a GIF of a teen character saying "Best. Mom. Evah".

The wait seemed to go on forever. The daily countdown ground on Penny but it didn't make the nervous, anxious energy of non-stop waiting go away. Special events like Halloween and her older brother Pat's birthday helped as a distraction, but the Jamboree was on Penny's mind at least half of the time between getting her schedule and finally getting to leave.

What did help were the small moments where the details of the trip came together. There was the day that their team received the lineup for their U15 tournament games; the week that her mom seemed busy on the phone every night trying to sort out the carpooling and accommodations to get Penny from Maple Creek to Regina. And of course, there was the day that their coach handed out the room assignments to her team .

Penny would be sharing a 2-bed room with three other girls, Li and Jenn, and fellow defence person (and Penny's best friend on the team), Siobahn; or Shiv as she preferred to be called. Everyone on the team thought it was a terrible nickname for the girl who regularly demanded penalty time when an opponent stopped too hard and showered snow in people's eyes. Nonetheless it had been her nickname since her first year when their orange Timbits hockey jerseys reminded Shiv of a prison uniform. Shiv's mom was a nurse at the Maple Creek urgent care center and wasn't able to take the full Jamboree off, so Penny's mom would be driving Shiv to Regina with them.

Penny, Shiv, and her other roommates were the handful of players that remained from their rookie squad, and 4 of the 6 third year veterans who would be graduating from the team this year. Penny knew that this meant they were responsible for an epic era-defining prank on the rest of the team sometime during the Jamboree and that kept her occupied as well.

The Senior Prank was a longstanding Beavs tradition. Borrowing from the lore of colleges and high schools across America, the Beavs' Senior Prank was a way for the outgoing players to leave their indelible mark in the memories of the years below them. Penny remembered last year when Fleur, who'd been Penny's good friend and team mentor when she'd been a rookie, and Fleur's group of seniors had offered to do all the laundry during the tournament. The Beavs' Home jerseys were solid white with just the emblem of the grinning beaver biting through a hockey stick sewn onto the front. And after they followed through their offer to do the laundry, the senior squadstill had stark white jerseys and everyone else skated their final home games in psychedelic rainbow tie dye jerseys.

As fond as Penny was of Fleur, she had to admit that last year's prank had paled in comparison to the first Senior Prank Penny had experienced when she was a rookie. That squad had taken things seriously until the coach had banned pranks until the end of the season. They had "intercepted" the official tournament schedule from the coaches and circulated an amended one that had their first game start a full 4 hours before games actually commenced. And fully 2 hours before the doors to the arena would be unlocked. Penny had been one of the dozen players who showed up for their pre-game warmup skate at 5am the first day of tournament play, only to find themselves locked out in the still-dark -24 degree weather. Parents were panicking and the players were huddled outside the doors, many still in their pajamas – when a van with the seniors rode by driven by one of their siblings and there was a blinding flash as the van stopped and the seniors took a picture of the scene. They then drove off with no fewer than four butts pressed against the van's windows. Just for posterity, they drove a victory lap a few moments later chanting "pranked – pranked – pranked – pranked" before driving back to the hotel for good. Penny remembered her mom being furious, but for her part, Penny had to admit it had been a pretty good one.

These were the shoes that Penny's class had to top. At the same time, she had learned her lesson back in her first season that it was possible to go *too* far in these things. Penny knew her year would pull off something epic, she just hadn't figured out how yet, and the waiting time until the event was a great period to think. And plan. And most importantly – plot.

The Jamboree kicked off every year with a formal dinner. Players from all years were expected to come in formal wear. Most opted for a dress or gown, though some broke the mold and went for a pantsuit and tie. Since joining the team in Penny's 2nd year with the club, the Beavs had gone to the formal dinner in their jerseys with dress slacks on underneath. As Coach informed them, "nothing is more formal to a hockey player than the uniform of their team." Penny wondered what legendary hard-ass coach was trying to emulate with all of these awful one-liners, but had long since given up trying. That aside, she shared the relief with her teammates that this approach spared them having to deal with any elaborate wardrobe issues for the evening.

This year's formal dinner featured a program including a speech by one of Canada's female Olympians – from a squad that brought home the women's hockey gold medal. Following a three course dinner anchored by Regina's best approximation of Chicken Kiev, the Olympian spoke to a hushed crowd *mostly* still awake and attentive.

"I want you all to know that I am terrified." She said softly into the microphone. The hush fell into a deep silence. "I have played in front of crowds of tens of thousands of people in over a dozen countries around the world. I have a gold and silver medal to show for my time with Team Canada's women's squad. But being here today, **talking** in front of people, terrifies me."

"So why am I here then? Why not simply decline Saskatchewan Minor Hockey's invitation altogether, and let another of the many talented, capable, *not deathly afraid of public speaking* sports personalities in this province come and be here today? The reason is simple. I'm here *because* I am afraid. Each time I am allowed to take a microphone at one of these events, show up, and actually speak to you, is a time that I overcome my fears and become a tiny little bit more of the badass woman warrior that everyone thinks I am when they see me on the ice."

She paused to take a deep breath and a sip of water. She flipped a piece of paper over in front of her on her podium, and continued. "I was scared to play hockey too. Back when I played junior there was *one* junior Saskatchewan female team. We played against two teams in Alberta and that was our entire conference." There was some hushed whispering of incredulity. "Girls didn't play hockey when I was a kid. Not in any organized way in this province anyway. My good friend's mom had to pay her own money to fund the team's league dues and we all had to cover our transportation, lodging and gear fees. That's right, we were so unsupported we had to *pay* for *everything* just for the right to play. No sponsorships, endorsements, or government grants, we got to play because our families made it possible for us to do so. And that made it terrifying! Think of the most you've ever had riding on a game. Standings? A medal? The ability to stay alive and play one more game this season? For us, every game we knew that we were only playing because our parents had given something up. A new car, a vacation, going out for dinners for a year, it was different for everyone. But they all had sacrificed for us to just be on that ice playing against other girls. But that was such a meaningful time for us because of that fear and the utter terror of disappointing people who'd put everything on the line for you."

Penny was listening with rapt attention. She sometimes felt the weight of other girls in sports and generally the people who'd come before them when she played, but the heaviness of that weight suddenly seemed much bigger.

"But I'm not saying this to complain, or frighten you." The Olympian continued. "I'm saying this to motivate you. Because fear can consume you, or you can consume it. There's an old saying my first Olympic coach used to tell us. Fear is like a pair of wolves inside of us. One wolf represents doubt, indecision, and the urge to run away. The other represents the desire to stand our ground to fight the things we are afraid of. The way we decide which wolf our fear is depends on which one we feed. When you feed the wolf of fear that represents fighting through being scared, it feeds you and gives you incredible power."

"Now," she took another sip of water, "I want each of you to close your eyes. No, really, if Olympic players can do this exercise at the end of our practices, you can too, so close your eyes. Now think of something you've been afraid of in a game. Were you afraid of getting hit by the puck? Of another player? Or of letting your team down? I want you to feed the fleeing wolf for a second and think of running away, of hiding. I want you to feel all the times you haven't wanted to go onto a shift, or didn't want to skate to the boards because you were afraid of a hit. Feel those moments. Own those moments. Now let them go. Now I want you to muster every time you felt terrified and fed the fighting wolf and overcame that fear and did something great. Now open your eyes. Every time you face fear in a game going forward, I want you to ask yourself which wolf is winning? YOU control them both, and you can determine whether you feed them, or they feed you!"

There was a thunderous applause from the assembled girls and coaches; over the roars you could hear some people clinking cutlery on water glasses and others pounding their fists on the tables. A standing ovation followed and a lengthy Q&A session from the players in attendance. It was nearly eleven when the event finally wound down and Penny and her teammates hopped on the shuttle bus back to their hotel. Penny fell asleep on the ride. Shiv woke her just long enough to get into their room, where she passed out on the bed, still wearing her jersey and pants from the evening.

The tournament play started the next day. There were so many games being played that the different age groups would be playing at three different arenas across Regina. Penny and her cohort of U15 girls were at one in the center of town. Penny was wowed (again) at the size of the facility when they arrived, and the quality of the rink. Her town's ice center had a single hockey rink that served as a skating rink, ringette rink, figure skating ice, and even occasionally curling rink. When they stepped into this building there were four different rinks **all under one roof!** There were two rinks set up for hockey and assigned to the tournament, and on the opposite side of the grand hallway that they entered into, a group of figure skaters was already up and practicing on one rink and curlers were shouting at their squadmates in the other. When Penny's team came in, there were already troops of players from other teams leaving the arena after morning practice.

The dressing rooms had skate-safe flooring and every dressing room had more than 1 bathroom stall. The one the Beavs were in even had a dedicated "changing" area with lockers separate from the communal sit-and-listen space you entered into. Penny felt humbled at her Maple Creek origins being surrounded by the scale of this new, modern facility that serviced a town with ten times the number of people. But she pushed that aside, remembering the wolf story from the night before. She fed the gratitude wolf and felt appreciation at the opportunity to be here playing in this fancy arena. She felt like a pro.

Her team would play two games each day on Thursday, Friday, and Saturday through a round robin . Then, the top 4 teams from their A group and the other B Group in their age range would play a third quarterfinal game Saturday night, followed by semi and final games on Sunday morning and afternoon (if they made it that far).

Game 1 kicked off an hour after they got to the arena. Instead of singing the anthem, the tournament organizers had a member of the local indigenous community read a traditional blessing, which was followed by a land acknowledgement statement from a member of the tournament committee. Each captain then met at center ice and read into a microphone a commitment to fair play and respect for the sport, officials, and tournament organizers before shaking hands and exchanging team pennants. Then it was go time.

The Beavs came out strong with their first line. Their center won the opening face off and Penny picked up the puck and skated it into the zone. She slid a dump pass along the boards that one of their forwards was already skating in to collect. She got there before the opposing defender and smartly passed it out in front of the net where the Beavs' center was just arriving to deliver a hard one-timer that shot off the opposing goalie's glove and out of play. There was a harsh tweet of the referee's whistle and Penny's line changed up. The second line scored a few seconds after play resumed. Shiv fired one in hard off the face-off and Li managed to get the blade of her stick on it just enough to change the angle and fool the goalie. Less than a minute in and the Beavs were up by 1. They held the lead for the entire game, finishing with a commanding 7-2 victory to open the round robin portion of the tournament.

Penny thought back to the first Jamboree she'd attended in her first year, and how the Beavs had failed to secure a single victory in that tournament. She'd missed playing in the second one because of a freak cotton swab injury to her eardrum, but she'd still been able to go with the team and participate in the event as a purely social occasion. The team had won a single game that second year, putting an exclamation point on their season series against the Moose Jaw Maidens with a repeat of the victory that won the Beavs a spot in the playoffs. Still, from a hockey perspective, the Beavs had improved but not by a wide margin in that second year and had been knocked out of the tournament during the round robin. Starting with a 7-2 win and with aspirations to do much better this year, Penny was thankful for the group of girls she was surrounded by and Coach who had come in with the vision that the Beavs could be more than a bottom-rung team and had put in the time to mold the club around her vision.

The second game later in the day was against a team from the North Saskatchewan league and the Beavs pulled off a dominant 4 – 0 victory. Credit for that victory lay squarely on Emma's shoulders. The offense had done their part putting 4 in the net over the 60 minutes of play, but Emma had put up 42 saves on 42 shots to keep her team alive and protect her shutout. Penny had never seen Emma seem so calm and composed in net. The backup-turned-reluctant-starter had struggled out of the gate this season following Bricks' graduation last year, but really come into her own this year and the extra time she'd spent doing positional drills had really paid off. At the end of the game, Emma's team each came by and rubbed her helmet for luck before skating in a line to shake hands with the other team.

Back at the hotel after their first day of games, the *real* Jamboree started. Penny's was one of several teams staying at the same hotel and the younger girls had all been invited to a "legendary pool polo party" by the U20 Junior girls. The U20 Juniors were called the Regina Rockets and they were far and beyond the coolest team at the tournament. They were there mostly as volunteers and to run skills activities for teams when they weren't actively in tournament play. The Rockets were a Regina based group who played against other U20 teams across western Canada.

They were the one and only team for girls over 16 in the province, and the *only* female team that regularly played teams in other provinces. Short of the Team Canada women's team, the U20s were the players all the other girls in the province looked up to.

Penny and her teammates got changed, any fatigue from the double game that day instantly forgotten. They headed to the hotel pool where the games were already underway and you could hear the shrieks and squeals of laughing girls from a good distance away. When Penny arrived, she saw that someone had setup a water polo net (like a volleyball net but a bit lower) across the middle of the pool and there was a roughly 10-a-side match going full tilt already. Outside the pool, the hot tub was packed and most of the usable space on the pool deck had young women sitting around on deck chairs and towels talking and laughing and having a great time. As Penny's group entered one of the Rockets spotted them and blew a whistle she was wearing. She cycled a few girls out of the game to give a couple eager girls from the Beavs a chance to join the game. Did that make them eager Beavers? Yes, yes it did.

Penny chose to pass on the water polo and managed to snag a spot in the hot tub as another girl was leaving. There was a lively debate going on between a couple of girls older than Penny who were playing a version of the old three-things-on-a-dessert-island game. The game had reached the point where the answers were a one-upmanship battle to see who could come up with the most ridiculous answer, and almost every answer was answered by a fit of giggles. Play seemed to be fueled by healthy sips from spill-free tumblers surrounding the hot tub, though there was no evidence of what they might have been filled with. Penny was offered one when she sat down, but she declined and chose to observe the game instead.

A loud round of annoyed groans brought her attention back to the pool. It appeared one of her teammates had done something to end up on top of the net, which had collapsed under her weight and was now sinking below her into the pool. The back and forth arguments over which side's fault it was quickly devolved into a splashing match that summoned all the girls sitting outside the pool in on the fun and for the next five minutes the room became host to the grandest water fight anywhere in Saskatchewan. It ended abruptly when they heard the shrill peal of a whistle and one of the other team's coaches sourly sent the whole room full of soaking wet girls back to their rooms.

When games resumed the next day, there was a noticeable change in the team's demeanor. During the warmups, players from opposing teams waved at each other and met at center ice to laugh about some shared hijinx the night before. The players were looser and the tournament took on a warmer feel that was more fun for the players involved.

Amidst this backdrop of renewed camaraderie, Shiv was the first one to notice something *else* different this game. "Psst, hey Goon." Shiv hissed when they came off a line change. Penny looked over. "Have you noticed the guy in the stands with the notebook?

Penny looked quickly where Shiv was nodding her helmet. Sure enough there was a man in a black zip-up windbreaker studiously making notes in a notebook. He had an emblem on his jacket but Penny couldn't make it out.

"That's a scout." Shiv said matter-of-factly. As if scout-spotting was we weekend pastime and she was the local expert on it.

Penny laughed out loud, but stifled it when it appeared Shiv was being serious. "Who in their right mind would be scouting the Saskatchewan Minor Hockey League's jamboree? The U15 division for that matter!"

Shiv looked her dead in the eye. "The new professional women's hockey league starting in a couple years is supposedly establishing farm teams across the country to bring the quality of play up before the league launches. We'd be the right age to be 18 when the league launches."

"Bullshit." Penny scoffed. But she looked back at the man taking notes and in the back of her mind, wondered if it was that crazy after all.

The same man was at their next game that day, and by then, *everyone* on the team *knew* that the Canadian Professional Women's League was scouting the tournament. Hell, everyone on *every* team knew it. Even the parents knew it. The absolutely-not-nonchalant excuses that some of the parents were making to wander near the man – who was sitting apart from everyone else by a good distance – just to see if they could catch a glimpse of what was going into that notebook, were absolutely juvenile.

The presence of the scout sent the players into a frenzy. Defenders who *never* went deep on the rush were suddenly pushing hard into the zone and letting go rockets from the point. Goalies were abandoning their basic butterfly stances altogether and going for big glove saves or dramatic diving rebounds. Even the forwards were leaving it all on the ice with shot after shot, crazy dekes and spin-o-rama backhand shots. What resulted was the worst game of hockey for the U15's that entire season. With the players going all flash no substance there was no cohesive play, little communication, and even less passing. More than once a player stole the puck or checked a player *on their team* just to get the chance at a breakaway or to make a big play themselves. Twice Penny was challenged by a player on the other team to drop the gloves; twice Penny looked at the bench hoping to see Coach give her their silent signal that a fight was acceptable; twice Coach shook her head and held Penny back. By the end of the game, the parents in the stands were actively booing the broken play and egos on display on the ice. The evening game ended in a spectacularly awful zero-zero tie. What's worse, the scout had left sometime in the middle of the third period and nobody had noticed him leave. The locker room seemed to agree after the game that they weren't likely to be seeing him again though.

Or so they thought. The next morning the players met for breakfast at the hotel's small eatery to have a team breakfast together. Maybe it was the team's poor performance the night before, but it was a silent and demure meal with players not making eye contact with one another. Never has a group of 12–14-year-old girls been so interested in the aesthetics of bacon, eggs and toast before. Emma was the first one to bring up the elephant in the room. "Did anyone, um, find something in their room this morning?" Emma asked between mouthfuls of scrambled eggs.

The table erupted into excited conversation. Girls rustled around and over half of them, mostly in the younger years, produced torn envelopes from various purses and pockets.

"What's this all about?" Coach asked from the head of the table. She held out her hand and eventually, hesitantly, someone handed over their stationary to her. Coach read the letter inside, stuffed it back into the envelope and returned in, not saying anything.

"Well?" Penny asked. She had not received a letter, and didn't think anyone in her room had either. "What's it say?"

Coach took a breath and was about to respond when a younger girl on the team couldn't hold it in anymore. "The scout that was at the game yesterday works with the Canadian Professional Women's League. They're setting up a U18 team based out of Regina next season and *we've* been asked to try out!!"

"No way." Shiv breathed.

"Holy shit." Penny agreed.

"When are the tryouts?" Li asked, some egg dropping out as she spoke.

"During the tournament!" Emma responded. "Tomorrow evening after the late game."

"Wow, they really want you to be at your best after a full day of other games." Penny observed sourly, clearly disappointed that she had been snubbed from the invitations.

"I don't think it will matter." Another youngster piped in. "I don't know about anyone else but I'm going to be *pumped*." That roused a small chorus of cheers in agreement. Coach finally quieted the group with a raise of her hands.

"Look this is all nice but it's also all a distraction." Coach pointed out. "It's great this opportunity has come up, but don't forget we are here for one reason: to win a tournament. You already let this thing go to your head yesterday and don't forget how *that* turned out." A choreograph of grimaces agreed. "So today, in our actual games that matter, we're going to play the same game we played all season and not let it distract us – understood?"

Nods.

"Good." Coach said finally. "Eat up, today's games will determine our standings for the knockout round that starts tomorrow."

The Beavs' came out swinging into their morning game, the fifth of the tournament. They handily dispatched the Regina Rattlesnakes in a game that sportsmanship demanded they keep at 9-0 after reaching their ninth goal towards the end of the second. The score held to the end, though the players on the bench spent a lot of the third period nervously fidgeting and glancing back at the scout, wanting nothing more than to keep showing off against this easy opponent while their coach kept urging restraint. The locker room *exploded* in loud conversation the moment the third period ended and they were able to get off the ice.

"Did you see?" "Was he watching?" "That was a sick move." The girls excitedly chattered about their exploits and the chance to show them off when it truly mattered. Coach hung back outside the locker room, taking a moment of her own to let the girls burn off their nervous energy.

Penny kept to herself during the discussions along with the other team seniors who hadn't received letters under their door overnight. Like the day after a draft, an unspoken courtesy was expected towards the players that *weren't* picked that you could be excited for you, but you didn't rub it in their faces. Penny instead spent the time doing her level best to thoroughly check her equipment. She retaped her stick and fully unlaced and relaced her skates, making sure the two lace ends were perfectly lined up and the same length. Penny cleaned the inner visor of her helmet cage with the anti-fogging mixture she made at home. Around her the girls continued to extol their performances and their chances to be picked for the new league and team, and that suited Penny just fine.

Eventually Coach made her way into the room and stood quiet until the discussions died down. She raised her hand, about the speak, when the door to the locker room swung open behind her. Three men in what Penny could only describe as hockey jersey t-shirts and oversized hockey pants bustled into the room, put a pair of portable speakers in the middle of the room and starting a pounding jock jam. The trio started dancing energetically and suddenly tore the hockey pants off revealing bright shiny blue thongs underneath. The girls looked on in shock and then starting giggling uncontrollably.

Coach tried to stop them but when they ignored her, she grabbed the phone running their music and hit the stop button hard.

"Hey lady, we're just here to perform ok?" The lead dancer growled. "We had a booking for a hockey bachelorette party – this room at this time."

"Does this *look* like a bachelorette party?" Coach snapped, waving an arm around at the girls locker room.

"Well, in fairness, we've seen some pretty weird bachelorette parties." The dancer replied. "I mean, Mike and I worked this one where the hens were all dressed up as firefighters and…"

"It isn't." Coach cut him off and answered her own question. "This is a room of *twelve to fourteen year old girls*." Finally the trio stopped, and all three looked very uncomfortable.

"Maybe we should just, uh… go?" The lead dancer suggested. The other two groaned as he motioned them hurriedly out of the dressing room. They took their speakers and not quite ran out of the room. There was a series of screams and loud laughter from the hallway. A second later the one he'd called Mike popped his head back in. "Um, can I grab our pants?"

"That might be a good idea." Coach said crossly. He did and disappeared. Coach addressed the room, who were trying hard to compose themselves but still laughing at the display. "I hope you're happy seniors." She looked at each of her third years harshly. "Not sure which one of you put this little prank together, but this is *hardly* appropriate even for a senior prank. And yes, I know about that little tradition. It's done, I hope you had your fun, maybe the squad next year will remember that these pranks are supposed to be done with taste."

The girls murmured acknowledgement and the first and second year girls looked uncomfortably at their senior peers.

"Well I was going to say that the team deserved to celebrate but I think that just about covered the celebration." Coach said. "Instead, let's just get changed and meet up in the lobby. We'll walk across the street and grab some food before coming back for the afternoon game. The dressing room is ours for the day so you can leave your kit here, I'll lock up once you're changed and presentable for lunch."

Efficient as always Coach left, leaving them to process what all had just happened.

Lunch was dominated by two topics: the scout and the failed senior prank. Penny was now excluded from both discussions but for entirely opposite reasons. Penny *hadn't* been contacted about the evening's scouting session but as a senior there was a sense that she *was* implicated in the failed prank. This left her in lonely company and her teammates *kindly* made sure that she was able to sit next to Coach so that she would be able to discuss the game at least. Coach was not much of a conversationalist though, so for Penny, the lunch passed in near silence. She just sat as an observer watching the rest of her team going on about both topics without her.

The final game of the round robin that evening couldn't end fast enough, and both sets of teams audibly groaned when the 1-1 tie went to overtime and then a shootout to decide the match. Tired and frustrated the Beavs won in the shootout but it was hardly their most defining performance to end the round robin on. After shaking hands the players *not* invited to the tryout hit the locker room, while the rest who'd received letters walked across the hall to the ice that the tryout was being hosted on.

Penny heard about it from Shiv later that night when the tryout girls got back. "It was weird!" Shiv exclaimed after she got out of the hotel's shower. Penny and Jenn, both excluded from the invite, were sitting together cuddled up in the pillows of one of the room's twin beds.

"How was it weird?" Jenn asked.

"Well, firstly they said they're doing a tryout for *every team's* prospects independently. If I was running them, I'd have everyone show up at once so I could compare them side by side." Shiv explained excitedly.

"Yeah, but in fairness, you're not exactly building a semi-professional farm team are you?" Penny's sass surprised even her.

"Me-ow!" Jenn joked and gave her a shove. "Lay off just because you didn't get invited."

Shiv looked awkward for a moment but her excitement won out and she rambled on. "We didn't scrimmage or anything. They said at this stage they're most worried about conditioning. It ended up being a long endurance skate. We all skated laps until we couldn't anymore and then when we were done he wrote something in his notebook about us and we were released. I think I made it maybe 45 minutes but that was it. The rookies were all doing better than I was to be honest." Shiv sighed and seemed to lose energy all at once. "I was beat. I *am* beat. Somehow I don't think I did that well."

"Sorry to hear that." Penny and Jenn said together. Then they joined their roommate in the land of nod.

Morning came and there were a fresh set of letters. This time each girl got one. It was inviting the entire team to hear the results of the scouting session in the hotel's small business center. It listed a phone number they should dial into at 8:30am exactly.

The girls, some who had only just been woken up in time to make it, crammed into the tiny conference room that had seating for eight. There was one old phone in the middle of the table and they had to get the front receptionist from the hotel to help them dial into the number. A polite and cheery (too cheery for 8:30am the girls thought) voice said they'd be joined soon and then the room was filled with hold muzak.

Everyone sat rigid and silent. The entire assembled group nervous about what was about to be shared. The line clicked after about two minutes, and a polite, and oddly familiar, voice filled the room.

"Thank you all for participating in our scouting exercise. Congratulations especially to the two girls who lasted the longest in the endurance skate last night, with time of one hour and twelve minutes and one hour and twenty one minutes respectively." The girls looked around at each other wondering who'd made it that long. Nobody was volunteering it was them. "We've reviewed the conditioning results along with the scouting reports from the tournament. We are happy to share that Penny, Emma and Jenn are the ultimate senior prank masters and you've all BEEN PRANKED! The scout was a plant, the letters and endurance skate were all fake! WE GOT YOU SO BAD! P-E-and-J forever bitches!"

The line clicked and the speaker phone filled the room with dialtone.

"What. The. Actual. Fuck." Shiv asked, channeling her inner Becks.

Penny, Jenn, and Emma opened the door at that point. Nobody had noticed in the cramped space they had been missing. Now as the doors opened and they stood there, cell phones at the ready, the combined team looked at them with glares and gapes of disbelief.

"SMILE!" The three yelled and snapped off a rapid fire group of photos on their phones. And then they ran, laughing hysterically as they did.

The Beavs pulled off a gold medal to cap off the Jamboree. That fact always seems to get lost when people talk about that Jamboree though. The fake scout and double-fake out with the exotic hockey dancers remain to this day the most epic senior prank ever pulled by a departing group of Beavs players. Quiet, bookish Emma had been the brains, Jenn had done most of the arrangements including convincing her brother to take his reading week break from University to play the role of the fake scout, and Penny had been the patsy whose apparent "exclusion" from the whole thing had sold it all. The decision to exclude Shiv had just been one extra step to sell the deal, and one that she found utterly hilarious. After the fact. Penny and her seniors had secured their spot in the Beavs' hall of pranking fame and for whatever else they may have contributed while they were a member of the team, that ensured them immortality for years to come.

17. Dumb Questions

One of the things you learn quickly in female hockey is how to humbly avoid the spotlight. As scandals about player abuse, fighting, and tv announcers cast shade across the men's game, the female leagues are largely left alone. The game of female hockey remains one of the purest forms of Canada's gam. As famous Canadian alt-rock band Rush once noted, "glittering prizes and endless compromises shatter the illusion of integrity"; by the same merit as boys and men's teams across the country are viewed through the political lens, the women's game remains out of the public eye and retains its integrity. The rare stories about the Canadian female program often focus on the compensation inequity between the women's game and men's game, which pose challenges as soon as you realize the issues inherent in comparing professional, paid players with equally talented but unpaid amateur ones.

Penny was never one to get very invested in any of the politics around the sport she loved. Penny wanted to play her game, her way, and unless you were on the ice holding a stick skating with or against her, who cared what your opinion was anyway? That was not, however, the view of the local Maple Creek Crier.

The Crier had been around since the early 70s and had never in its existence enjoyed a year that wasn't a tumultuous battle for survival. The Crier's staff fluctuated between one and three, depending on the year, and they (exclusively for lack of any competition) covered everything that qualified as news in Maple Creek and the surrounding small rural communities. And yes, there are communities smaller than Maple Creek Saskatchewan.

The Crier had been through a difficult conversion in the last decade. Like many printed publications, the Crier had seen their subscriptions and sales drop off as consumers favored news they could consume on their phones and tablets over something they could sit and flip through over a morning coffee before having to recycle. The Crier had made the jump to online and social media with the same grace as a gazelle fighting to escape a crocodile in the middle of a river. Look for gazelle crocodile battle on youtube if that doesn't bring an image readily to mind.

The local high school student who had helped the Crier go online had really done the best they could with what they were given. The bad decisions started with the Crier insisting that the new website reflect the heritage and feel for the local community, by which they meant that the website should have a verdant green background that evoked a sense of the expansive green Saskatchewan prairie, with bright gold text representing the golden wheat that was the town's main agricultural product. Gold on green for every story, heading, and advertisement. Glinda and Elphaba sported less green and gold in a Texas homegrown production of Wicked. The decisions just got worse from there. They wouldn't sell any advertising that would clutter the site, they would charge a subscription fee for people to access the stories.

Suffice to say the transition to online media did not go well, and once again the Crier came a razor's edge away from going out of business. In the end they fixed the problems and managed to stay afloat, though with the door opened for yet more problems. A mere few months after the re-launch of the Crier online, the web erupted with a hashtag movement in support of women around the world. The Crier came under fire a few weeks into the social media storm when one enterprising young woman noticed that the Crier had, in its nearly fifty-year tenure, never employed a woman. It didn't exactly matter that the Crier had never said no to an applicant male *or* female – they'd never been in a position to do so – but regardless the reason behind it, the fact that they'd been an all-male institution became something the local community took issue with.

The duo running the Crier at that moment tried to recruit a woman to join their team. If things had stopped there, it might have been another flash in the pan and the issue could have died off with public interest in the hashtag. But it didn't. While they struggled to recruit their diversity hire, they also made it a priority to produce more "female friendly" content for their readers to show their dedication to the local community. That couldn't have gone worse for them.

In a single week they started Monday's special "Women's Stories" section with a 2 page story on finding your right cup size the first time, brought to you by the senior gentleman who ran the lingerie department at the local department store. Tuesday doubled down with "Family Meals sure to Please" featuring a survey of local kids and husbands on their favorite weekday meals. Wednesday kept the momentum going with "Beating Tough Stains without Bleach" and other laundry advice borrowed verbatim from the Tide website. Thursday scraped the bottom of the barrel with "Beauty tips from local Babes" shared by the girls from the town's one and only gentleman's club, and Friday gave up all hope and featured "Surviving your Period" with a local (male) sex ed teacher as the local expert they found to interview. The efforts were so poorly received that a mashup of the week's headlines became a meme that circulated with the hashtag #soclueless.

Learning from their mistakes, the Crier followed the series up 2 weeks later with a new special section "Stories About Women". This is how they came to be interviewing Penny after the Beavs' latest home game.

Penny had never been interviewed before, honestly never really *thought* about being interviewed. The media was so outside the sphere of minor female hockey that when Coach told the team they needed someone to talk to the Crier about the Beavs' season, Coach might as well have been telling them there was an alien overlord looking to talk to them. Penny had been the only one who'd volunteered.

Penny spent the night before her interview researching common hockey media interview questions and how the pros answered them. She spent a good chunk of her evening on youtube looking up past interviews to see how the process worked. Penny made a short list of questions she would be ready for. What helped your team win or lose today? How do you think you played in this game? What does playing for this team mean to you? Penny wrote out answers to each of the questions on cue cards to help her practice what she would say.

It helped that Penny's team won the game the next day. Penny felt like she'd had a solid game and the girls had some good plays for her to talk about. As she walked off the ice she spotted the thirty-something man in the faded "Maple Creek Crier" t-shirt and went over to him.

"Hi there, you're Penny?" The reporter asked. She nodded. "Ok I'm Bob with the Crier. I'm hoping to ask you some questions. After this I'll be recording and you'll be on the record, ok? If there's anything you don't want to answer, just say "no comment" and we'll move on ok? Great." He talked with a machine gun cadence that left Penny feeling breathless just listening to the man.

"Ok Penny, first question. What jersey size do you wear?" Bob held up his cell phone between them and pressed a red circular "Record" button as he started talking.

Penny blinked. "What *size* jersey? Um, medium?" This was NOT in the shortlist of questions Penny had prepared for today.

"Medium?" Bob looked at her, eyeing her as if he didn't believe her and was about to ask her to check if that was true. "Do your team wear the same size as the boys' teams or do you have your own sizes?"

"I don't order our equipment." Penny stuttered. "But I assume there's men's and women's sizes just like normal clothes. I suppose I'd be wearing a women's medium."

"Oh, ok that makes sense." Bob said, sounding completely disinterested. "Moving on, how do you do your hair before a game so that it doesn't get in the way of your play?"

"I just put it in a ponytail?" Penny answer/asked. "Not that it ever 'gets in the way of my play', but it's something easy and it doesn't come loose when play gets physical."

"Thanks for that." Bob nodded eagerly. "For the readers at home Jenny,"

"Penny." Penny corrected.

"Right. For the readers at home, do you have a special someone in your life?"

"My mom, my dad, my brother Pat who brings me to the games. Really, my whole family is special, and so are the other girls on my team of course." Penny nodded to the locker room.

"Sure there's nobody *extra* special, maybe *romantically* special?" Bob pressed.

"Do many fourteen-year-old girls have someone romantically special?" Penny blurted back. This interview was moving from the realm of "strange" to "completely bizarre" in Penny's mind.

"Ok last question." Bob was clearly struggling with this as well. "What made you want to play hockey as opposed to figure skating or ballet or…"

Penny cut him off. "Or a more girly sport?" She finished for him. "I have 3 brothers who all played hockey. I come from a hockey family. We eat. We go to school. And we play hockey. That's what our family is about. It was never a decision or choice I made, it's as much a part of me as my hand or my name." Penny finished off with a stomp of her skate on the rubberized floor below her.

"Ok no more questions." Bob said and turned off the recorder. "Thanks Penny. Good game." He turned to leave.

"Yo, reporter guy." Penny called to his back. He turned again to face her. "What the hell?"

"What?" Bob asked, perplexed.

"You don't think people want to hear about the *hockey* we play or the *game* we just won? They're just going to want to know that some *girls* played hockey today and they wear clothes just like boys and maybe they have a boyfriend and secretly want to be a jazz dancer?"

"DO you secretly want to be a jazz dancer?" Bob perked up and his thumb quivered expectantly back over the record button on his phone.

"God – NO! You're hopeless!" Penny rolled her eyes in exasperation. This time it was her turn to spin her back to Bob and walk off.

"Women." Bob shook his head and put his phone away and left.

Penny went in the locker room and the room immediately fell silent. She walked over to her spot on the wall and sat down. She started the regular post-game ritual of removing her equipment, helmet first. Twenty other pairs of eyes watched her. Penny smirked and wondered how long she could keep pretending she hadn't noticed.

"WELL?" Becks broke the spell first. "How did it go?"

"He was a tool." Penny replied, "He wanted a hockey barbie and got a hockey *player* instead. Total waste of time." Penny went back to removing her equipment, starting to unlace her skates now.

"I dunno, I thought it was pretty enlightening," Shiv observed. She was leaning against the wall beside the locker room door. She paused a beat before explaining. "I had *no idea* you secretly wanted to be a jazz dancer." The room erupted into laughter and Penny joined in. The whole thing *had* been a joke. The write-up that ran two days later, was better than Penny expected. In the end, Bob wrote the piece as a recap of the team's win that afternoon. Penny's interview was only mentioned at the end of the piece, and only one sentence. "People want to hear about the hockey we play and the game we just won." The article closed with a call for better media coverage of youth sports in general. Penny leaned back when she finished reading it and smiled at a job well done.

18. The Playoffs: Quarterfinals

Penny Davies' third and final year with the Saskatchewan Minor Hockey League's Hungry Beavers U15 female team had been an up and down affair from the outset. Penny had been ejected and suspended for 2 games for a questionable hit in her second game of the season. She'd been paired up with fellow veteran Jenn, a forward-turned defender who Penny had clashed horns with before the two had settled their differences by Jenn becoming Penny's first girlfriend. There'd been the ongoing bitter rivalry with the Winnipeg Witches' Maja Carlsson, with Penny having had to fight the big Swedish immigrant twice in the regular season. And her group of seniors had pulled off the most epic Senior Prank in Beavs history before winning their age group at the annual Minor Female Hockey Jamboree in Saskatoon.

Today, however, none of that mattered. It also didn't matter that her team had ended the regular season in the top spot in the league for the first time ever. None of it mattered because today was the first day of the playoffs. The Beavs were three best-of-three rounds, or six wins (or losses) away from a historical championship or bitter defeat. Penny tried to remind herself it also didn't matter that she'd missed the team's first playoff run last year because of a fluke off-ice ear swab injury that had taken the better part of the summer to fully heal. Lastly, Penny knew that it didn't matter that this was her last guaranteed year of play, and if she didn't get onto the provincial U20 Junior team, her hockey career ended with this playoff run. That most definitely didn't matter, but all those things together added gravity and intensity to an already nerve-wracking start to the post season.

Penny, for her part, had tried to avoid thinking or worrying about the playoffs until they got here. The Beavs had qualified for the post season a full month before the end of the season, thanks to their strong position in the league's standings. As a result, it was hardly a surprise that they were going to be in the playoffs but that had just meant that after the initial excitement passed, there was that much longer to stress about the upcoming games. Coach had been a godsend through the final stretch keeping Penny and her teammates too busy and exhausted with extra practices and hockey homework to have much free time for worrying.

Penny realized after her first shift that it had been 3 years since she was last in a playoff game, and that had been with her Ringette team. Everyone on the ice was working on level 11. Familiar opponents from the regular season were skating faster, making passes they would've missed during the regular season, and taking harder shots than Penny had seen before.

Their first-round opponents in that playoff run were the Dog River River Dogs. The Dogs had been a scrappy team in the regular season. Coming from a town about the same size as Maple Creek, they had a similar work-over-talent mentality to their game and ground you down with their work ethic over sixty minutes of play. Here in the playoffs however, they seemed to have thrown that playbook out the window and were going for a fast zone entry and then getting as many shots from wherever they could before chasing the puck back up the ice.

Their normally physical play had been pared back to hardly any, with the Dogs letting the Beavs chase the pucks and control the boards, opting to bottle play up in the center of the ice and pick up turnovers when they managed to block cross-ice passes.

The Beavs were responding with changes of their own. Coach was shuffling their lines and had Jenn playing switch as a "fourth forward" whenever the puck was in the other end. The Beavs were playing the open lanes along the boards and working to move the puck up the ice faster than the Dogs could transition, trying to create odd-woman rushes and scoring opportunities.

Penny found herself a defensive team of one for most of the first period, play after play grabbing the puck from the corner or behind the net and rolling it along the boards to the blue line where there was a free winger ready to pass it on to the Dog's blue line. Penny got some decent one-on-one battle time on the faceoffs, but both teams were playing it clean and careful so the only faceoffs were coming off of deflections out of play or goalies holding the puck.

Despite the upped tempo Penny was *bored*. This might be hockey, but it wasn't *Beavs'* hockey, and definitely wasn't Penny's hockey.

Late in the first, Penny's heart leapt when the puck squirted loose from the Dogs' end of the ice and a trailing forward picked it up at center. Penny was the lone defender back-checking and that set up a one-on-one between her and the forward in defense of Emma's goal. Penny got paired up with the forward at her own blue line, skating backwards as the forward skated towards her, Penny keeping her feet moving and her body between the forward and the goal. The forward deked once and Penny stayed right with her. She deked again, and this time Penny planted her feet and while the forward was shifting her weight to deke a third time, her momentum carried her directly into Penny's body. The puck slid under Penny's legs as the forward collided with her. Penny had been expecting the hit and had her arms and stick up in front of her torso to absorb the hit; after the initial collision Penny shoved the forward back away from her with both her arms and stick engaged. The forward was caught off balance suddenly moving backwards, tripped over her own skates and fell to the ice with a satisfying *ooof*. Penny turned to chase down the puck when she heard the tweet of the referee's whistle.

Penny rolled her eyes and turned to see the black and white official skating towards her. "You, off." The ref stated firmly, pointing to Penny.

"For what?" Penny asked, although her feet were already started to move her in the direction of the opening penalty box.

The ref made a pushing motion with both hands balled into fists. "Cross-checking." She told Penny, and then repeated the statement and motion louder facing the benches and crowd. There was a groan from Penny's bench and she watched them switch up players to the first PK line; with Shiv stepping up to cover Penny's normal spot on that line.

Penny got to spectate the final seconds of the period and skated across the ice to join her team heading to the locker room at intermission. She was right behind Emma in the hallway and patted her helmet. "Great saves," Penny told her, "Thanks for bailing my ass out of that BS call." Emma's helmet nodded but she didn't reply.

Coach was leaning against the outer wall of the locker room when Penny and Emma came to enter. She put a hand on Penny's shoulder. "Hold up there Goon." She said softly. Emma closed the door behind her.

"What's up Coach?" Penny asked. "Did you have a chat with the refs about that bull cross checking call?"

Coach ignored her question. "Why'd you play the body on that breakaway instead of just taking the easy poke check?"

Penny had to shift her train of thought before responding. "I didn't really think about it. It just seemed like the right move to make." Penny answered.

"Would you do it again?"

"Probably." Penny said quickly. "It stopped the breakaway even if it did pull a penalty."

"Hrm." Coach chewed on that but didn't say anything else. She gestured to the door and let Penny go through first.

Nervous energy filled the room, and Penny felt a weird vibe from Coach after their discussion. But there was nothing further she said about it. Coach let the girls work out their own jitters for that intermission, and for Penny that meant she slid her headphones in and cranked up the music. Kesha's "Die Young" followed by Katy Perry's "Firework" had her bouncing and ready to rock for the second period.

Back on the bench, Coach started Shiv's second line that period, followed by the rookie defenders of D-line 3. When the ref's whistle blew and Coach signaled the third line change, Penny and Jenn got to their feet ready to swap out. "Shiv, swap on line 1 with Goon. Go on with Jenn."

"Yes Coach!" Shiv shouted and jumped to her feet. Penny spun around and looked at her coach in frustration. Coach's steel blue eyes looked back stonily. Penny opened her mouth to protest but Coach was already raising her palm in their long time 'red light' signal, meaning Penny needed to reign it in. Penny spun back around angrily to continue spectating and sat down on the bench in a huff.

The play picked up in the River Dogs' end. Penny watched Li get tossed from the faceoff circle and Shiv cycled in to take her place, cleanly winning the pass and getting it back to Li. Li used her fancy footwork to spin away from a check and gain the inside of the Dogs' defensive box for the first time that period. Jenn was back where the faceoff had been and slapped her stick urgently on the ice as the *four* Dogs covering the front of the net converged on Li. Li did a 270 spin and knocked the puck cleanly between one of the defenders' legs and perfectly onto the tape of Jenn's stick. Jenn didn't wait. She let a hard wrister go through the open ice at the side of the net. The goalie, partially screened by all the players directly in front of her, raised her glove to catch the puck but never got a good view of it and overshot where the puck was going. The puck sailed through the space between her arm and torso and into the back of the net. The red light went off and the buzzer went and Penny joined her team in cheering their 1-0 lead. Penny pounded Jenn's glove as she skated by, very impressed by the rare goal from her girlfriend.

The same lines stayed on to finish their shift, and as the seconds wore on Penny heard Coach's voice in her ear. "Now that we've got a lead you need to help us keep it. *Anyone* comes in our zone, make them feel it? Understand?"

Penny gritted her teeth and grinned. "YES COACH!" She responded with enthusiasm. She got to her feet now.

"Shiv, change." Coach shouted and Shiv cycled off the play she'd been skating up to join and onto the bench. Penny hopped on the ice and got into position.

The Dogs were scrambling. They still hadn't managed a line change since the goal and Penny could see their defensive box was getting wider and wider as the Beavs players happily cycled the puck around the neutral zone in long, quick tape-to-tape passes like the ones they'd been practicing coming into the playoffs. Penny took Shiv's position at the far corner of their passing box along the Beavs' blue line and joined the fun. The girl nearest Penny's adopted position was one of the Dogs' star forwards, and Penny could tell that she was getting increasingly frustrated each time she lunged her stick out towards the passing lane the puck was transiting and missed. Penny decided she could probably press a few buttons here.

"Passing left!" Penny called cheerily the next time she got the puck, a second later doing exactly that across to one of the Jess's.

"Passing up!" She called the next time. The forward scrambled to where that would put the puck but didn't get there in time.

"I don't need *pointers*." The forward growled at Penny.

"Nope, you just need this here puck." Penny laughed as she received and sent off yet another pass. "Oh, except you just missed that one."

"Fuck you." The forward snapped.

"Already got a girlfriend, thanks." Penny blew her a kiss.

"Shut UP." The forward stumbled trying to reposition her body and collapsed down onto a knee.

Penny took and sent another pass while she was down. "No skate sharpeners in Dog River?" She pushed.

The forward shrieked in frustration and threw her body at Penny. She knocked Penny to the ice with a big body check and straddled her, trying to claw through Penny's face mask with her still gloved hands.

"Ah!" Penny cried out, deliberately. "Don't hurt me!" Penny tried to put her arms up over her face defensively but the other girl just knocked her hands away.

"You little shit I'm gonna rip you apart. Shut your smart mouth! When I'm done with y----" The forward growled but was cut off. Two officials had skated over and grabbed her. She protested at them, shouting obscenities all the way to the penalty box. Penny gave her a tiny wave as the door closed, and noticed that the other team's coach was hanging her head looking like the classic Captain Picard 'facepalm' meme.

Penny was called back for a line change, not realizing she'd been on the ice over a minute during the entire exchange.

She sat for a while as Coach was juggling up the power play lines, and the Dogs' forward losing her cool gave the Beavs' a 5-minute major power play. This time Penny didn't mind being benched. She was starting to understand Coach's strategy against the Dogs and knew that this wasn't her time to fit into that plan.

The period ended 2-0 following another Beavs' goal in the last 30 seconds of their major penalty. Penny only had one more shift that period and she didn't end up doing much more than back checking in her own zone, alone the entire period except for Emma in net behind her. The two fist-bumped when the buzzer went and then went to the locker room.

A curt and abrupt speech from Coach at the intermission reminded them there was still a period of play left and to not get comfortable. The team had to remember their fundamentals and keep playing *their game*. Ten seconds of coaching done, Penny got her jam going with Meredith Brooks' "Bitch" followed by DJ Khaled's "All I Do Is Win". Penny didn't realize she was singing out loud until the entire locker room started joining in, and the repeated chorus continued all the way to the bench.

"All we do is win – win – win no matter what!" The girls chanted over and over.

Penny hit the ice for the third period along with her usual first line mates this time. She smiled as she and Jenn did a quick down-up-down-down-

down stick clap routine that they'd seen on a TikTok from one of the members of the Czech women's national team and adapted to make their own. That always drew some attention and sure enough Jenn pointed to the Dogs' bench when they were done where a full half of the girls were pointing and whispering to each other about the routine.

"Stick sisters for life!" The two shouted and raised their sticks, then quickly got into position following a harsh glare from the refs.

Puck drop, the Dogs won the face off and their center fired a quick pass across to her winger. Penny was already on it and tied the puck up in the winger's feet as soon as it arrived. The two battled stick and foot for possession, and Penny soon felt Jenn's presence behind her, and another stick joined the battle followed by another on the opposing team. After a furious cycle of shoving and kicking at each other's skates, the whistle went. Penny glanced at the score clock and grinned, seeing she'd managed to eat up 32 seconds of the period with that move.

The next faceoff the Dogs had more luck. They won the puck again and managed to skate it over center before dumping it into the Beavs' zone. Their coach called for a line change and all except their center skated to the bench while the center chased the puck down in the Beavs' zone. Penny's line was also called for a change but she wasn't going to leave Emma to a 1 on 0 and went after the center while her own line went in the opposite direction.

The center beat her to the puck and held it behind the net. Emma was furiously looking behind her left and right, head on a swivel waiting for the first indication of where the forward was going to move. Penny beat the incoming Dogs' fresh legs and chased the center behind the net. That forced her to skate out the far side and Penny was hot on her heels. She tried to make a tight turn back in towards the net, but Penny had caught her now and leaned her body heavily against the center's side, making it nearly impossible for her to turn her feet. "Get out of my zone." Penny growled in her best impersonation of Harrison Ford in "Air Force One". Instead, the girl opted to pass the puck towards a winger who was just approaching the zone. She overshot though, and the puck bounced off the board just in front of the winger and bounced free of the zone behind her. There was a pounding of sticks-on-boards from Penny's bench and Penny used that interruption to get off the ice.

During Penny's play break, the Dogs managed to gain the zone and slide one past Emma on a sneaky but well executed reverse wraparound and made it a 2-1 game. Penny was next on the ice with half the period gone and the score holding at 2-1. 8 minutes and 14 seconds to go. That forward she'd drawn a penalty from in the second period was lined up against her.

"I owe you one." The forward told her. "And I always settle my debts."

"Ask the Lanisters how that worked for them." Penny suggested as the puck dropped. She and the forward got tied up in each other's limbs and equipment, and eventually ended up on the ice. Neither one really had an advantage in the situation, and as the play continued down the ice without them both girls had to scramble back to their feet and try to catch up.

Penny remembered Pat's advice from nearly two years back. The forward was the River Dogs' best scorer, and her team wasn't exactly at risk from anyone else on their team. She decided it was a matchup worth leaning harder on. As Pat would have said, one Penny for their top forward was a smart trade for a game or two.

Penny caught up with the smaller girl and every chance she got gave her an extra bump with her hips here or a bonus tap with her stick to the back of the legs there. The forward was getting more and more frustrated and finally snapped at Penny. "Do you wanna go?" The forward demanded at the next whistle. Both benches were calling the girls back but neither really seemed to care.

"Think you can handle this?" Penny asked. She looked over and saw that Coach was nodding and giving her a closed fist signal in front of her.

"Oh, I've been waiting all game." The forward said. They were drawing a crowd now along the boards in the River Dogs' end.

"I'm worth the wait." Penny winked. And that did it. The forward threw her stick and gloves to the ice and lunged at Penny. It was clear she'd never been in a fight before, but Penny knew that didn't get her any special treatment. The forward tackled Penny around the waist and tried to drive her back to the boards. That made her helmet perfectly positioned for Penny to grab by the sides and pull up and off her head. The girl swore and spit splattered Penny's neck and the top of her jersey the girl's now exposed face was so close to her.

Penny didn't even bother with the jersey. The girl was still holding the sides of Penny's own jersey and not doing anything to protect her face. Penny's arms were both free so with her stronger left arm she pulled back and let loose five quick jabs directly to the girl's nose. On the fifth jab Penny felt a satisfying, if somewhat sickening, *crack* and the other girl's nose erupted in a torrent of blood. With her adrenaline fed senses Penny even heard the *splat* as the first big gush of blood splattered on the ice between them. The other girl let go and doubled over, using her hands to cover her face and trying to catch as much of the blood as possible. The Dogs' trainer was already on her way out of their bench with a towel to help with the cleanup. Penny mechanically picked up her equipment where she'd dropped it and let the official lead her off the ice. Her bench was pounding away in appreciation at the win and Coach gave her a quick nod as she walked through the bench and out of the rink. Penny could hear the *well done* even if she hadn't said it out loud.

Seven minutes in the locker room later and the rest of the team came in jubilant with the victory. The game had ended 3-1 following an empty netter in the last minute which rookie Jada had managed to put in from her own end of the ice. It had been a little dicey before that when the Dogs' had gone on a late delay of game penalty, but the empty netter had shut them down pretty good to end the game.

Game 2 was in Dog River the next day with the team bus leaving at 5:30am so the team didn't overdo the celebrations. Most of the players made a point to come by and congratulate Penny on taking their star forward out of the series, even if it did mean that Penny would have to watch the next game from the stands.

The second of the best of 3 games against the River Dogs followed a three and a half hour bus trip the next morning. Penny found a seat in the stands with a couple of her teammates' parents who had made the trip out to watch. It wasn't Penny's first time having to sit out a game suspension, but she certainly felt the most frustrated and useless of all the times she had.

The arena was a small one, smaller than the rink in Penny's hometown of Maple Creek. There were only six rows of bleachers in the spectator area, and they only ran the length of one side of the rink. The couple dozen spectators in attendance had lined themselves up on the end of the ice their team started the first period in. Penny craned her head to look over at the other side of arena to see if she could see the forward she'd fought in the stands. So far she couldn't see them anywhere.

The first period started and the game began slowly. A few younger siblings had signs they were pressing against the glass cheering on their bigger sisters. The parents around Penny were far more energetic than the players, sipping from their Tim's or Starbucks coffees and discussing their family's plans for the off-season.

"Oh you mean the five months of the year our family is allowed to have a life outside hockey?" One mom joked, the others laughed.

Penny had always found summers dragged and she couldn't wait for the camps to open at the end of summer. Family vacations and the short soccer season always just felt like distractions from the giant hole that not having any hockey to play left in Penny's life. She reflected sadly that, in all likelihood, once these playoffs were over that was going to be the new normal for her.

Her team scored their first goal at the midpoint of the period. Jess (another rookie)put it in and did the kneeling sharpshooter celly pose she'd been practicing. She saw Shiv and Jenn waving to her from the bench after the goal celebration, and Penny appreciated the gesture of trying to keep her included. The rest of the period continued at a sleepy pace with well over half of the possession time spent in the neutral zone trading the puck back and forth between the teams. The final buzzer elicited a relieved groan from the parent section.

Penny joined the other spectators during the intermission out in the lobby getting herself a pop and some chips from the vending machine. She tried not to wonder what her team was doing in the locker room now. She imagined Coach was probably giving the team an earful about dragging their asses out there. That's what she'd be saying anyway. Penny sipped her pop and noticed a pair of parents in Dogs' jerseys across the lobby cocking their heads together and looking at her. Penny looked behind her to see if there was someone behind her they were focusing on, but when she looked back they made a show of not looking her way anymore. Penny shrugged and went back to her seat with her team.

The second period was the best period for the Dogs that Penny had seen in the playoffs. They came out with energy and enthusiasm, and Penny thought they seemed to be having *fun* for the first time all series. Their improved mood translated to faster skating, better follow up on their pucks, and much more confident passing. Penny hated to admit it, but from her seat in the stands it was clear the Beavs were on their heels. Struggling to match the Dogs' tempo they were getting themselves in trouble and getting sloppy with their discipline. The Beavs drew three penalties and it was only thanks to an outstanding performance by Emma that the team kept their lead through to the end of the period.

Penny was breathing heavily from the stress of being on the sidelines by the time the buzzer went for the second intermission and she was able to catch her breath.

Instead of following the majority of people out to the lobby she stayed put, not needing to warm up and still with over half of her pop left. While she was watching the Zamboni clear the ice, one of the two parents in the Dogs jerseys she'd seen earlier walked up to her.

"You're that suspended player who got in the fight in the last game, aren't you?" The man asked. Penny thought his tone was unnecessarily aggressive, and then she saw the number on his jersey.

"Yes." She replied as neutrally as she could.

"I was supposed to be watching what will probably be my daughter's last game in this league today." He told her, gritting his teeth and she could see his eyes were watery. "But thanks to *you*, that's not happening."

"Where is she?" Penny asked, trying to avoid focusing on his veiled accusation.

"Oh, not even here with her team, where she should be. She and her mother are still in Maple Creek. At the hospital." Penny's heart sank. He continued on, "Her nose was broken and they needed to wait for a doctor who could properly reset it." He finished. "Which is absolutely ridiculous considering fighting isn't even allowed in this league. I don't understand how you're here, she's still there, and you are still allowed to play in this league at all." His body sagged with exhaustion and a few tears fell from his eyes. "She's a good girl, she's not like…that. She just loves to play so much. And for it to end like this…" He took several deep breaths before he was able to finish, "I hope you're proud of yourself."

Penny felt like she'd been gut punched. She just sat there.

"She should be!" A voice called from behind her. Penny looked back to see Shiv's mom flanked by two other parents from the Beavs walking down towards them. Shiv's mom advanced on the dad, absolute fire in her eyes. "How dare you? You can't just verbally attack a player like that."

"But she attacked my daughter…"

"Who dropped the gloves at the *same time*." Jenn's dad glowered, catching up to Shiv's mom. "I was actually there. Were you?"

The other dad fell silent and looked like a kicked puppy. He turned to walk back to his side of the rink.

"Hold up there!" Jenn's dad shouted. "You need to apologize to this poor girl. You're a grown man. Act like it."

"Sorry." The dad mumbled, barely audible.

"We didn't *hear you.*" Shiv's mom yelled.

"I'm SORRY." He said very loudly and clearly. He couldn't bring himself to meet Penny's eyes when he did though. He turned and hurried off before things escalated any further. Penny felt shattered.

Shiv's mom came over and put a hand on her shoulder. "He shouldn't have done that. Hockey dads are the worst." She quickly glanced at Jenn's dad who was giving her a falsely hurt look that quickly dissolved into a shrug of grudging agreement.

Penny had the third period to sit and stew on that. The other girl really should have been able to be here. This could very well be the end of her team's playoff run and her time in U15, and Penny had taken that away from her. She hadn't *meant* to, but Penny had definitely pushed her to the fight and been the one who'd broken her nose. She thought back to the rules Paul and Pat had taught her, particularly about fighting a willing opponent. It'd been a *smart* move but definitely not a sportsmanlike move. Penny was going to have to live with that.

Her team held on to their 1-0 lead to the end of the game and won the series. Penny hurried down to ice level and opened the door the referees came and went from to get on the ice. She joined her team in the celebration of their victory. It was their first playoff series win as a group, and she was happy for her team but found her excitement bittersweet. The cost of victory had been high. She and her team may not be the ones paying it, but Penny had been forced to confront the dark side of the consequences of playing her game, and she didn't like the look of it. As she followed the team to the locker room and listened to everyone chattering excitedly, Penny hoped none of them would ever end up having to face another player's parent like that, and very relieved that she wouldn't be seeing the Dogs or their fans again.

19. The Playoffs: Semifinals

The bus ride home from round 1's series victory started off as a giant party. The South Saskatchewan Minor Hockey League's U15 Hungry Beavers – the Beavs – had just knocked out the Dog River River Dogs to secure their first Series 1 playoff victory in over a decade. The girls weren't old enough for champagne, but that didn't stop a couple of rookies from bringing a pair of bottles of non-alcoholic sparkling fruit drink and cracking them open as soon as the bus left Dog River's city limits. Although they had no intention of *drinking* the stuff, instead they shook the bottles like crazy before popping their plastic corks and then sprayed the fruity beverages all over everyone and everything present.

It was utter ecstatic pandemonium for about thirty seconds, with girls standing up in their seats and dancing under the spray until the carbonation ran out. Then the rookies started pouring what was left over each other's heads and tried to feed sips to each other with one player holding a bottle while another sat, mouth open, trying to catch the dribbles while the bus bounced across the terribly maintained south Saskatchewan secondary highway.

Then the moment passed, and people started to get cold. And wet. And sticky. A few spots where the spray had hit the roof dripped down on top of players below who had nowhere to go on the cramped bus. And the jubilation started to fade.

To a girl, the players on the bus would say they were happy if you asked them. But the general mood on the bus was anything but. The players were tired from the early start and the second of 2 three hour bus rides that day. They also had a lot to process after the victory over the Dogs. The series hadn't been particularly challenging, but Coach had made clear during the intermissions of their 2nd game that the Beavs were going to need to find the next level competitively if they were going to have any hopes in the next two rounds. They were also in uncharted territory. The team had suffered an early first-round knockout the previous year, and that was the only experience with series-based post-season hockey any of the girls had. The magnitude of their achievements so far brought a new weight, the weight of expectation they all carried to make it worth something. And *nobody* wanted to be the one letting their families, Coach, or the team itself down.

"It's the Witches!" Emma cried out when they were halfway back. Two dozen heads turned to look at her. "Their goalie just posted," she explained. "They beat Battleford in two. So we'll be against them in the semis."

Penny's heart started to race. The Beavs had split their regular season series with the Witches, each taking 2 wins from the other in their 4 matchups to date. The Witches were a talented but inconsistent team, and they had a very offensive play style that the Beavs' veteran defenders managed to shut down pretty well. But the Witches had a sniper who could bury it top corner from the point, and the best goaltender in the league. Even counting the games the Beavs had won, they'd never put more than 2 pucks past the Witches' goaltender in a single game. And they had Maja Carlsson. If there was a competitor in the league for biggest, baddest bitch aside from Penny, Maja Carlsson was the contender. She and Penny had gone a round twice already that season, and neither were satisfied with the tie their current record sat at. Maja was one of the few girls Penny'd gone up against in her career who'd had enough skill to pop Penny's helmet off and she'd given Penny her only black eye of the season owing to a wicked left hook. And now she and Maja had up to 3 more meetings.

Penny had fought one of the River Dogs' forwards in the Quarterfinals and gotten the pair of them suspended for their second, and ultimately final, game of the series. That one Penny had instigated by goading the Dogs' star forward into dropping the gloves. She expected the problem with Maja was going to be keeping both girls' gloves *on*.

That gave Penny's full brain even more to chew on as she let herself drift off for the final hour back home.

"So the Witches." A statement. Pat shoveled another mouthful of chicken casserole into his mouth as he said it. Penny waited while he chewed. Mouth still half full, he continued, "Isn't that the one the blond Scandinavian chick is on? The tall hot one?"

"I really wouldn't know." Penny slid a piece of broccoli around on her plate trying to get some of the creamy cheese sauce off the florets.

"Come on, you're dating your defensive linemate – I figured you'd have *some* opinion." Pat swallowed a mouthful.

Penny's face flushed red as it always did when one of her family mentioned her first girlfriend and implied assumptions about her sexual preferences. "Yeah, but it's not like that, it's…" She trailed off. She couldn't really explain it herself so trying to explain her feelings to anyone else was always a losing effort. Yes, she was dating Jenn. Yes, the two had been together for a few months and yes, both *were* girls. But Penny didn't find herself *looking* at other girls, or really guys for that matter. She hadn't gone looking for what she'd found with Jenn, and she definitely wasn't looking for it with anyone else right now.

Pat moved on. "Anyway. Swedish girl. You fought her before yeah?"

"Twice." Penny nodded.

"I really wish you wouldn't do that." Penny's mom let her fork clatter on her plate. "I did not agree for my daughter to become a thug when you started playing this sport." She looked harshly at Pat and Paul. "Not that I should be too surprised."

An awkward silence fell over their Sunday night dinner table. Penny pushed her chair back, having had enough of everyone else's opinions on her life. "I'm not hungry anymore." She said firmly and hurried off to her room before the tears started coming out.

"So the Witches" seemed to be the theme of both practices before the series started the following weekend. Coach did her best to focus her team on the Witches' weaknesses they'd shown in the previous matchup. She'd managed to find a couple of videos on the Witches' social media that the team watched, seeing how their plays came together and the position of the goalie for different types of shots. Two practices didn't make for a lot of time to adjust their game though. The team practiced a few specific skills and shots that might help them out in the next round, but mostly they just tried to stay loose by playing games in practice and cracking nervous jokes through their drills.

Saturday afternoon's Second Round – Game One arrived very quickly. The Beavs were visitors for game one and because the Witches were based further away, the team drove out Friday night and stayed in a hotel before their game. This was a relief for the team after the rough early morning departure for their second first-round game the previous Sunday. They were able to get a proper sleep, eat breakfast as a team, and get in some mental downtime before they had to load up and game ready just after noon.

The Witches' arena was generally agreed to be the worst in the league. The arena dated back to the 50s and was lit, if one could call it that, by big brass parabola lights suspended from the low ceiling. The rink was notoriously difficult to play in because the ceiling was barely 14 feet high, so more pucks ended up hitting the ceiling off deflections or high clears than went out of play over the boards. It hadn't made it around the web quite the same way that Lang's rink had, with its stowable staircase players had to use to get on and off the ice, but it was still pretty terrible. The players focused on all of the different ways it completely and totally sucked to keep their minds off the upcoming game in the locker room.

Penny stayed out of the discussions and instead put her headphones in and let the music get her into the zone. Twisted Sister. "We're Not Gonna Take It". Damn. Fucking. Straight. Penny gritted her teeth as she did and recalled the brief conversation she'd had with Coach while the others were doing their pre-game skate.

"What do we do about Maja?" Penny had asked.

"Simple." Coach replied.

"Well this I gotta hear." Penny said.

"You're going to kill her with kindness." Coach said.

"What the f---" Coach cut Penny off.

"Every time she gets up in your face, I want you to thank her for every bit of shit she's giving you and ask for more. It's gonna be hard, but if you want her focused on you... that's how to do it without getting either of you kicked out of the series. And we need you on the ice." Coach instructed.

Penny realized she was grinding her teeth now and forced herself to stop. The momentary irony made her laugh out loud as she noticed that she was listening to "We're not gonna take it" to get ready to take everything and more that the Witches' toughest player had to offer. The abruptness of the laugh caught several of her teammates off guard but Penny waved their inquiring glances away with a dismissive hand.

The team stomped their way to the benches and it was "big game time" Penny thought, once again borrowing Paul's expression. She hit the ice for her warmup laps and stopped dead in her tracks, along with half of her team. A few of the girls that didn't stop bumped into ones that did and more than a few Beavs' ended up on the ground.

Across the ice, the Witches were just entering. Wearing white sleeved home jerseys… with garishly bright rainbows covering the rest of the jersey. There was no logo, and Penny noticed on a few of them they had numbers (each player had a different color for their number) but no names on the backs of their jerseys either. She heard a few girls around her cough to stifle laughs.

The teams lined up at their respective blue lines a few minutes later, and an explanation was presented. A representative from the City read a special pre-game ceremony speech:

"We acknowledge that we are gathered on ancestral lands, on Treaty One Territory. These lands are the heartland of the Métis people. We acknowledge that our water is sourced from Shoal Lake 40 First Nation." She began.

"Our team have adopted special jerseys for their very first playoff run. We have a fairly new team in the league, and they felt it was important to mark this occasion in their club's history. I am grateful to be able to give thanks to the non-binary indigenous artist who designed these jerseys and provided us with the following explanation of their inspiration and meaning:"

"In keeping with the traditions of my people in knowing and caring for the land, creatures, and people in it, the rainbow has always been a powerful symbol. Traditionally it was viewed as a sign of our spirits giving renewal to the land and its people. As we renew our look for this team's first playoffs, I also draw inspiration from the rainbow as a symbol of Pride and the LGBTQ+, of which I am also a member. Together, the power to unify and renew expectation and overcome prejudice is an important message for me."

The Witches started clapping their sticks on the ice and the Beavs followed suit a second later. Their captains did a ceremonial puck drop with the city official, shook hands, exchanged team pennants, and got back to their benches.

Penny started with the first line. The opening faceoff was instantly called back on a bad drop by the ref. Always a bad omen to start a game. The second one was deemed an ok drop, but the Witches cleanly won the face off and gained possession. Jenn managed to pin the winger who took the puck against the boards, and this kicked off an entire shift of gritty battles along the boards and the blue lines with neither team managing to gain the other's zone before an offside brought the second shifts on. Penny caught her breath and it dawned on her that Maja hadn't been on the ice with the first line. Surveying the ice, she wasn't on the second line either. Penny leaned back and tried to peer through the glass to the Witches' bench to see if she could see where Maja was at, but the glass between the benches was so scratched and dirty it may as well have been frosted glass. There was no seeing through it. Penny shrugged the oddity off and shuffled around with the girls around her to get in the right sequence for who was on the ice next.

The Witches scored late that shift. Emma had struggled to control a rebound off her chest and lost the puck during the scramble in front of her until the buzzer went off and the goal light came on behind her.

1-0 Witches.

Penny and the first line were put right back out there and given the simple orders to "make something happen." *Thanks Coach.* Penny thought with a Jamaican accent and a sardonic glance at Jenn. And now, Penny saw getting on the ice, Maja was out.

The puck came straight to Penny off the faceoff. *Let's make something happen* she thought to herself, and fired a hard slapshot at the Witches' goal from just on their side of the center ice line. The goalie hadn't been expecting the shot, but had no problem stopping it with her stick. She got ready to pass it off to one of her defenders, but a rushing Li and Jada bearing down on her made her opt to cover up the puck for a whistle.

Li skated the long way around to get to the faceoff circle, and as she looped around Penny said simply, "Park yourself in front of the paint." Penny nodded but Li didn't see as she'd already turned to get into faceoff position.

The puck came loose towards the Beavs' players but on the opposite side of the faceoff from Penny. She didn't wait to see her teammates and what they were doing with the puck, but rather did as Li suggested and shouldered a Witch out of the way to get to center ice in front of the goalie.

"Maja!" Penny heard called from behind her. The big Scandinavian girl looked over from where she was covering the far side boards and nodded. She saw it was Penny. Penny saw her notice her. The two locked eyes, Maja's icy blue Swedish eyes narrowing and Penny's steel grey eyes widening as the two summed each other up. *Kill her with kindness.* Coach had instructed. Penny's what-the-hell mindset kicked in and she lifted her hand off her stick, stood up and full on waved at Maja as if the girl was her best friend.

A puck shot in and hit Penny's hand as it was waving. Penny cried out in surprise and pain but noticed the puck was sitting between her skates. Several things occurred to Penny in a single moment then. One – I should hit the puck. Two – I only have one hand on my stick like an idiot and the other hand just got nailed with the puck, that's a problem. Three – Maja was already skating towards me and I'm about to get hit no matter what I do right now. Four – if I touch the puck the ref might call that a hand pass. And so Penny weighed those facts and made up her mind.

Maja bore down on her like a bull, and Penny thought she could hear the big girl *grunting* as she breathed heavily with exertion. Penny brought her stinging free hand into her body in a protective motion. "Maja!" She called as the bull was about a body's length away. The bull hesitated a second. That was enough. "Here you go!" Penny shouted and used her skate blade to slide the puck *towards* Maja. Maja just looked at Penny in utter confusion and then her body collided with Penny's and both girls crashed to the ice to the side of the net.

The puck Penny had kicked slid safely past Maja and was now sitting in no woman's land between the goalie and a handful of other players. Penny was on her back under the stinking, sweating mass that was Maja Carlsson and couldn't tell what happened next, but before the big girl had fully removed herself from atop Penny, the red light went off behind the goal and the goal buzzer sounded. Penny saw her teammates skating over and two of them pulled her to her feet and gave Maja a few guiding shoves away from Penny. And then Penny was in another mass of bodies as her team embraced to celebrate the goal.

Both coaches seemed to agree that the tying goal meant it was time to sit their power girls for a bit as neither Penny nor Maja saw ice time for the remainder of the period. Coach did find a moment to come find Penny and give her a pat on the shoulder for the good work on the screen and on following the Maja game plan so far. Penny had clued into the bigger picture strategy back in the first series and wasn't too upset about the invitation to sit and cool her heels for a bit.

The second period reached a new pitch in the game's energy. Both teams were adjusting to the lenient refereeing and were finishing their checks against the boards with new gusto. Every faceoff seemed to involve a shoving match between the centers while their teammates dug the puck loose. Even the goalies were shining with big glove saves and aggressive shoving and stick slaps at anyone who got near their creases.

Maja was out on the ice for every shift Penny was. The big Swedish girl had Penny marked like a Sharpie. Every time Penny touched the puck Maja was there with a stick to the back or shoulder check making sure Penny had no room to breathe. Penny was getting frustrated at being unable to make any play without battling the big Witch first. Keeping a smile on her face and tossing a "great puck battle" or "really felt *that* hit" at the other girl after every exchange was starting to drive Penny mad. And adding to her frustration was that Coach was telling her what a great job Penny was doing after every single shift. Penny got it, Maja was focused on her and the other 4 skaters on the ice were free and clear to make plays while Maja was busy harassing Penny, but it didn't make it easy.

Especially since the other 4 skaters *weren't* making plays. While Penny was taking a pounding and effectively nullifying Maja, her teammates were struggling. The high energy, physical match wasn't the Beavs' normal hockey. Coach's regular mantra of hard work and solid fundamentals was starting to buckle under the pressure of the Witches' frantic energy. There were too many breakaways being given away by broken up passes and the Beavs were getting hit with heavy checks whenever they entered the Witches' end of the ice and then getting called on icing or creating a turnover at the blue line.

The Beavs were living the period in the neutral zone for the most part, except when they had to skate after the one or two player breakaways the Witches were getting off those turnovers.

The Witches put up two goals in the second, while the Beavs only managed to get two shots on goal the entire period. Penny spent most of the period on her back or on the ice so felt very isolated from the game the rest of her team was playing. Her body ached and groaned with every motion as they went to the dressing room for intermission though, and emotionally she felt completely spent from the battle of wills with Maja through the first 40 minutes of the game.

Coming back for the third, down 3-1, Coach tried to rally her team. She tried to inject energy and enthusiasm in the girls who were still playing in the club's first semifinals round in over ten years. But the whole team seemed to have accepted the game was lost at the end of the second.

The third period was one of the worst Penny had seen the team play since her first year on the squad. The Beavs spent most of the period on the penalty kill following bad mistake after bad mistake. Becks had blown a skate on one of the Beavs few good offensive rushes of the game and taken out the Witches' goalie, earning her an interference call. Lots of loose and poorly controlled sticks found three Beavs down for tripping and hooking calls. And Penny finally lost her patience with Maja in the third. The big girl had been shoving Penny after the play was called dead and the two ended up in a weird not-quite catfight of pushing and slapping each other for a couple seconds. Their gloves had stayed on and neither had thrown any punches so they earned offsetting roughing penalties but that just added to the Beavs' penalty infraction minutes for the period.

Emma remained solid in net and kept the Witches' power play team unrewarded in the third, but the game ended 3-1 for the Witches. Penny, along with the collective body of the Beavs' team, breathed a sigh of relief when the final buzzer went and they were able to go to the locker room and change. It was by far their worst game of the season. Coach, thankfully, recognized where the team's headspace was at and didn't come down on them. She simply let them go home to think on the advice, "every good team has a bad game, we'll get back to ours at practice this week."

There were a few snippy comments between the players as they hurried through their preparations to leave. The opposite, Penny thought, of the "I am Spartacus" moment way back in her first season, players were making little snipes at mistakes their colleagues had made that had hurt them that game. Penny knew it was the frustration finding an outlet but she got out of there as quickly as possible.

Game 2 followed the next weekend. Two good practices that week and a team dinner the night before exorcised any of the team's remaining regret over their performance in game 1. It also helped that they were at home for game 2. The local news outlet, the Maple Creek Crier, had run a *front page* story about their playoff run on the Friday too. Much better than the puff piece interview they'd done with Penny earlier that season, the Crier even got comments from previous members of the club about how much it meant to them for the team to be doing so well in the post season. Altogether, it was a week of renewals that left the team raring to go for the weekend.

As they arrived for game 2, the Beavs were met with a final surprise waiting for them outside their locker room. Bricks and Fleur, alumni from the years ahead of Penny's group, were hanging out waiting for the team. For some reason, they were wearing baker's toques, but that just added to the surprise of the moment.

"About time you all got here." Bricks observed when they arrived.

"This group always was a group of slackers." Fleur agreed wryly.

Penny was there with the first group of girls arriving and gave Fleur a playful shove.

"Yeah well, you only ever had to play for a *regular* season." Shiv snarked. "Our seasons are a bit longer."

"Good ol' Shiv." Bricks laughed. "Still causing shit everywhere."

"So, what's with the hats?" Penny asked.

"Oh, we're just here doing a delivery." Fleur said. "Some baked goods for your competish to welcome them to town."

"What, nothing for us?" Jenn asked, playfully hurt.

"You get *us* instead!" Bricks said.

The alums joined the team in the locker room for the pre-game and the team excitedly told them about their exploits in the first series. When it was time for the pre-game skate the alums went out to the spectator area and the team headed to the ice.

It was clear immediately that something was wrong. The Beavs team was doing their usual laps in their end but there were no Witches on the ice, save their coach and Captain. Both were on the ice near their bench at their blue line and were in a conference with the officials. Penny flagged Li's attention and the two of them skated over. The Witches' coach jabbed angrily at a piece of paper in her hands and Penny just caught the end of what she was saying "—absolutely unacceptable."

The referee made a placating motion with her hands and Penny arrived as she responded. "Look, I'm not saying it's tasteful…sorry no pun intended… but there's no rules for fan conduct before the game."

"Fans!" The coach exploded. "They were *alumni* of the team. That makes the team complicit."

"No, if they're not actively on the team, it doesn't." The referee managed to maintain a calm composure. "Besides, your team are old enough to check ingredients. I assume there were no allergies or other issues we need to get the medical staff involved over?"

"No but…" The coach could see she wasn't winning this argument.

"Ok, then your team has three minutes to get to the ice before you get a delay of game penalty, and ten minutes before you forfeit."

The Witches' representatives turned to go.

"What's going on?" Penny asked the ref.

The Witches' captain spun angrily and jabbed a piece of paper into Penny's hands. "As if you didn't know." She glared. "I think I'm going to be sick again."

Penny and Shiv looked at the paper. "Looks like some fans gave the other team some cupcakes along with that at the bottom of the packaging." The ref explained, trying to keep a straight face. But she turned quickly and skated off, laughing along with the other officials.

The paper started with big bold lettering, "GOOD LUCK WITCHES FROM THE TOWN OF MAPLE CREEK". Then in regular font below, "We hope you enjoyed these homemade vanilla cupcakes." Below those text was a photocopy of a black and white cartoon beaver, lying on its back with its legs spread wide and pointing at its prominent butthole, with the caption "Vanilla comes from HERE!"

Below that was a screen capture from Wikipedia, explaining how artificial vanilla flavoring comes from Castoreum, a secretion from a special beaver gland located… indeed… immediately next to its anus.

"Oh. My. God." Shiv gasped. "That's…"

"Diabolical." Penny agreed with admiration. She looked up at Fleur and Bricks in the stands, in their white baker's toques, doubled over in laughter.

"Daaaaamn." Shiv observed. "I think they just one-upped your senior prank without even being on the team."

"Fucking. Legends." Penny agreed, and they rejoined their team to wrap up their laps.

The Witches got their team to the ice before they had to forfeit but not before incurring a delay of game penalty. That elicited a new tirade from the Witches' coach but it didn't gain them anything. The Beavs' started the game on a power play.

Coach wanted Penny to get more involved on the offense this period, leaving former forward Jenn to trail as the back-checker. Penny took on the role of muscling the puck across into the Witches' end of the ice and holding her corner while the first line offense took it from there and got the puck onto the net. Their efforts paid off just over a minute into the game and a nice tic-tac-toe passing play buried the puck in the top corner to give the Beavs a 1-0 lead.

That ended the penalty as well as Penny's first shift. She watched from the bench as the Witches got their first line out on the next shift and Maja made her thoughts on the early goal felt by Shiv and Becks. Both girls took big hits while playing the puck against their boards, but thankfully both were back to their feet quickly and they kept battling.

Maja's line was short shifted after holding the zone for two scoring chances and they swapped out. The Beavs managed to get their third line offense out but Shiv and Becks were pinned in their end unable to get the puck cleared for a change. Emma was confidently directing pucks and traffic away from her net and was holding her game well. One shot took an awkward rebound off Becks' skate and bounced wildly around Emma's feet, but she dove on top of it not even trying to get a glove or stick on it and forced the play to stop.

The Beavs' defenders skated slowly to their bench and changed up, putting Jada's third line out along with their usual third line offensive pairing now. The Witches had Maja and the first line back out there again, barely 30 seconds of play time after their previous shift had ended, and Maja ran over the Beavs' center off the face off to gain the puck and take a point-blank shot at the net. Emma had been coming across the net and went fully into the splits and managed to snag the puck out of the air. Maja swerved tightly away from the net, avoiding running Emma over as she made the save but clipping Emma in the side of the helmet with the blade of her stick.

Emma's head snapped sideways and she fell awkwardly to the side from the strength of the impact. Penny and the couple other girls that had seen the contact shouted angrily but Maja circled around from behind the net and looked right at their bench as she shrugged, as if to say "What, I didn't do anything". During the play stoppage that followed, Emma took her helmet off and had to readjust it, which gave her a good chance to inform the officials about what had happened, which of course they hadn't seen. They took the puck and nodded a few times at Emma as she finished with her helmet and the players got ready to resume play.

Penny and Jenn were out there now as well, and Penny had definitely seen what had just happened on that play. But Coach wanted her focusing on her offense and *not* sending messages to Maja, no matter how much the girl might deserve it. A quick glance back and Coach holding up her palm in their long-standing signal confirmed that for Penny.

Maja was focusing on Li now, and Penny shifted into position as Li's shadow. While Li used her fast feet and faster hands to create scoring opportunities, Maja pursued her and tried to hit or physically intimidate the much smaller girl every time she touched the puck. Except between her and Li was Penny. Li skated back around the boards to get a shot that had gone wide; Maja came in from the opposite end of the net with speed getting ready to shoulder Li to the ground… and then there was Penny colliding with Maja from the side and leaving Li loose to try a wraparound. The next shift Maja parked herself in front of her own net except when she came forward to try and poke check the puck off Li's stick. But as soon as she stepped out of the crease, there was Penny to knock her stick aside with a leg or lift Maja's stick with her own. That left Li with wide open angles to shoot at the 4 corners of the next and two player's creating a screen on the goalie.

That Li and the first line forwards didn't manage to score wasn't critical at this stage of the game. The fact was they were getting chances, and chances that were being created by Penny's rival on the Witches team being completely nullified by Penny's smart offensive checking.

At the halfway mark in the period, the Beavs held a 1-0 lead and had dominated possession time in the Witches' half of the ice. Whatever the ex-Beaver bakers had done with those cupcakes, there was no sign of the Witches' domination that had been there for game 1.

156

Then the penalty problems started again. Jada pulled the first one just after the 10 minute mark and went to the box for a sloppy high stick against the Witches' goalie.

On the PK, Becks picked up the next one by closing her hand on the puck in the crease after Emma had been caught out of position and there'd be a loose puck scramble in front of the net. The play had saved a goal and the Beavs breathed a sigh of relief after the refs conferred and decided on the 2-minute minor instead of a penalty shot. That still left the Beavs on a 5 on 3 for nearly a minute and a half with *two* defenders in the penalty box.

Penny, Shiv and Jenn were picked as the 3 Beavs to take the ice and help Emma weather the storm. The puck dropped just to the left of Emma. Jenn lost the faceoff and it went back to the three Witches lined up along the Beavs' blue line. They passed it back and forth and the three defenders took turns blocking the shooting lanes with their sticks down on the ice as the puck moved from the corner to the center to the corner of the Beavs' zone and back.

Not Maja, but another Witches defender picked up the puck at the corner and lined up a slapshot. Penny dropped her whole body trying to block the puck, but the Witch had faked it! Penny was down and out and watched the puck instead of speeding at her body, lazily slide down the ice to the corner boards Penny would be covering if she wasn't lying on her belly.

Penny cursed and scrambled to her feet, knowing already it was too little. The Witch in the corner passed the puck perfectly to a forward skating in towards Emma. The point-blank shot Emma managed to get a pad on and the puck shot out in the opposite direction of the shooter… and straight onto the stick of another uncovered Witches forward Shiv was struggling to get into position to cover. The Witch gave her no chance. The loose puck was on her stick and there was a wide-open net behind where Emma was down on the ice from her first save and the Witch sent the puck home to tie the game.

Penny cringed when the goal horn went. She knew on a 5-on-3 she'd hardly be at fault for letting the goal happen, but she still felt like a fool for having been tricked by the fake point shot. But it didn't matter, Penny and Shiv were left out along with 2 forwards to finish off the 1:28 of 5-on-4 penalty killing they had to do now that Jada's penalty had ended on the goal.

Penny put her physical game to work and managed to get two good full-ice clears off of solid checks in her own zone before Coach called her line back and swapped in Jada and Jenn. Penny felt much better after that solid performance and shutting down the Witches' chances to take the lead.

Emma got put to work for the remainder of the penalty kill but also seemed determined not to have any repeats of the 5-on-3 and was forcing stoppages every time she touched the puck. It made the penalty kill drag on and on but also prevented the Witches from getting any sort of rhythm going.

Following that kill, both teams were completely gassed. The game degenerated into the teams dumping the puck from center and then icing it out of their zone, getting possession off the power play and repeating all over again. It was a slow and painful end to the period but both teams just wanted to get to the locker room.

Refreshed and rested from the intermission, the teams came back and played the second like it was the final game of the series. Which for the Beavs, it would be if they lost.

Penny and Maja were given a chance for some bench time as the coaches both opted to focus on their offensive players and give the hard checking d-liners a break. The matchup between Penny and Maja had been a zero sum affair thus far that game anyway, so keeping them both off the ice was a chance to shake things up in their lines.

The outcome of that choice was a change, though neither coach would likely have predicted it. Both the Beavs *and* the Witches scored four goals that period. The goal buzzer went off a total of 8 times before the teams went to their locker rooms with the game tied 5-5 after the second.

Penny would have liked to believe that her limited ice time that period was proof that she was key at keeping the team's defense going, but she'd learned at the very start of her career the team's performance said nothing about her own; and vice versa. From her perch on the bench, Penny would have had to say that if there was any *one* thing that caused the change it was that both goalies seemed off their game in the 2nd. But whatever the cause, both teams were burying every other shot on goal and the game was set up for a 5-5 tie to start the 3rd period.

And the Beav's season was on the line now. Win or go home.

Big Game Time.

Penny and Jenn started the third backing up Li's first line forwards. Their first shift was spent digging the puck out of the boards, turning it over, getting it back, and getting caught back up in the boards. The puck didn't leave the neutral zone the entire shift and it was over a minute into the period when the puck flipped up into the Witches' bench for the game's first whistle.

Penny realized she was humming "Radioactive" by Imagine Dragons, which had been playing on her earphones when she shut them down to come onto the ice. She had a moment of perverse enjoyment as she imagined herself as the fluffy pink care bear from the music video, taking down Maja the reigning "monster" with her super powers. Except in this game Penny wasn't winning with her muscles or even her eye laser, she was winning over Maja with skill and mental focus.

The tight checking game continued through three full shifts and neither team had much to show for a gritty, physical five minutes when Penny and her line were next on the ice. Their shift lasted all of ten seconds. The puck shot into the Beavs' corner off the faceoff and was picked up by a member of the Witches. Penny followed the puck in a second later and collided full on with the Witch player who was still struggling to gain full control to skate or pass the puck out of the corner. The Witch went down, Penny grabbed the puck and the referee blew her whistle.

Penny whirled in confusion and the referee motioned her off.

"What did I do?" Penny asked as she skated past.

"Boarding. Consider this a 2 minute warning, could've been 5 for that hit."

"What the f---" Penny's protest was cut off by the slamming sound of the penalty box door in front of her. She couldn't even sit down she was so angry. She pounded on the glass of the penalty box and shouted at the referee, but to no use. On the ice, they could barely hear anything but muffled shouting anyway. No matter the calls, you just wanted the refs to be consistent throughout the game. Whether tightly controlling the play or letting the game find its own organic flow, you couldn't mix things up at the start of the 3rd in an elimination series. Penny was sure she'd thrown hits *identical* to that one a dozen times in game 1 and so far in this game, but there hadn't been any issues. And that wasn't counting all of the questionable hits Maja and the Witches had laid out on Penny and her teammates, like that non-call on the stick to Emma's head in the first. To get called on this *now*... Penny seethed.

She tapped her skate anxiously as she watched the penalty kill unfold. Shiv and Jenn were a solid pairing anchoring the PK and Penny pounded the glass in appreciation each time they sent the puck the full length of the ice, which they were doing regularly following the Witches' dump-and-chase attempts.

In the dying seconds of the penalty, the Witches lined up one final rush pushing 5-skaters strong in a line across center ice and skating hard into the Beavs zone. They managed to stay on-side and Penny watched the Beavs collapse into a defensive box around Emma. The Witches' goalie started pounding her stick on the ice. 5 seconds...

Penny grasped the handle of the door.

The Witches passed the puck from the wing to the center, who deked away from a poke check and set up a 3-on-2 facing down Emma.

4 seconds.

Penny tightened her grip, and held her breath.

The Witches' center let loose a cannon shot dead on at Emma. Emma got a glove on it but it shot up in the air. Players swarmed the crease watching it come down...

3 seconds.

Penny tensed.

The puck came down and there was a mad flurry of sticks and bodies. Emma butterflied in her net and took up as much of the space as she could while the battle in front of her ensued.

2 seconds.

Penny lifted the handle.

The puck came loose from the horde, sliding up the ice towards the blue line.

1 second.

Penny pulled the door open.

Maja. The Witch covering the blue line skated to where the puck was going to cross over the line, hoping to keep it in. She leaned forward, outstretching her stick... but missed.

The penalty countdown disappeared. Penny shot out of the box and picked up the loose puck at center ice. She turned and skated towards the Witches' goal on a full breakaway. She skated as fast as she could. She didn't even look at the puck below her, a decade of being on the ice let her hands feel the puck against her stick and where she needed to adjust to keep control.

She zoomed into the Witches' end and deked once.

She deked twice, lining up her shot...

And a stick came crashing down across hers, splintering Penny's stick into several pieces. Penny looked over to see Maja bearing down on her, and she had only a second to process what had happened to her stick before Maja shoved her with both hands and the stick between them. The move pushed Penny off balance. Penny stumbled sideways then backwards and collided with the metal post at the side of the Witches' net. She fell on her side and cringed at the pain that erupted in her ribs. She lay on her back for a second, winded and disoriented, when she heard a whistle go off.

The Witches' goalie took off her catcher and offered Penny a hand up, which Penny accepted appreciatively. She got to her feet and saw, to her incredulity, that the same ref who'd called her on the cross-check was pointing with an open fist at center ice. Penny had earned her team a penalty shot. Two games of getting under Maja's skin and she'd finally made her mistake. The big blonde girl argued her way to the bench as she was also assessed a 2 minute minor for cross-checking; in addition to the penalty shot for the slash on Penny.

The ref met Penny and the other players at center ice and explained the penalty shot process. Anyone on the ice could take the shot. Penny looked at who else was out... and saw Jenn was there. Jenn, who'd anchored the first line forwards that Li was now in charge of for 2 seasons. Jenn, the best shot on the team after Li. There was no question.

"You take it." Penny told Jenn, locking eyes with her.

"It was your penalty, goon." Jenn replied flatly.

"And I want you to win us the game with it." Penny responded.

Jenn could tell there was no arguing and the other Beavs on the ice were nodding agreement. Jenn nodded once and went to center ice.

The players lined up by their benches to watch.

Jenn grabbed the puck and started skating. She started with a long lateral glide that took her far to the left side of the ice. The goalie was out a full ten feet past the edge of her crease and was following Jenn's movement.

Jenn turned and crossed over center ice to the far side, moving forward so that the move took her almost to the right face off circle. The goalie skated backwards and to the side following her. And fell over.

There was a collective gasp of shock. The Witches' goalie had caught an edge on the ice out front of her crease and full on bailed in the middle of the penalty shot. Jenn needed no encouragement. She made a wide looping skate to get around where the goalie fell and neatly passed the puck into the back of the net. Buzzer. Light. Cheers.

The Beavs were up 6-5 with 12 minutes to go in the third.

The combined failed power play and penalty shot goal broke the Witches' spirits. They held the Beavs' power play off for the full 2-minute penalty kill, but in the dying seconds sent a puck over the glass earning themselves *another* 2 minute minor. Maja was benched for the rest of the game after being released from her penalty, and Penny tried not to look (which is to say, she stared relishing with great pride the tirade Maja got from the Witches' coach). Penny helped keep the puck deep in the Witches' zone for the two powerplay shifts and then Coach gave Jada's line a lengthy shift so the PK crews could catch their breath.

The Beavs didn't pick up any further goals on either power play, but they took 4 minutes off the clock while keeping the puck in the Witches' end of the ice the whole time. Working the clock, protecting their lead just as Coach had instructed.

Jada's shift went out with just under 8 minutes left. Back at even strength Jada and her crew replayed the first 2 minutes of the period with a chippy, physical matchup along the neutral zone boards that didn't really go anywhere for anyone.

Penny and Jenn swapped out when the clock hit 7 minutes, and managed to catch the tired Witches squad without a change. Penny, Jenn and the forwards got into their cycle position in the Witches' end and started passing the puck back and forth in their best approximation of "keep away". This particular skill was one they'd focused an entire practice on that week, and each girl was trying to collect the puck and pass it on to another player as fast as they could.

When they finally missed and shot a puck too far, forcing an offside when Jenn tried to send it back in, the Witches' line was so tired they literally stumbled their way to their bench. There was 5:15 left on the clock.

That turned out to be Penny's last shift of the game. The Witches earned another penalty around 5 minutes left and that sealed the fate of the game. They managed to put together a late game 6-on-5 pulling their goalie and gained a few shots on the Beavs' goal but the Beavs kept the Witches against the board and the shots weren't dangerous. Emma handled them with ease until the final buzzer went securing the 6-5 Beavs' victory and tied them 1-1 with the Witches in the best of 3 series. Fleur and Bricks hung around with the team in the locker room after the game which helped the team keep their minds on that day's victory, and avoid, at least for that afternoon, worrying about the final game coming up tomorrow.

The next day came fast. The Beavs had to load up on a bus at 9am the next morning and get back to the Witches' town for their afternoon game that would decide the series. It was a quiet bus, a polar opposite of the riotous sparkling cider spray down that had started the series 2 weeks ago. Those 2 weeks could have been 2 months for how long it seemed to everyone on the bus.

Penny opted for a more mellow playlist for the bus ride and mostly thought about the exchange of penalties from the previous game, both the cross-check she'd been called on and the penalty shot she'd been awarded. Honestly both calls bothered Penny because neither seemed like the right decision for a playoff game. Penny had tried to discuss it with Coach after the game but Coach had been dealing with some fallout from the alumni girls' baking prank and had been unavailable. So instead, Penny listened to a mix that expressed her mixed feelings.

Genesis – Misunderstanding, Santa Esmerelda – Don't Let me Be Misunderstood (Kill Bill Remix), Kim Stockwoord – Jerk, Rolling Stones – Satisfaction, Justin Bieber – Sorry, Bryan Adams – Please Forgive Me, and just for the poetic aptness, Brittney Spears – Oops I did it Again. The music set her mind straight for the game ahead and she left the bus feeling centered and ready for the third and final game of this second series.

When the Beavs arrived, the Witches' retribution for the cupcakes was jarring and obvious. Instead of the usual piece of paper taped to the door, someone on the Witches had found a beaver pelt and hung it by the tail from the door. The Beavs gathered round and were silent for a moment, not sure what to make of the grotesque gesture. A few Witches could be seen down the hallway snickering at them. Suddenly Shiv said what was on exactly *none* of their minds. "Awwww, how cute!" And she proceeded to step forward and rub the pelt behind the ears and give the broad tail a high five. "Don't forget to slap your beaver for good luck!" She shouted loud enough that the Witches could hear. Then she went into the locker room. A collective shrug went through the Beavs and they high fived the tail of the pelt on their way into the dressing room.

Despite Shiv's brilliant turnaround of the beaver pelt, which the Beavs brought onto the bench and made their unofficial mascot for the game, the third game started badly for the Beavs. There was no single play or player that was the cause, but the Witches were just hitting the ice with a completely different tempo. They were winning the face offs and beating the Beavs to the loose pucks. They were completing their passes neatly and forcing the Beavs to do a lot more skating to keep up with their plays. The first goal felt inevitable when it slipped past Emma's shoulder around the five-minute mark. The second came off an almost identical play with eight minutes and change left in the period. The Beavs on and off the ice were already breathing hard and feeling a sense of shock at the difference in the teams from yesterday's game to todays.

The first sign of relief came with barely five minutes left in the first. Maja and the Witches' first line ended up against Jada and her third line group for the Beavs, and it was a lopsided battle. Jada was trying to battle Maja for the puck along the boards and Maja took offense to the tiny, junior defender getting inside her personal space. She tried to swing her arm back to get Jada off of her, but between the size difference and Jada being positioned directly behind her, Maja ended up elbowing Jada directly in the face mask. Jada went down, probably harder than she needed to Penny thought, but nevertheless she was on the ice and the refs called the penalty.

Maja did *not* agree with the call. Instead of skating to the penalty box like she was being instructed she stood her ground and argued that Jada took a dive. One of the linespeople skated over and grabbed her by the arm, which Maja pulled away angrily and unleashed a string of profanity that brought the head ref over to have a chat with her. And still Maja wasn't done. The ref did an excellent job of keeping her cool and trying to defuse the situation but Maja was simply beyond a state where she could be reasoned with.

The Witches coach got off the bench and with the help of two of her linemates, more or less tackled Maja and guided her, still shouting, off the ice to the penalty box. Back on the bench, the coach ended up in a long discussion with the head official. In the end the calls weren't explained, but 5:00, 2:00 and another 2:00 went up on the penalty board and two more Witches went to the penalty box. The Witches ended up with 3 players on the ice after everything got settled for a 2 minute 5 on 3 for the Beavs.

With Maja and half the Witches starting lineup in the penalty box, Coach opted to sit Penny and let Jenn anchor a heavily offensive power play. This gave Penny a moment to look over at the box and see Maja *still* shouting through the glass completely ignoring the efforts of her team to calm her. Penny shook her head, thinking how much Maja in that moment reminded Penny of how she'd been at the start of her 2nd season. She wondered if this would have been her fate – blowing a gasket in the playoffs – if she hadn't met Coach when she did and learned how to keep the monster in the box when it wasn't time to let it out to play.

The penalties cost the Witches badly, and the Beavs were able to score once on the 5 on 3 and again on the remaining power play. The period was over before the 5 minute major was finished, and the Beavs had tied the game at 2.

The second period Maja was not even on the bench. Both teams seemed to be settled now into a pitched back and forth battle that raged from one end of the ice to the other, trading near misses but failing to move the scoreboard in either team's favor. The shifts were short and players were still skating the full length of the ice up and back at least twice every shift. The Beavs seemed to have abandoned any transition game elements and simply jumped out of their zone right onto a rush into the Witches end of the ice every time they forced a turnover. The Witches were relying on the two wingers staying on a deep forecheck and picking up long lead passes that let them go 2-on-2 with the Beavs' defenders.

Both tactics were working and each team was getting quality scoring chances. Nobody was finding the net though. Penny had ripped a rocket from the point that Li had redirected and managed to find the back of the Witches' goaltenders glove; she also ringed one off the crossbar from the blue line but it deflected uselessly out of play from there. That was pretty much how it was going for her whole team that second period. Their only saving grace was that the Witches were struggling just as much.

The second expired with the score still tied at 2.

The nerves in the locker room at the intermission were intense. Many of the girls were staring ahead contemplating both what it would mean if they lost the next 20 minutes, and what it would mean if they won.

Penny felt the weight of the moment and keyed up the song she had selected the previous night for this final intermission. Taylor Swift. Antihero.

The steady beatline and acoustic guitar combined with Taylor's dulcet voice washed over Penny and melted the stress. Penny knew the song had become something of an anthem to female athletes everywhere with its message about self-sabotage and overcoming the expectations of others. It had for her too.

Lining up for her first faceoff Penny looked at the girl across from her and spoke the chorus, "it's me, hi, I'm the problem, it's me." And then she hip checked the girl, stole the puck, and passed it over to Li.

Maja was still nowhere to be seen. Penny caught up with Li and got into covering position behind her. A Witch was coming in at Li from the side, Penny saw her and managed to get between them knocking the Witch over before she could stop Li's entry into the Witches' zone. Li skated in and let a shot go point blank against the Witches' goaltender. She had a fast glove hand which snatched the shot barely after it left Li's blade, but she held it for a whistle.

Penny and Li high fived on the bench, and a second later the goal horn went off. They looked back at the ice and saw that Shiv had fired one on net right off the faceoff and it had found its way home. They high fived the lineup as they skated by and hugged at taking the lead for the first time in the game.

Shiv and Becks stayed out for the rest of their shift and then Jada and her line got absolutely decimated by the rough third liners of the Witches. Jada's defensive partner went down with a possible wrist injury and had to go to the locker room for assessment by their trainer. The Witches seemed to be sending a message that if the Beavs were going to score, they were going to hurt for it. Penny smiled. This was Penny's game.

Penny stepped onto the ice after Jada's line finally limped to the bench and grinned widely. The Witches won the face off and cycled the puck back into their own zone. They crossed the ice with a wide pass and then quickly sent it up the boards to a waiting winger near center ice. Penny had seen that pass so many times these past three games she knew where it was going as soon as the back pass happened. That meant she was perfectly positioned to flatten the Witch who was unlucky enough to receive the long lead pass and steal the puck.

"It's me! Hi!" Penny said exuberantly as the Witch fell to the ice.

The puck got turned over again quickly and Penny skated back into her end to head off the Witches coming the other way. Penny managed to get a stick in between one of their long cross-ice passes and poked it loose to center ice. Li's winger grabbed it and made for the Witches net but Coach called Penny and Jenn for a change.

The Witches were pushing hard when Penny got out next with 14 minutes left in the third. She took over with the puck in her own zone and scurried to get into position to break up the rapid cycling of the puck between the Witches. She managed to pin one of the Witches against the boards but the girl kicked the puck free with her skate rendering the effort useless. Penny released her and chased the puck around the back of the net. Another Witch was coming deep to collect it and Penny got to the puck half a second earlier, turned her body, planted her feet and braced herself. The Witch collided full speed against Penny's side and Penny gave the girl a strong push with her shoulder which caused the Witch to lose her footing. Penny backhanded the now uncontested puck as hard as she could and shoveled it out of her zone. Unfortunately, the puck ricocheted off the low roof of the Witches' arena and that brought a faceoff right back into the Beavs' end to the left of Emma.

Penny was left out to battle for the puck off the faceoff and this time managed to tie up a Witch and the puck along the boards for a lengthy period of time. Jenn got in behind Penny and two more Witches joined the scrum so that a full half the players on the ice were engaged in sliding the puck up and down the boards a few inches at a time.

The Beavs managed to get the puck forward across the blue line and it was pushed back across by a Witch but they got caught offside. Penny and Jenn were back on the bench.

The Witches landed themselves a penalty a few seconds into the next shift. The Beavs got a flurry of shots off but the Witches managed to collect a long rebound and started a breakaway. The Beavs tried to rally back in time but it was 1 on 1 Emma vs. the Witch. Emma made a valiant effort but the Witch slid the puck in five hole and scored.

The short-handed goal gave the Witches the same turbo boost the Beavs' short hander had done the previous game. The Beavs struggled through the last eight minutes of the third period against a renewed Witches squad that could smell the blood in the water. The Beavs found themselves trapped in their own end for the last three minutes without any reprieve. Penny blocked three shots in her last two periods, body aching from the exertion of all the game's physical demands on her. Emma played the best three minutes of her entire career shutting down 11 shots in give minutes.

The buzzer finally went and Penny let herself collapse to the ice. A tie. All of that leading up to... a tie. To have to play overtime now.

She skated over to the bench. 5 minutes of abbreviated intermission had already been added to the board and was counting down until the start of the 10 minute sudden death overtime period.

Coach was at the boards surveying the twenty exhausted girls around her. Many were doubled over, sitting on the bench itself, or kneeling near the boards.

"Girls, times like these there are no words to make you feel less tired or sore. This team is beatable. You've done it. You held the lead most of this game. If you want to get to the finals, you need to play through that pain and fatigue and go take the victory. One goal! Go do it!"

A few heads perked up but mostly exhausted nods were all the girls could muster. Penny looked over at the Witches and was relieved to see they seemed to be in as bad shape as they were.

"Hey Coach." Shiv said breathlessly. "Grab that beaver."

Coach took the beaver pelt down from behind the bench and tossed it over.

"Hey girls, let's go out like we came in this thing!" She threw the pelt on the ice in front of her. "SLAP THE BEAVER FOR LUCK!" She gave the tail a hard slap with the blade of her stick. Slowly, one by one the others did the same with increasing energy as more and more of them did. As the girls grouped together afterwards, they rhythmically clapped their sticks on the ice, getting faster and faster, until they shouted as one, "GOOOOO BEAVS!" They pointed their sticks skywards, did a circular rotation and then split apart.

Overtime began with Penny on the ice. Jenn grabbed the puck from the faceoff and circled it over to Penny. Penny passed it forward to Li. Li skated the puck into the Witches end. She was instantly swarmed by three Witches and lost the puck. Jenn caught the girl who stripped the puck off Li and managed to turn it back over. Li found some open ice and collected a pass from Jenn. She passed it to Penny. Penny spun away from an incoming Witch and avoided a check. Penny had a bit of space and stepped the puck up to the slot between the two faceoff circles. She saw Li starting to loop around the back of the net. Penny caught Li's eye. Li suddenly stopped directly behind the net. Penny fired. Wide.

The puck hit the boards beside the net and bounced, but Li's stick was already there to collect it. The goalie was getting out of her butterfly position from Penny's shot and tried to get across but Li completed her wraparound to the far side of the net and slid the puck in behind her. The light went on. The horn wailed. The ref pointed aggressively at the puck in the net. Twenty seven seconds of overtime and it was over. Penny couldn't believe that had worked, but didn't have time to process before she was caught up in the entire team swarming around her, Li, and the rest of the on ice skaters. Penny's brain found itself back in the moment and she jumped and cheered and screamed along with her team.

They were going to the finals.

20. The Playoffs: Finals

Penny closed her eyes and pressed "Play". Nikki Yanofsky's "I Believe" rose to life in her ears. The once anthem of Canada's 2010 Olympic games and the soundtrack to so many of the Golden Goal replays Penny had watched when she was a little girl immediately brought her back to that feeling of triumph the whole country had shared in that moment. Penny looked around at the girls around her as the song slowly built up to its piano-backed first chorus "I believe in the power that comes from a world brought together as one."

Jenn, Penny's first girlfriend, was standing and bouncing on her skates, shaking her helmet around as she stretched her neck.

Siobahn, Shiv, Penny's longest and best friend on the team, was bent over pulling the laces of her skates tighter and adjusting the knots.

Emma, the goalie who'd stepped up to fill Bricks' pads this season, was doing her usual pre-game psych out staring into a void a few feet in front of her and seeing how long she could go without blinking. A seriously badass staring contest of one.

Li had a small red book she was reading with tightly embossed gold mandarin characters on the cover, which Penny knew from asking her over the years was a collection of inspiring Chinese poetry.

The music in Penny's ears notched up another step as the chorus peaked. "I believe together we'll fly, I believe in the power of you and I."

Becks, Jada, and the rest of her team were going through their pre-game routines just as Penny had watched them do for the last three years. This moment and its intense familiarity gave Penny so much comfort and confidence as she looked at the 20 other young women around her. Three years building up to this *one* game. The first two games of their final series with the reigning league champion Regina Rattlesnakes had been split one apiece. This third and final game in the best of three series would determine one way or another how the Beavs season was going to end. And through the scheduling oddities of the best of 3 series in her league, the Beavs were hosting the game as the "visitors" in their own rink.

"I believe the time is right now. Stand tall and make the world proud. I believe together we'll fly. I believe in the power of you and I."

Coach motioned it was time to get to the ice, Penny stowed her phone and headphones and got to her feet. "This is our time, right now!" Penny shouted at the top of her lungs, startling several other members of the team in the process. "Let's GO!" She started a light jog towards the door, which Coach swung open in front of her. Her team followed and they stomped through their hallway, under the arch of the bench entrance, and onto the familiar yet alien visitors' bench. As they entered Penny heard the twangy rhythm of the Arrogant Worms' "We Are the Beaver" being blast out of the rink speakers, and she had to laugh. There were a wall of hands reached out in front of her as she passed through the chute, with all the younger siblings in attendance trying to high five the players and Penny fist bumped as many as she could while she walked by.

There was a roar of applause that drowned out the music and she looked back through the glass to see the small arena's stands were packed for the first time Penny had ever seen. Parents, friends, teachers, siblings, everyone and anyone who the girls knew in the town and even some strangers who'd gotten caught up in the Crier's surprise coverage of the final series, had come out to see the team play their final game. And now they were all on their feet, clapping, cheering, whistling and stomping their feet to create a wall of human noise that swept over the players when they got onto bench.

The team stopped, stood, and waved for a few moments before hitting the ice for the pre-game skate. Then the black and green home jerseys of the Rattlesnakes appeared on the other side of the rink, and all the work to get here, all the fans in the stands, the music blaring over the speakers, and the weight of the game disappeared and it was go time. The song faded out, "We are the beaver, we are the beaver, we are the beaver."

The opening whistle went and the puck dropped at center. The Beavs won the puck and it was passed back to Jenn. Jenn picked up the pass at her blue line and passed it up to the winger. The puck easily slid past a Rattlesnake skating at Jenn to check it away.

The Beavs picked the puck up along the boards. The puck carrier ran into a pair of Snakes at the entrance to their blue line and was knocked onto her back. One of the Snakes grabbed the puck and passed it up. Another Snake picked it up at the Beavs' blue line and skated it across into the zone. Penny and Jenn skated backwards as a 2 on 2 developed in their end of the ice. Emma followed the play closely, adjusting her body to the movements of the puck carrier.

The Snakes forward passed it to her winger as she reached the right faceoff circle. Penny reached her stick out as long as it would go and managed to poke the puck with the very tip of her blade. It was enough to send the puck away from the Snakes' winger's waiting stick and into the boards. The Beavs were skating back with speed but another Snake got to the puck first and quickly passed it back to the winger that Penny was covering. Penny made wide sweeping arcs with her stick and tried to keep her body positioned between the winger and Emma.

The winger turned away from Penny and passed the puck back to the blue line around center ice. One of her teammates was waiting and made a nice redirect pass back to the center who'd started the rush in the first place. Jenn stepped up to pressure her but the center was ready for that and did a fancy fake turn then took off the other way after Jenn had committed her body to the wrong direction of movement. That left the center alone, ten feet from Emma. Emma glared and stared at the Snake, getting her glove up and ready.

The Snake let a shot go that whistled past Emma's glove and collided with the post with a *diiing*. The puck shot away from the net and into the far corner. Emma smiled coldly at the look of disappointment on the other player's face.

A Snake chased the puck and got tied up with Jenn and another Beav in the corner, and the Snakes decided to execute a line change. Penny's line was called back to do the same.

18:22 left in the first period.

Penny caught her breath. She glanced back at Coach and saw she was chewing on the cap of a sharpie, something Penny hadn't seen her do before. Big stakes for Coaches too, Penny thought, and this was not how the Beavs had wanted to start the game.

The Snakes got two more solid scoring chances on that attack after the 2nd lines took over. Emma shut the first down with a lightning glove save on a point blank shot that was headed top shelf. The second she didn't even see but the puck had shot off her leg pad when she was down in her butterfly position and she'd been able to clear the rebound with her stick before anything else happened.

15:41 left in the first period.

When play finally calmed down a little and got whistled dead in the neutral zone, Coach skipped the third line altogether and put Penny and

172

the first line right back out there. The Beavs' center got tossed from the faceoff and Penny stepped up to take it. The puck dropped and she pushed her shoulder into the opposing Snake while sweeping away with her stick at the puck between them. Penny managed to slide the puck back through her legs and heard someone on her team pick it up. For good measure, Penny pushed the Snake off her with her shoulder and then pushed *off* of her to join the line of Beavs players about to cross the blue line into the Snakes' end of the ice.

Three on two the first pass came to Penny, Penny was the most central of the three players, and passed it across to the left wing immediately after receiving the pass. One of the Snake defenders committed and pressured the left winger on the boards, forcing her to dump the pass along the boards to the right winger. She picked it up in the corner and Penny watched as the second defender chased the puck. That defender laid a solid hit against the Beavs' player, something Penny was sure would've been a penalty in the regular season but not now in the final game of the post-season. The winger took the hit pretty well and managed to get to her feet before the Snake defender and pass the puck back to Penny… who found herself all alone in the middle of the ice in front of the Snakes' goaltender. The girl glared at Penny and positioned herself a few inches back towards her net. Penny glared back and heard her bench screaming "time". She didn't have room to deke, and had nowhere to pass. Penny looked straight at the goalie's glove, and the goalie twitched the glove a big higher in the net. Then Penny, still looking at the glove, *passed* the puck towards the net softly, trying to keep her body as rigid as possible through the motion.

The goalie held Penny's eyes for a second more then looked down at Penny's stick, where there was no puck. She saw the puck slowly coming towards her five hole, and decided to jump on the puck. Except it was too late. The puck had already slid underneath her, and the goal buzzer went. Penny had scored! Her team caught up to the play and hugged her and bounced up and down in excitement. Then Penny led the bench fly-by and made sure to swing by and tag up with Emma for keeping the game 0-0 as long as she did.

13:52 left in the first period. 1- 0 Beavs.

The Snakes swarmed. Penny tapped her stick nervously on the bench as she watched the Beavs collapse into their zone to defend against a new rush. Shiv and her line were out there doing their best, but the Beavs' steady, positional defensive play was taking a beating from the pure adrenaline the Snakes were pouring out against them.

Emma made a big save with her stick-side blocker and rebounded the puck the length of her end of the ice. Exhausted defenders thought it was going to go all the way out of the zone but their hopes were dashed when a Snake grabbed the puck before it made it across the blue line and passed it back into play. A quick tic-tac-toe pass took the puck from the right side of the net, to the point, to the left and then a point blank shot was saved by Emma going flat out on the ice. She couldn't bring in the rebound though, and was still scrambling to her feet when a Snake grabbed the puck and passed it back across to the right side of the net which now lay wide open. The Snake that collected the pass lined up a huge shot and fired. The puck collided with Shiv's falling body and there was a scream. Shiv lay on the ground moaning and grabbing her wrist, stick useless beside her, while the puck lay with her body between it and the empty net.

Emma scrambled to get back in position. Shiv cried out again in pain. Becks, Shiv's defensive partner, and two Snakes fought for the puck beside her.

Slap. A Snake's stick collided with Beck's, missing the puck slamming Beck's stick blade into Shiv's body.

Slap. The puck got a clean hit and flew into Shiv's stomach, rebounding back to its previous position.

Slap. A Snake missed the puck and Beck's stick entirely and hit Shiv square in the metal cage of her helmet.

Coach screamed at the referee to whistle the play dead on the injury, but if they heard her they didn't act.

Slap. Becks slipped from someone contacting her back and steadied herself with her stick... pressing the blade into Shiv's arm as she did and forcing another scream of pain.

Shiv moaned and forced her body to move. She log rolled *towards* the play and succeeded in trapping the puck under her body.

Another two or three slaps and jabs for good measure came from the Snakes, but they were unable to free the puck before the referee finally whistled the play dead. The Beavs' trainer already had the bench door open and rushed out onto the ice.

The arena fell silent except for the sound of Shiv sobbing and crying as the trainer assessed her injuries. Coach summoned the referee for a conference and they spoke in harsh but hushed voices as Coach reprimanded the woman for not protecting her player.

A round of clapping started from the crowd and the benches joined in bashing their sticks against the boards as Shiv got unsteadily to her feet and was helped by the Trainer and Becks off the ice. Penny saw the trainer lock eyes with Coach, and trainer shook her head slightly. Penny felt an icy ball in the pit of her stomach. Shiv's season was over. Penny tried to pass a sympathetic look to Shiv but Shiv was too busy concentrating on keeping one foot in front of the other to notice.

11:04 left in the first period. 1-0 for the Beavs.

Penny and Jenn lined up for the faceoff in their zone. Li was at Center and won the faceoff, passing it back to Jenn. Jenn turned away from a check and found some clear ice to skate the puck out of the zone. That earned her a thumping tribute from the Beavs' bench.

Li and her forward linemates skated out and the Beavs entered Snakes territory 4 on 2, with Penny backchecking at her own blue line. Jenn dumped the puck deep around the boards, sending it to the far corner where the Beavs' left winger collected it. Jenn took up position on the point to hold her position on the boards.

The winger skated out of the corner with both defending Snakes pursuing her. The winger got cross ice a pass across to Li but Li got the puck caught up in her skates and struggled to get control of it. By the time she got a shot off, the Snakes' goalie had plenty of time to reposition and prepare for the shot. A whistle blew the play to a stop and it was time for a faceoff in the Snakes' end.

Li lost this face off but the puck went wild and ended up alone behind the net. Penny chased a Snake down the left side of the ice as the other girl went to grab the puck. Penny knew she was going to lose the race by about two strides so adjusted her approach. The other girl did beat Penny to the puck, got the puck on her stick and was about to start skating it out from behind the net when Penny's shoulder and the full weight of Penny Davies behind it collided with her side. She crashed into the boards with a loud *crunch* and lost her footing, going down hard on top of the puck. Penny dug for it and managed to pop it loose. She heard the beaver-tail call of one of her teammates asking for the puck and Penny blindly passed it in the direction of the request. She didn't see Li hop *over* the body of a defender trying to block the pass, but she did see the puck bury itself in the netting beside her for the Beavs' second goal of the game.

Penny tried to skate around to congratulate Li, but the fallen Snake player smashed her skate with their stick. Penny fell and landed awkwardly against the netting of the goal. A whistle went and the celebrations paused. The referee came around behind the net and assigned the first penalty of the game to the Snakes player for the trip.

Penny joined her team for the fist-bump flyby of their bench and then her line went off on the change.

9:36 left in the first period. 2-0 Beavs. Beavs on the power play.

Jenn stayed out with the first power play line while Penny and the rest of her line took a breather. The Snakes were doing a good job of bottling up the shooting lanes and seemed content to let the Beavs have possession of the puck so long as they couldn't get any good scoring chances with it. The four Snakes girls formed a tight box of 4 in front of the net and they were doing a good job of getting their sticks down flat on the ice and in front of anywhere the Beavs, forced to the outside, might shoot through.

With 40 seconds gone on the power play, Becks took a big windup and fired. She was aiming to get the puck high and over the sticks blocking her line of attack, but failed and ended up with a rolling knuckle puck that rebounded uselessly off the nearest defender. And rolled back out past Becks and into the neutral zone. Where a *speeding* Snakes forward escaped from their defensive box and picked it up for a breakaway.

Emma came far out of her net to challenge the girl. It was clear none of the Beavs were going to be able to get back in time to be of help, so this was a wo-mano a wo-mano matchup. Emma adjusted her position once, then twice as the attacker deked in a tight line towards the net. The attacker slowed and started gliding about twelve feet from the net and Emma locked her pads down against the ice and prepared to catch the shot. The attacking Snake didn't shoot, but instead dragged her stick far across, behind where Emma had gone down into her position, and managed to slide the puck behind the goaltender.

The Snakes' bench erupted in an explosion of noise and there was scattered applause from the Snakes' parents and family members in the stands. The player that had scored the goal stood and blew exaggerated kisses at the audience as if she'd just won Miss America, and then her team tackled her in celebration.

8:45 left in the first. 2 – 1 Beavs. 1:10 left in the Snakes' tripping penalty.

Coach kept Penny benched after the first power play line came back in. Instead she put one of the team's second-year forwards into Penny's slot in the 2nd power play lineup. Despite shaking things up a bit, the Beavs on the ice were facing an obvious change in momentum after the shorthanded goal. The Snakes continued to play their frustrating, patient defensive screen while the Beavs turned into their own worst enemies, sloppy and too-hard passes missing their targets and ending up in turnovers that got sent down the length of the ice, or that just careened off the boards and out of the zone with no help from the Snakes at all. The first power play of the game landed the Beavs exactly zero shots on goal, and one given up short hander.

Penny and her normal first line got back on the ice at the first play stoppage following the power play. The faceoff at the Snakes' blue line had no clear winner, and ended up with both centers in a heap over the puck where it had been dropped and two players from each team digging away to get it loose. Penny managed to gain possession and slid it away from the melee where the faceoff had been. Jenn slapped her stick for a pass but Penny looked over at her and shook her head. Instead, Penny carried the puck into her own zone and back behind her own net. Aside from one forechecking Snake Penny was largely uncontested in her own team's end, and that gave her players time to get back into their position and everyone a few seconds to breathe and take stock of where they were.

The forechecker pushed the issue and chased Penny, coming around one side of the net to get to her. Penny skated out the opposite side of the back of the net and passed the puck forward to Li at center ice. Li picked it up and now she and her forward line moved it in across into the Snakes' zone. Penny and Jenn held the line at center ice, not interested in a repeat of the giveaway goal on the power play.

Li and her wingers managed to get off two good shots before a third shot was deflected out of play and that ended the first liners' shift.

6:36 left in the first. 2-1 Beavs.

The third line got stuck on the ice for a long, grueling shift of board battles. The puck moved a few feet at a time from one neutral zone board battle to another. Both team's lines were getting worn down by the physical play and lack of progress, and they were each trying more and more desperately to make *something* happen. Jada won the puck from a late shift board battle and sent it high into her own zone. One of the Beavs' defenders reached their stick up to try and bat it out of the air, and managed to clip a Snake in the side of the head in the process. That earned her a penalty and the Beavs went to the PK for the first time of the game.

4:51 left in the first. 2-1 Beavs. 2:00 Beavs high sticking penalty.

Coach was not pleased. Even though the offending player was in the penalty box on the other side of the ice, the players on the bench got a harsh verbal lashing reminding them about the importance of not taking undisciplined penalties. Penny was thankful she was on the first PK line and only had to hear the first part of the reproach.

Two minutes later Penny thought back that maybe she should have heard the whole thing. The goal was only *sort of* Penny's fault. It had come in the dying seconds of the penalty kill and Penny's line was back out for their second shift on that PK. Penny had been covering the crease and the Snakes' center had positioned herself right out front of Emma. Penny had been battling her, pushing her back out of position each time she managed to get into a screening spot, and then Penny had seen a pass coming at the other player and pushed her hard. Success – the Snake player missed the pass, then stumbled and fell... right into Emma who was crossing her crease following the puck. Both girls went down in a heap with Emma struggling to get back to her feet. While she was down, the puck that Penny's player hadn't been able to shoot got picked up by a Snake, who easily buried it with Emma out of commission.

As far as a goal review went it was a quick conference between the refs followed by a lengthy discussion with the Beavs' coach. Being a minor hockey league game, it was hardly as if there were video review officials in Toronto, or any video to review at all for that matter, to challenge the ruling. It was a good goal. Any hopes that Coach had of a goaltender interference call were negated by the fact that Penny had been the one who'd pushed the Snake player down on top of Emma. The consequences were on her and her team, and the consequence was a tied game.

3:02 left in the first. Tied at 2.

The goal did count as a power play goal and so ended the penalty. Penny, along with the third line defender who'd earned the penalty with the high stick, got to sit and watch their team struggle through the final three minutes of that period. It was not pretty. Emma faced as many shots in those final three minutes as she'd done the entire rest of the period, power play included. She somehow managed to keep them *all* out of the net but there was no question that she was the only reason the Beavs went into the first intermission holding onto a tie. The whole bench waited for her to skate off before anyone else went to the locker room, waiting to rub her helmet in appreciation of her effort.

The first period in the books, 2-2 tie.

Coach hit the dressing room with fire in her belly.

"What did I just witness in those last 5 minutes?" She demanded after all the players had assembled. Most players struggled to meet her eyes as she scanned the room.

"You let in *one* goal and bam, game over, let's stop skating and forget every one of the fundamentals of our game?"

Nobody answered the rhetorical question.

"Discipline. Hard work. Movement. Speed. Four simple concepts we've been working on all season. All out the window! Make no mistake *they* earned that first shorthanded goal, that was skill and we need to respect that they have the ability to pull those plays off. But *we gifted them* that second goal between the sloppy penalty and whatever shit that was Davies pulled in front of the net."

Penny felt eyes burning into the back of her brain. She was glad she was wearing a helmet in that moment.

"We won the middle of that period. You were the better team out there for a full half of the first twenty. So get yourselves sorted and get *that* team back on the ice for the second. Understood?"

"YES COACH!" The room yelled.

Coach then stepped out of the room and let the players be with their own thoughts. Emma was already zoned out, and Penny popped her earphones in and joined her. Aerosmith, "Dream On", drowned out the rest of the room and let her slip into herself for a few moments. Penny had the song on her playlist because of its use at the end of the Disney movie "Miracle", about the 1980 Olympics' Miracle on Ice. It had been one of Penny's dad's favorite movies, and she remembered seeing it at least five times before she had seen her first animated Disney movie. Penny had thought of the Snakes as her team's Soviets since she'd started playing hockey. They were the dominant league leaders, the team nobody thought could be unseated. And *dammit* she wanted to be on the team that did it.

"Any word on Shiv?" Penny asked when they were back on the bench. The trainer had rejoined them for the second period but Shiv had not.

"I gave her some painkillers but her parents have taken her to the hospital to get xrays done." The trainer explained. Penny wasn't surprised, but she felt like that was another blow anyway.

"They'll take care of her." Coach interrupted. "Just focus on your game Davies. No more dumb ass moves in our own end got it?"

"Yes Coach." Penny confirmed.

Penny and the usual starters kicked off the second. The Rattlesnakes came out calm, relaxed and loose. They took their time coming to the face off circle and were all jokes and smiles with each other. The Beavs were all business. After the puck drop it was obvious there was a tempo shift too. The Snakes had lost a bit of the killer instinct they'd showed at the end of the first period, and were working a tight 5-player wide neutral zone trap followed by dumping the puck and chasing it into the Beavs end rather than skating it in and taking shots.

The Beavs were hungry and were chasing down every loose puck and trying to muscle their way through the wall of bodies in the center ice zone but were mostly turning the puck over to chase it back into their end. Three shifts in and neither team had secured a shot on goal or show much offensive life.

"Davies," Coach announced from behind Penny after her second useless shift, "our forwards don't have the muscle to break through their defensive line. Next time you get the puck, I want you to skate it out – no passing you hear?"

"Got it Coach." Penny nodded.

Next time she was out on the ice she did just that. Jenn collected a dumped puck from behind the net and passed it out to Penny. Penny saw Li at the blue line waiting for the pass and two Snakes turning in Penny's end to chase down the puck. Penny took off up the boards.

She crossed out of her own end, leaving the two Snakes offside behind her. Her next obstacle was a forward holding her side of the boards ahead of her. Penny got to just outside stick range and bounced the puck lightly off the boards and past the girl. Then she let her momentum carry her straight on through the forward. The other girl made the mistake of trying to lay a hit on Penny, allowing Penny to do what she did best and *deflect* the girl's attack in a different direction. As they came past, Penny pulled her shoulder back and opened up her body until her torso was almost sideways to the other girl. The Snake player, who'd been angling for a shoulder-to-shoulder contact with Penny, stumbled and glanced off Penny's arm but ended up with most of the force of the move carrying her into the boards, meanwhile Penny skated past and picked up her pass to herself with only a minor bump.

Now she was in the Snakes' zone, alone, with the puck. She glanced to her side and saw Li, the left wing, and their Snake escorts skating across the line following Penny in, but they were both well covered. Penny looked at Li. Li looked at Penny. And the two turned and started skating directly at each other, leaving Penny skating away from the opposing net with the puck.

As they converged, Penny dropped the puck from her stick. Li skated past her and grabbed the puck. Penny skated directly into the defender that had been chasing Li, and both went to the ice in a big collision of bodies, pads and sticks. That left Li open. She deked once and put the puck up and over the goalie's shoulder for the Beav's third goal of the game.

Penny couldn't get up though. She grabbed her thigh and rolled back and forth on the ice in pain. She saw the trainer was coming out but waved her off. Penny got to her feet and dragged her pained left leg under her body relying on her right leg to do most of the work. She limped on her skates to the bench and collapsed onto the seat. Li and the others celebrated and came in behind her, looking concerned.

The trainer started looking at Penny's leg, and Penny explained between deep breaths that her left thigh was in extreme pain. The trainer did her best "does it hurt when I do this" workup and then agreed Penny needed to get a proper looking at off the ice. The trainer helped her limp down the tunnel and into the locker room, worried looks from her teammate's disappearing behind Penny.

In the locker room, the trainer had Penny expose her lower body down to her undershorts. She winced at the big bruise developing on Penny's thigh and prominent swollen lump rising away from Penny's leg. She gave Penny a pair of painkillers which Penny forced down without waiting for the cup of water she went to fetch. Penny lay back on the uncomfortable benches and put one hand up against her forehead. In that position at least the leg pain wasn't as bad.

"Not *again*." She groaned. Referring to the previous season where she'd missed the Beavs' playoff run altogether due to a perforated eardrum.

"Good news bad news." The trainer said. "I'm pretty sure it's not broken, but it's gonna hurt like hell. I'm going to give you an ice wrap and see how the swelling is in 30 minutes, that is, unless you'd rather a family member drive you to the hospital for an xray to make sure."

"What if the swelling is better in 30 minutes?" Penny asked, a glimmer of hope in her eye.

"If you can handle the pain and put weight on it, we can probably get you back out there." The trainer told her, tone not matching the fact that she'd just made Penny's entire *life*.

"Ok! Let's do that!" Penny exclaimed. The trainer got to work on the ice wrap.

While Penny gritted through the pain coming from her leg, now expounded by the stinging pricks of icy cold, she tried to hear what was happening in the game. Whistle. Oooooh from the crowd. Whistle. There was the unmistakable blast of the goal horn. Someone had just gotten a goal. More whistles. The pain was beginning to subside a little when she could hear the long blast for the end of the period and a few moments later her team started to come into the room. They tried to give Penny a wide berth but in the tight confines of the locker room that wasn't really possible.

"What happened?" Penny asked Jenn when her friend came and sat by her feet. "Where's the game at?"

"Whoa!" Jenn said with an admonishing tone. "You first. You going to make it?"

"Yeah, probably not even broken." Penny told her. "I'm gonna go back out there after the break."

"Hah, what?" Jenn laughed, taking in her pantless friend who looked like she had last Tuesday's leftovers cling wrapped to her leg.

Before Penny could respond, Coach was in and the chatter died down.

"Girls listen up." Coach said. "THAT was Beavs' hockey. I don't care about the scoreboard right now, that fourth goal was a gift from the officials and those happen. We're down by 1 but we are playing *our hockey now*. However the next 20 minutes goes, you all keep playing the way you have been and I'm proud of this team no matter the final score."

The energy level in the room rose noticeably and the girls started talking again. Coach wasn't quite done though. "When we get back out there, leave it all on the ice. Work your asses off and let's WIN THIS THING!"

The girls made noise in any way they could and roared and cheered at that.

"So we're down by 1?" Penny asked Jenn once calm had descended.

"Yeah, 4-3, they got a penalty shot awarded late in the period on a questionable tripping call." Jenn explained.

"Damn." Penny breathed.

"We're not done yet." Jenn said. "Well, not all of us." She nodded to Penny's leg. Penny gave her a good-natured kick in the ribs with her good leg.

183

Penny pulled her hockey shorts on with the ice pack still taped to her leg. She pulled on and laced her skates and then stood on the leg again. She winced but still threw an exuberant thumbs up to the trainer. "I'd still recommend taking it easy, but you won't listen anyway, so I'll just say, give 'em hell." The trainer smiled. Penny flashed her a giant grin and stomped as convincingly and non-limpingly as she could after her team to the bench.

When she stepped onto the bench her team was turned to the tunnel and clapping. Penny thought for a second the ovation was for her, but then she noticed they weren't looking *at* her but *past* her. Penny turned and saw Shiv with a wrist splint on standing behind the glass. Penny shouted in excitement. Shiv pointed and started to wander off to a corner of the rink where she could watch from. The pain in Penny's leg seemed to lessen further seeing that her friend was ok.

Coach did swap Penny to the second line for the third, but Penny was just glad to be back. She watched the puck drop and her team quickly gain the zone and put a shot into the glove of the Snakes' goalie. Another good faceoff win set up a long cycle of the puck around the zone that ended in another shot that went wide and out of play.

Penny's line swapped in and lost the faceoff. Penny let Becks chase the puck down on the forecheck while she held the corner of the blue line. Becks made a really nice poke check and stole the puck from the Snakes. She passed it back to their center who cycled it around to Penny. Penny fired it right back at the center who moved awkwardly and took the puck off the heel of her stick, sending it careening wildly towards the net. The goalie hadn't been expecting the puck coming her way and tried to get down, but the puck took a bounce in front of her that brought it up and over her leg pad and into the net.

Penny braced herself as her teammates swarmed her and patted her helmet. Every bang on her head sent shooting pain down her leg, and she tried to look happy about tying the game. She skated to the bench but instead of doing a flyby signaled for an immediate change and sat.

"You ok?" Coach asked.

"Surviving." Penny gritted, trying to ignore the pain that was much worse now than it had been in the locker room.

"Good work on that assist." Coach told her. Penny nodded.

16:10 left in the 3rd period. Tied 4-4.

Penny did a quick mental calculation. 970 seconds left. Third line was out and the Snakes were double shifting their first line which made for a tough matchup. The Beavs were completely on the defensive in their end and struggling with a reinvigorated Snakes offense. The Snakes weren't bothering with any finesse at this point. Get the puck, gain the zone, fire on net from whoever and wherever it was touched first. They ended up with a lot of shots, but not a lot of shots *on goal*. Most of the shots went wide or high and the Beavs were easily able to pick them up and clear the zone before losing possession and repeating the whole sequence over again.

The Snakes were showing their fatigue though, and Penny wondered how much longer they could keep this up for. Her own team was taking a beating but for the most part, they were having to do about *half* as much skating as the Snakes were doing right now.

Emma deflected a puck out of play and the Beavs got their first line out against the Snakes' second. This was a more fair matchup that favored the Beavs. Penny gripped the pommel of her stick tightly and watched her team break out from their own zone and develop a 3-on-1 in the Snakes end of the ice. Li carried it in at center and skated hard for the net. The Snakes defender was close on her. At the edge of the crease, Li did the *hardest* hockey stop Penny had ever seen, showering the goalie with snow shavings while also tossing the puck backwards… to Jenn who was just crossing into the zone! Jenn didn't even stop to control the puck, she lined up a slap shot and *fired*. Li ducked. The goalie squinted but her eyes were still covered with water droplets and she saw the puck too late. It sailed into the open glove side of the net and the Beavs were up 5-4.

The goalie slammed her stick on the ice and two Snakes players converged on the front of the ice to get into Li's face. Thankfully the rest of the Beavs' on the ice were already arriving to celebrate the goal and got between Li and the others before anything developed from the menacing glares they were sending at the short forward.

11:03 left in the third. 5-4 Beavs.

Penny put in another short shift after Li's victorious line got back on the bench. The Snakes were pressing hard and Penny and the Beavs were on their heels in their own zone the entire shift. Penny got tied up in the corner with a battle for the puck. She and the Snake she was marking both jabbing for it. The Snake however, was the same one Penny had collided with on Li's goal back in the second. After making no progress in either direction for a few seconds, the girl used her free glove hand to give a little punch to Penny's thigh. Penny cried out, but managed to stay upright. The girl hit her again this time harder. Penny's leg buckled under her and she went down hard. She ended up on top of the puck and the other girl's stick jabbed at her body to get at it, finally prying it free from under Penny's chest. Penny felt helpless and angry at losing the battle and tried to play the puck from the ground but ended up tripping the girl instead.

With 10:36 left in the third and the Beavs up by 1, Penny had earned her team a 2 minute penalty kill for her efforts. She looked apologetically towards the bench as she was led off.

In what felt like a bizarre decision, the Snakes pulled their goalie for the opening faceoff of the power play. Penny puzzled over that coaching decision as she watched the power play unfold. With 6 attackers to 4, the Beavs were in a perpetual state of shot blocking. Penny was pleased to see Jada on the PK getting her body on the ice in front of the puck, something she'd been struggling with all season. To Penny's immense relief, the Beavs weathered the two minutes with a number of shots on goal but no goals given up.

As Penny's time expired she hustled onto the ice and started for her bench, when Emma sent her a long clearing pass from the Beavs' own net and right onto Penny's stick. With all the Snakes in the Beavs' zone and the net still empty from the power play, Penny had an empty net! She turned to skate the puck in but her leg nearly buckled under her as she did. Penny winced and instead of skating the puck up and making an easy ten-footer she fired from half-ice and limped off the ice.

The puck had gone wide. Penny's shot had missed. Penny hobbled her way back of the player lineup and found the trainer. "I think I'm done." She sighed. "I'm turning into a liability out there."

The trainer nodded gravely. "Your call. But there's nothing more I can do for you treatment wise, you might as well be with your team to the end."

"You just try and get me off this bench." Penny challenged, but lay back on the seating area and raised her injured thigh up.

8:04 left in the third. 5-4 Beavs.

Penny lay injured at the back of the player bench. Shiv pounded on the glass with her good hand while her painful one hung splinted and slung in front of her. Coach rallied the Beavs in their defensive efforts. From the ice area Penny heard a shot ring off the post and the crowd reacted in relief. That must have been close, Penny thought.

There was a rattle of player vs. boards and the crowd booed. A few moments later Jada came in and sat next to Penny holding her side and got some attention from the trainer. Penny gritted her teeth. Jada, Shiv and herself made a full half of the Beavs' d-line out of commission! Poor Jenn and Becks were going to have their hands full for… she craned her neck to try and see the score clock… the final 5 minutes of the game.

At this point, when Penny retells this story in the future (and she will many times), people will complain that it's a terrible ending. If it was a popular movie like Mighty Ducks or Miracle the Snakes needed to tie it up with a special teams spectacular in the dying seconds to force overtime and then Penny would need to fight someone and then the Beavs might win the game in the final round of a shootout. All of those things would have been exciting, it's true, but real life isn't often like the movies.

The Beavs did go on to win the game, holding on for the last five minutes against an exhausted Regina Rattlesnake's team that just fell apart from fatigue and frustration to end the game. There were some hits thrown against the Beavs' players and some mean words shared, but Penny's game ended in that 11th minute of the 3rd period and the game was decided by the 5-4 goal just past the 8 minute mark.

Emma made some great saves, that much is true, but Penny couldn't see them from where she was on the bench. Penny's game at that point onwards was one of sound only. Trying to piece together a picture of what happened on the ice from the slaps and thuds of the puck and the crunches of players hitting and being hit.

Goon Girl: The Minors

When the final buzzer rang, Penny sat up and the girls on the bench around her threw themselves over the boards and rushed Emma en masse. They threw their gear up in the air and gloves and helmets rained around them. The mob collectively knocked itself to the ice. Penny, Jada, and Shiv followed more hesitantly a few moments later, getting there after the initial eruption but in time for the hugs and laughs and congratulations.

A hundred tiny moments came out of the next few minutes, as Penny embraced and was embraced by all of the members of her team. The team's parents started to come down onto the ice with cell phones and took pictures of the girls celebrating.

When the jubilation died down, both coaches came together at center ice and lined their players up on the blue lines.

"Ladies and gentlemen," Coach said as loudly as she could, "The South Saskatchewan Minor Hockey League U15 Female champions for this year – the Maple Creek Hungry Beavers!" A roar of cheers erupted and the coach brought forward a trophy which she presented to Li as the series MVP with five total goals over the last 3 games.

Each girl had a chance to take the trophy and do a victory lap of the ice. Parents were more than happy to wait around and take pictures of their daughter when it was her turn. Penny skated her lap slowly and painfully. Her body was barely holding together after the difficult 8 game post season and everything she'd put it through over the last three weekends. She skated past the end boards and saw Pat, Paul, Peter, her dad... and even her mom there waving and cheering! Penny stopped and pressed a hand against the glass. "Thank you" she called through to them. They kept on cheering.

That championship was the first in the Beavs' history, and Penny's first in any league she'd played in. She felt excitement, pain, joy, sadness at it being over, but mostly, complete and utter physical exhaustion. While she sat in Pat's car on the ride home, stroking the gold medal hanging around her neck and thinking of everything that had gone into getting to that moment, she fell deeply and peacefully asleep.

Manufactured by Amazon.ca
Bolton, ON

35414996R00105